The Day After Never

Legion

Russell Blake

Books@RussellBlake.com

ISBN: 978-1793435545

Published by

Reprobatio Limited

Chapter 1

Four riders, their jackets beige with trail dust, hunched low in the saddle as their steeds picked their way along a rocky trail that traced the mountainside. To their left was a straight drop to the silver thread of a creek hundreds of feet below. Their sunburned faces squinted beneath their hat brims against the late afternoon sun, and their shoulders slumped from fatigue, AR-15 assault rifles resting against their saddle horns or dangling from shoulder slings.

The lead rider, a rail-thin man with a black handlebar moustache and ebony eyes, held up a gloved hand and reined in his horse. The others stopped behind him, and he swung down from the saddle and handed his reins to the nearest rider, his eyes locked on a fork in the trail ahead.

His boots crunched against loose gravel as he picked his way forward. When he reached the fork, he stopped, rifle in one hand, and stared at the ground with focused intensity. His eyes narrowed and he crouched to study the loose shale. Then slowly he swiveled and straightened before walking back to the men.

"No way of tellin' which trail they took. Both been used since the last rain," he said, and spat a brown stream of chewing-tobacco-colored saliva by his boots.

The rider who was holding his horse's reins frowned. "Damn, Leo. No part a this is gonna be easy, is it?"

1

The rider held out his hand, and Leo took the reins from him.

"That's why they pay us the big bucks, Doug. If anyone could do it, they'd a sent anyone."

Leo hoisted himself back onto the buckskin stallion and twisted toward his men. "We'll try the one on the right. See where it goes. If it comes up empty, we'll double back."

Doug glanced up at the sky. "Gonna be dark in a few hours."

Leo shrugged. "True. Nothin' we can do about that. We'll make camp where we can when it comes time. For now, we ride."

The men grumbled but fell in line behind Leo. It had been a long week in the rough, but they were resigned to the job they'd been tasked with – it would take as long as it took. They had no idea exactly where the enemy's encampment was, but based on Ellen's description, they were confident they were somewhere in the vicinity.

These trackers were the best Elijah had, and his instructions had been clear: trace the route of the escapees who'd murdered his father, pinpoint their home base, and report back. Elijah would raze the earth once he knew exactly where to direct his wrath, and he'd delivered a powerful sermon to a packed crowd that cited Old Testament-style destruction as the only possible punishment for taking one of the Lord's angels from the earth before his time.

The prophet's death had come as a shock to the community, but Elijah had stepped into the vacuum and taken charge, directing the able-bodied men in the congregation to prepare for a battle between good and evil to avenge the murder of their beloved leader. Almost immediately he'd called Leo and his scouts to the church and directed them to do whatever it took to find the killers – and not to return to Denver unsuccessful. Leo had accepted the challenge and saddled up within the hour, and had been riding hard ever since.

A figure on the mountainside above lowered his binoculars and crept over to where a man and woman with assault rifles were following the progress of the riders through their scopes. When he reached them, he whispered, his voice barely audible, "Everyone ready? You know what to do."

The pair drew themselves up. "Where?"

"The bend. Hundred yards up the trail. Good cover, and we'll be in place before they make it."

The two followed the lead gunman along a trail to where their horses were standing by a grove of trees. Their green camo jackets and pants made them nearly invisible in the brush, and they'd blacked out their faces to avert any glare from the moon. They moved in silence, their expressions grim, rifles clutched at the ready as they made their way past their animals and continued to higher ground. They'd been dispatched to watch the trail in case any of Elijah's fighters had managed to follow the tracks from the highway – an unlikely possibility, but one they had to guard against while Elliot decided how to proceed. Their vigilance had paid off, and with any luck, the men on the trail below were the walking dead.

Leo's horse stiffened beneath him an instant before the first shots rang out from the trees. The stallion's instinct saved Leo, and rounds snapped past his head as he threw himself from the saddle and rolled to an outcropping of rocks at the edge of the ravine. The other riders weren't so lucky, and two screamed as bullets tore through them, their flak vests no match for the onslaught of fully jacketed rounds.

Doug squeezed off a three-round burst one-handed as his other clutched at where the ceramic plate that protected his chest had shattered from the sniper fire, but the shots went wide, the shooters ghosts in the shadows of the tall pines. More shots exploded from the tree line, and he tumbled from the saddle and hit the ground like a sack of cement, dead before he finished bouncing. His rifle skittered harmlessly down the trail.

The tracker behind him swung to the ground, unfazed by the blood streaming from where a bullet had struck his unprotected shoulder, and emptied his magazine at the trees as he ran for cover. Dirt fountained in the air around him from incoming fire, but he made it to a fallen log and ejected his spent mag and slapped a fresh one in place.

The last rider's horse had frozen in place at the gunshots, but then threw him from the saddle and raced back down the trail, away from the battle, its eyes panicked and its breathing harsh as it galloped as fast as it could. The rider lay stunned for a few moments and then scrambled for the ravine as bits of gravel showered him from ricochets.

Sniper fire peppered the riders' positions as they returned volley after volley. The man who'd been hit in the shoulder was squeezing off methodical shots from behind the log, concentrating his fire on the likeliest sniper positions, when a round blew through his temple, killing him instantly.

"Leo!" the surviving rider called from the gorge, his feet barely maintaining a hold on the treacherous surface. "You hit?"

"Shut up, moron," Leo hissed from down the ravine, out of sight of the other rider due to the shape of the sheer face.

"They've got us pinned down," the rider tried again. "And I've only got one mag left."

Leo didn't respond.

More shooting from the trees pocked the area in front of the rider, and he cringed behind the ravine edge, weighing his options. The shooting abated, and he swung his rifle over the ridge and fired at the trees, and when his magazine ran dry, he replaced it with his last one, hauled himself onto the trail, and took off at a run, spraying the forest with three-round bursts as he sprinted for safety.

Six slugs slammed into his back and thighs, and he tumbled forward, his legs suddenly useless. He struggled to roll over so he could continue shooting at his attackers, but his arms refused to obey his commands as he gasped for breath. The pressure on his chest felt like a piano had landed on it. Another shot echoed across the trail, and the back of his head shattered in a spray of bloody emulsion.

"Hold your fire," the lead lookout called.

The trail fell silent, and the three sentries surveyed the carnage. The horses had all bolted, leaving the dead man in the middle of the track, and the rest out of sight in the ravine. The lead lookout edged to his companions, his eyes never leaving the trail.

"That all of them?" he asked.

"I think so, Bill," the woman replied. "But we can't be sure. Someone could be playing possum until we show ourselves."

Bill nodded. "Could be."

"So?"

"We wait."

A half hour went by with no sound, and eventually Bill sighed and looked to the others. "Cover me. I'm going to work my way over there and then come down the trail. You see or hear anything, let them have it."

He took off at a jog, hunched over as he moved through the brush. When he was out of sight of the killing zone, he cut over and emerged onto the trail, peering down the barrel of his rifle. He took cautious steps until the dead man was in sight, and trained his gun on the crumpled form of the rider by the log as he approached.

Bill could see that the man was dead as he neared, so he pivoted and headed to the ravine to peer over, leading with his weapon. At the edge, he swept the drop with his gun and spotted a third body ten yards down the mountain face, twisted unnaturally between two boulders. Seeing no danger from the corpse, he moved to the rock outcropping where the lead rider had taken cover, his finger hovering over the trigger, his breath hissing through clenched teeth.

Spent brass littered the rocks, glittering in the late afternoon sun, but there was no body. He peered over the outcropping and scanned the ravine below, but didn't spy anything. Frowning, he called over his shoulder.

"Come on over here and see if you can spot the last guy."

The man and woman joined him and, after five minutes of searching, stood together uneasily at the trail's edge.

"He must have worked his way down the side of the gully," the woman said.

"But the question is, which way?"

"Back the way he came, don't you think?"

Bill's frown deepened. "Maybe."

The other sentry took a final look down the ravine. "How do you want to play it?"

Bill indicated the trail leading down the mountain. "You two take that direction; I'll take this one. He can't have gotten that far."

They split up and searched the ridge, working their way along and studying any irregularities in the terrain with their scopes. The sun had begun to fade in the cobalt sky by the time they reunited where they'd left their horses, and Bill's expression was dark as he debated his next step.

"I'm going to ride to town and tell Elliot what happened. Take the horses and keep looking for him farther down the trail."

The pair departed and Bill mounted up, his thoughts racing. He rode flat out and was at the springs in less than half an hour.

Elliot was already waiting for him outside his cabin. "Heard the shooting."

Bill nodded and gave him a short report. When he finished, Elliot's scowl wrinkled his face.

"He's on foot," Elliot said. "That's at least one piece of luck. If your men don't find him by nightfall, we'll organize a search party at first light. We have to intercept him before he can give away our location."

"It's a long walk back to Denver. A lot can happen to a man on foot out there," Bill observed.

"We can't depend on luck. If we don't find him, our fate is sealed."

Bill hesitated. "I'm sorry we let you down."

Elliot looked away. "You couldn't have foreseen this. Sounds to me like you did everything you could."

"But not enough. Obviously."

"Don't worry. You were right. It's a long walk back to Denver," Elliot said, but when he turned back toward the cabin, his lips were a thin line and his eyes were hard as flint.

Chapter 2

Leo hunched forward in the saddle as night fell. His horse sedulously plodded north toward home. He'd caught a break after traversing the ravine's face and climbing onto the trail beyond where his men lay dead – the stallion had come at his whistle, obviously frightened but conditioned to obedience. He'd ridden the poor animal as hard as he'd dared through the darkness until finally stopping for a few hours of rest as dawn's salmon glow colored the eastern sky.

From there he figured that he'd worked up a sufficient lead to where he didn't need to run the horse into the ground. Still, he'd stuck to the trails along either side of the highway to Denver, just in case Shangri-La had somehow managed to communicate with any conspirators along the way. He gave the few outposts along the road a wide berth, preferring caution over convenience, and rode mostly at night, secure that he was the most dangerous thing on the highway, given his skills.

Still, the return journey wore on his nerves, and the combination of sleep deprivation and having lost all the members of his team was coming to bear. The horse was doing the best it could, but he calculated that at most he was only making twenty miles per day; at that rate it would take another four to make it back to Denver and give Elijah the news.

Earlier that day, the ride had been worse than any he'd taken before. Around noon, with the sun high in the sky, he'd spied a group of scavengers riding up the highway from his cover a quarter mile toward the foothills. He'd taken to sleeping near the deserted buildings that lined the road, worried that someone might spot the horse and come to investigate – another reason he was getting precious little sleep. A dust cloud had followed the men south, and he'd reckoned they were likely part of the neo-Nazis who'd laid claim to Colorado Springs, or worse, outcasts from that group, considered too dangerous and reckless for even their depraved lifestyle.

Leo had watched them through his binoculars, holding his breath as the filthy riders worked their way down the highway, their horses' ribs like washboards from malnutrition. On the way south from Denver, Leo and his group had avoided both Colorado Springs and Pueblo lest they attract unwanted attention, or worse, in the event the murderers in Shangri-La had watchers there. While that was unlikely, they hadn't wanted to take the chance; a group of four men from Denver with well-fed mounts and full saddlebags might have been too appealing to the local miscreants.

The danger was just as great on the return trip, but Leo wasn't worried – he remembered the trail they'd followed on the way down and could manage it handily, even at night. The only possible hazard would be a misstep from his horse since a broken or sprained ankle would effectively strand him in the middle of nowhere with predators all around.

The scavengers had continued past his position, and when they'd shrunk into dots on the horizon, Leo had set the binoculars down and exhaled with fatigue. Sleeping during daylight hours was hard duty with nobody to stand watch, which meant he was rarely fully asleep for any sustained period.

"I'll sleep in Denver," he'd muttered to himself, and caught himself on the final syllable. He'd noticed that he'd taken to holding punctuated conversations out loud on the ride, and feared he might be losing his mind from the sleeplessness and stress. It was one thing to curse occasionally with nobody around to hear it, but another entirely to fall prey to mumbling like a delusional hobo.

Now, only a few more days from Denver, he was going to have to be especially careful not to slip up. Tomorrow or the next night he would pass Colorado Springs, and if he made it without mishap, he would be home free. The thought cheered him, and he patted his horse's neck with a grimy hand. "Almost," he said, reasoning that he was talking to his animal to reassure it, not to himself. That he had to make the distinction troubled him for only an instant, and then he settled back in the saddle, scanning the horizon for campfires or any other hints of life.

He made it to Denver on the fourth night and, after being stopped by a patrol, was escorted to Elijah's headquarters beside the convention center/church, where he was brought a meal while he waited for his master to arrive.

The young preacher's eyes were rimmed with red and his face puffy from sleep when he entered the room where Leo was seated at a table, feasting on his dinner.

"Well?" Elijah demanded.

Leo delivered his report in a wooden tone, so tired he could barely manage to form words. When he was done, he held Elijah's gaze before dropping his eyes and returning to his meal. "Sorry if I eat while we talk. It's been three weeks since I had any real food."

"No problem, Leo. You've done well. But..." Elijah's tone softened. "You didn't actually see Shangri-La?"

"No. But it had to be nearby. Otherwise why set up an ambush?"

Elijah nodded absently, but his eyes were reptilian in the candlelight. "A fair assumption. But still, only that." He sighed. "Where exactly is it?"

"Do you have a map?"

"Of course." Elijah snapped his fingers, and one of the stewards by the door hurried away to fetch the desired item. He returned with a dog-eared highway map of Colorado and set it in front of Leo. Leo unfolded it and studied the topography, and shook his head in wonder.

"Hard to believe this is all gone, isn't it?"

Elijah tensed at the comment. "This isn't a trip down memory lane. Where is Shangri-La?"

Leo frowned. "Ellen had said that it was in the mountains west of Pueblo. We followed her directions to the trail she'd described, and then worked our way into the mountains. We picked up tracks almost immediately, so from there it was merely a matter of following them."

"Yes, yes," Elijah snapped. "All very interesting, but I didn't ask for a blow by blow of how you located it. I asked where it is."

Leo hunched over the map and pored over the surface until he sat back, the cracked nail of his index finger defining a point. "Here. Amber Hot Springs. Has to be. There's nothing else close."

Elijah glared at the map like it had bitten him. "You're sure?"

"Well, it makes sense. Remember how Ellen said they'd managed to rig up some power? The hot springs would be the only realistic source. Especially if they hoped to make it through the winter there." Leo paused and nodded, the lines in his face deepening with each bob of his head. "I'd bet my life on it."

Elijah sat back, obviously lost in thought. Leo resumed eating, and the only sounds in the room were the wet crunch of Leo's mastication and his hoarse breathing.

After several moments, Elijah stood and smiled at Leo.

"You've done well, my son. My father will be avenged. At dawn, we will prepare an army and march against that cursed place. We'll burn it to the ground, and those responsible for his death will be brought to justice. The Lord has willed it. We shall make it so."

Elijah stood and marched briskly to the door, where the stewards had been watching the scene impassively. He paused at the threshold and then slowly turned to face Leo.

"Get some rest. I'll want you at the head of the procession tomorrow. You've earned the honor."

Elijah left, taking his entourage with him, leaving Leo alone with his food. He blinked at the blurry map and rose. He barely made his way to a divan in the corner before he passed out, weeks of sleepless nights hitting him with the force of a blow.

Chapter 3

Houston, Texas

Snake paced the length of his chambers as he listened to Nate, one of his lieutenants, deliver his report. Snake's face was a mask of rage as the man described the treasonous behavior of the leaders of one of the largest factions of his gang.

"Word is that they had a meeting two days ago to discuss what to do. Nothing was decided, but the fact that they're even talking about it is…a problem."

Snake clenched his hands at his sides. "Go on."

"They're worried that by killing the Illuminati ambassador, you've subjected all of us to risk. What it comes down to is they don't trust your judgment or your leadership."

"They didn't take it any further than that?" Snake asked, as though the clear and present mutiny weren't enough.

"Not yet. I argued on your behalf, obviously, but they've already made up their minds." Nate paused. "I pretended to be on their side, of course, by the end. I had to, or they would have killed me. But I'm still not sure they trust me enough to tell me their plans."

"Of course," Snake said. He stopped in front of a floor-to-ceiling bookcase that he kept in the room because he liked the look of it, not because he'd ever read any of the dusty tomes on the shelves. "Here's what I want you to do. Call an emergency meeting for just before dawn. Only the lieutenants and their most trusted officers. That way they won't have enough time to prepare."

"For…this morning?" Nate stammered.

"Yes. From what you've told me, it isn't smart to leave this any longer." Snake resumed pacing. "Your loyalty will be rewarded. Now go. I need to think through how I'm going to handle this."

After Nate shouldered through the door, Snake bolted it shut and then stormed across the room to his desk, eyes blazing. He sat down, extracted a translucent vial from one of the drawers, and filled the bowl of a glass pipe resting in an ashtray with the contents.

Two minutes later he exhaled a long stream of white smoke and closed his eyes as his veins constricted. The meth hit his heart and the inside of his head like a sledgehammer, and he bolted to his feet and began pacing again, the pipe forgotten on the tabletop.

That those scum would dare to challenge him was only the latest in a string of dangers to his tentative reign. Only this wasn't some fringe element – between the lieutenants and the men they commanded, it represented a substantial portion of the Crew. Worse, they were some of the most influential fighters he had, and it would substantially weaken the gang if he were to lose them.

He shook his head to clear it and wiped a sheen of sweat from his brow. He needed to think. Not act impetuously.

Perhaps the meeting wasn't a good idea? He had no plan other than to confront them. But what then? Have them all killed? It wasn't a bad idea, but with his ranks already depleted and many of his men agitated and unhappy, summary executions, while satisfying, might further weaken his grip on power.

He walked back to the table, his hands shaking, and considered the pipe. No, no more drugs until he'd thought things through. The men would arrive in less than five hours. How to deal with a group that collectively could overthrow him without much resistance?

The area around the Crew headquarters glowed from fires burning in oil drums set up in what had once been the huge church's parking lot. Over a hundred of the top officers were gathered outside on a wide, flat promenade that led to the building entrance, where they huddled in groups, talking in low voices. Snake appeared on the roof with his two bodyguards and stared down at the assembly, rifle in hand.

"I called you all here this morning to let you know that there are going to be some big changes. Now that we're free of the Illuminati, we're going to reclaim our territory to the north and down by the border and run things our way, not the way they wanted. By the time we're done, we'll be the strongest gang in the country. Nobody will dare go up against us, not even them." He glared at the men, his face hard and angular. "I know some of you have been grumbling about how I've been running things. So this is your chance to leave. Anyone who questions my authority from here on out will take a bullet to the skull, understand? I'm only warning you instead of doing it because I understand you might have your doubts. That's fine. But for this plan to work, I need you to come together, and I can't afford anyone who isn't going to back me. We can't go to war with a group of traitors sabotaging us."

Silence settled over the men, and Snake raised his rifle and slowly swept the crowd. The crosshairs settled on a tall, muscular Latino man with many of the same types of tattoos on his face as Snake's, and he fired a single shot that plugged him between the eyes.

The man collapsed and Snake lowered his weapon. "I know he was the instigator of the mutiny, so he had to pay the price. The rest of you can make a choice: stay or go. If you decide to go, you won't be hurt as long as you leave now. Just get out of here. But if you stay, by the time we're done taking back what's ours, you'll be powerful beyond your wildest dreams, with anything you want for the asking. So the question is, do you want to cut and run and try your luck on your own, or be part of a new Crew that will be stronger than ever?"

The officers had seen more than their share of brutality and death, so witnessing one of their top leaders gunned down had no visible effect on them. Several of them turned to their fellows and began murmuring; Snake stood like a statue, his gun leaning against his hip, barrel pointed at the sky.

A shout rang out from near the back of the crowd over the hum of conversation. "How do we know you'll keep your word and let anyone who wants to go leave safely?"

"If you leave, that'll be the least of your worries. You'll be marked men. Don't forget that there are plenty of groups that would tear you to pieces if they weren't afraid of reprisals from the Crew. Making it out of Houston will be the easy part."

More grumbling, and then a pair of dark-skinned men with shaved heads split from the others. "Everyone's watching. You gave your word," the taller of the two said.

Snake recognized them. Jay and Mike, cousins, both of whom had been incarcerated for rape, aggravated assault, and violent home invasions before the collapse. They were responsible for one of the areas down by the refineries and had reputations as ugly as their scarred faces.

"That's right. Do what you have to do." Snake looked around. "Anyone else? Now's your chance."

Four more men broke ranks and joined the cousins. Snake resisted the impulse to gun them down and instead stared at them without reaction. "Okay. That's it? Good. You six – grab your shit and get out of my town. If you're still here at noon, you're fair game. Hit the road."

Snake watched the men as they edged away from the crowd, wary of a trick. When nobody shot them in the back, they picked up their pace. Snake turned and called to Derek, his second-in-command. When he approached, Snake leaned into him.

"Follow them to the city limits. When they cross out of Houston, kill them. I didn't promise them they'd be safe outside town."

The lieutenant grinned, revealing several gold-capped teeth, and hurried away to carry out his orders.

Snake straightened and regarded the assembly. "All right. The rest of you stayed. That means you're part of the winning team. I want you to make the same offer to your men I just did to those cowards. Anyone who doesn't like the way things are can leave. But if they stay, they need to be committed. Report back to me by nightfall and let me know how you did."

He eyed the officers and frowned. "We don't need some mystery men a thousand miles away giving us orders. We're the Crew. We take what we want; we don't beg for it or crawl on our stomachs. The Illuminati lied to us about everything — about fixing the refinery, about more gold for reinforcements, all of it. I don't know about you, but I know what Magnus would have done if he'd been lied to. I did the same. So now we're free agents again, in control of our future. And our first order of business is going to be to consolidate our power in our territory. No more fragmentation. This is going to be scorched earth, and you're either with us or against us. By the time we're done, nobody will dare defy us. Not the cartels, not the Illuminati, not anyone. Now get some sleep and then put out the word. I've got work to do."

Snake spun and marched back to the bowels of the church, his message clear. It was a calculated gamble, but the only card he had to play. That more hadn't left was the only surprise, which told him that there were still traitors in the ranks. But he could deal with those on a case-by-case basis — the crisis was averted for now. His informants would keep him apprised of any further dissension, which he would crush with an iron fist.

Assuming those who had remained hadn't done so to attack him from within.

He had to assume that might be the case, but there wasn't much he could immediately do about it. His only option was to watch and wait and, when somebody tried something, to gut them like a fish.

Chapter 4

Seattle, Washington

Lucas rode alongside Lyle, one of Sam's top gunmen, their horses' hooves clattering on the pavement of a large boulevard that ran from downtown into what had once been the surrounding residential area. Lucas's planned departure within a day or two of the victory over the Chinese had proved more aggressive than practical, and he'd reluctantly agreed to stay a week to help the locals organize against a repeat appearance of the Chinese on the horizon, even though he was anxious to get on the road and return to Sierra and his new family.

Art and Lucas had met with the community leaders, such as they were, who'd been of distinctly different mindsets over how best to proceed. The one commonality was that they were all in shock from the intensity of the battle that had cleared the invaders from the city, and were still trying to come to grips with the prospect of sudden self-determination. Art had proposed a city council to act as the steering committee for defense and policing, and Lucas had agreed to meet with some local holdouts who'd rejected the idea of working under a central authority.

He was on his way to see one of the most prominent – a man named Levon, who held sway over a significant area of the inner city and who, before the Chinese had appeared, had successfully held off the gang who'd ruled the town. He'd appeared at the first big meeting with the other leaders and had dismissed any discussion of bowing to the will of a group. Art had tried to make the man see reason, but Levon had stormed off halfway through the summit, and it had only been through Sam's seeking him out at Art and Lucas's urging that he'd agreed to meet again to discuss how to proceed.

"Getting close," Lyle said, glancing around at the run-down buildings.

"Good," Lucas said. "Got better things to do than chase down every gangster in Washington for a powwow."

"I hear you."

Lucas was annoyed at having to delay his return home, and being sent as a peacemaker wasn't improving his mood. Two days had passed since the battle for the city, and Lucas was anxious to be on the move rather than serving as a figurehead for the reestablishment of order in Seattle.

Lyle slowed his horse and leaned toward Lucas. "Up there on the next corner. You can see his lookouts."

Lucas eyed the slouching group and grunted. "Where were they when we were fighting the Chinese?"

"Good point."

They approached the corner, where four young men were lounging on a stoop, fiddling with a variety of assault rifles. One stood as they neared, and Lyle caught his eye.

"We're here to see Levon."

The tough looked Lyle over and shifted his attention to Lucas, who met his stare with one of his own. After a tense moment, the youth pointed down the street. "Next block. Middle building. 218."

Lucas spurred Tango over to where two muscular men were standing with crossed arms outside the shell of a furniture store. The one on the right pointed to a lamppost.

"You can leave the horses here. Levon's waiting for you inside." He eyed Lucas's M4 with a squint. "No guns."

Lucas shook his head, his expression stony. "Nobody touches our weapons. If your boss has a problem with that, we can come back with a thousand heavily armed men to discuss it," he said, quickly tiring of the gangsta bluster. "Go tell him we're here."

The man glowered at Lucas for several beats and then turned to enter the building. A few minutes went by before he returned and faced him again. "Levon says it's okay. Tie the horses there. We'll watch them."

Lucas and Lyle swung down from their steeds and walked them to the lamppost. Lyle cinched his reins to the pole with his free hand. In his other he clutched a vintage Thompson Model 1928 submachine gun he'd used to great effect during the battle with the Chinese.

They entered the building. Levon was seated in the rear, behind a simple metal desk, leaning back in a ragged executive chair. He indicated two seats in front of the desk.

"Sit."

Lyle did as directed, but Lucas remained standing. "Too much time in the saddle. Think I'll keep my legs stretched."

Levon shrugged. "You wanted to talk?"

Lucas nodded. "We want you to think about joining the council so you have a voice."

"Already got plenty of voice around here. I can't see any reason to shuck and jive with those clowns," he replied evenly.

"There's a big one you're missing," Lucas said.

Levon's eyebrows rose. "That right? Do tell."

"Town's going to get civilized whether you like it or not. Has to, in order to fight off the next wave of Chinese when they come. If you're not a part of that, you're against it, and there's way more of us than you."

Levon snorted. "You seem pretty sure of yourself for a guy who rode into town a few days ago."

Lucas refused to let himself be goaded. "And cleared that town of an invasion force nobody else was able to take on. Including you. So the question is, you want to be on the receiving end of that, or part of it? All the same to me either way."

"That a threat?"

Lucas shook his head. "Quite the opposite. It's an invitation to power. Because once the council is organized, that'll be where it lies.

Rogue operators will get mopped up, just like the old days."

"I was around during those days. Not all got mopped up."

Lucas shrugged. "You want to spend the rest of a short life running from the inevitable, that's your call. But you were invited." He looked to Lyle. "We're done here."

Levon shrugged but said nothing.

Lucas threw a final glance at him. "Invitation's open. You want my opinion, you're making a mistake by turning it down. You can help rebuild the city instead of running game on it. That offer won't come up again."

"If I want your thoughts, I'll ask for them," Levon snapped.

Lyle and Lucas walked back to the storefront, their boots crunching on debris, Levon's glare searing into their backs. Outside, Lucas murmured to Lyle, "Friendly, wasn't he?"

"You had to try."

"Sure."

They made their way back to the horses and mounted up. Lucas was turning Tango around when gunfire from a block away shattered the calm. He ducked low in the saddle as several bullets tugged at his trail coat, and a round skimmed his plate carrier at the base of his left ribs. He goaded Tango across the street to where a row of rusting cars would provide some cover. More shots rang out, and Lyle moaned and fell from the saddle, hitting the pavement hard. His horse continued on without him, and Lucas leapt from Tango's back, braced his M4 against a burned-out Suburban, and scanned the street for the shooter.

Movement several hundred yards away caught his eye, and he squeezed off a couple of rounds. He didn't hit anything, but caught a glimpse of a pair of men running to where two horses were standing by an intersection. He took three more shots, and one of the figures fell forward. The other kept going, and Lucas moved to Tango while the gunman was more intent on escaping than on taking another potshot at him.

He remounted and spurred Tango forward, still peering through the scope. The other man was on his animal and tearing away at a gallop, his focus on getting clear of the area rather than shooting it out.

Lucas slowed when he reached the fallen man, who was lying facedown in a lake of blood, his shirt stained red where a shot had drilled between his shoulder blades. After a glance at the man's cheap rifle, he continued along the street, trying to keep the rider in sight. The man's horse turned a corner, and Lucas coaxed Tango faster, eyes fixed on the building behind which the rider had disappeared.

He guided Tango through a snarl of wrecked vehicles that littered the street and slowed as he reached the intersection. When he was a few yards short of it, he pulled Tango to a stop, cocked his head, and listened. Hearing nothing, Lucas dropped from the horse's back and moved to the corner and looked around it. Three blocks down, past yet more wreckage, he saw the rider make another turn and vanish. Lucas swore and climbed back into the saddle, and the big stallion thundered around the corner and down the street in typically fearless fashion, his hooves like hammers on an asphalt anvil as he navigated around the steel detritus of a vanished civilization.

Lucas leaned forward, presenting as small a target as possible, and let Tango run however he liked. When they reached the point where the rider had turned, Lucas repeated his prior dismounting and cautiously studied the unknown area around the corner over the M4 sights. This time there was no sign of the rider – just an endless procession of ruined cars abandoned where they'd gridlocked and run out of gas. Lucas could imagine the scenario as the virus had ravaged the city and panicked survivors had fought to get out, sitting behind the wheel as their tanks had run dry, nothing moving, trapped in a mobile prison of their own devising. He'd seen the same scene countless other places, but for whatever reason, here in Seattle, with buildings stretching as far as the eye could see, he could feel the ghosts of the past weighing heavy in the air.

The distinctive bark of a Kalashnikov rattled from down the street, and chunks of brick blew from the building façade. Lucas pulled back and waited for the shooting to stop. The sound of this rifle was different than the one that had waylaid them, which had sounded more like his smaller bore M4 to his ear, whereas the AK had a deeper tone due to its larger caliber.

There was a lull in the shooting, and Lucas debated his options. Forward lay the unknown – the layout of the streets was a mystery to him, and the identity of the shooters was a question mark. That they'd had the foresight to make a stand here didn't augur well for him, and he could see nothing to be gained by fighting it out. Worse, he had to assume that the longer he stood his ground, the more he was inviting his aggressors to circle back around him, which he would have done in the same situation. That there was more than one gunman was obvious from the two rifle types. The real question was how many more were in the party.

"Come on, boy," he whispered to Tango. "We'll figure out how to get out of this."

Lucas led Tango down the block and steered him left, opting to try a different direction than he'd come. If the ambush were Levon's doing, he didn't want to give the gangster's men another shot at him, and to retrace his steps would have been suicidal. Lyle was dead, and there was nothing waiting back at the furniture store other than a bullet with Lucas's name on it, so he pushed south, moving as quickly as he could, keeping Tango to a slow trot while sweeping the street with his rifle.

At the next corner he made another turn and noted that the neighborhood was degrading further. Remnants of graffiti marred the buildings, and the abandoned cars were older than on the other arteries. Here the empty stores were mostly laundromats and liquor stores and pawnshops, their windows staved in long ago by the desperate and the opportunistic.

He paused at the next street, and seeing nobody, mounted up, the value of stealth now offset by Tango's greater speed and agility. The problem was that while the big horse could move faster than Lucas could ever hope to, he had no idea where he was, and there were no landmarks Lucas could see to guide him back to Art's headquarters.

"All right. Steady, boy," he said with a glance at the sky. Based on the position of the sun, barely visible through a marine haze that hadn't lifted since they'd arrived in the waterfront city, he calculated that headquarters had to be off to the right, so he pressed Tango forward, eyes roving over the broken windows with laser intensity, wary for any hint of threat.

Chapter 5

Sacramento, California

A horse with a single rider leading a pack mule picked its way along the highway to Sacramento's main entry, where a barrier erected by one of the most violent gangs on the West Coast – the Blood Dogs – blocked the road east. Three guards were loitering in the shade of a Greyhound bus that towered among the cars and trucks clogging the road, a tarp strung from its front entrance as a makeshift overhang flapping in the breeze.

The rider approached, and the guards reluctantly rose with their assault rifles in hand to greet him. The road into town was usually deserted. Sacramento was one of the more dangerous enclaves of what once had been civilization, due to the Blood Dogs' dominance over the city, and few were desperate enough to brave the journey over the mountains from Reno or Carson City to see if the gang's reputation was deserved.

One of the men, his face scarred on one side from acid that had been thrown in his face as a last-ditch defense by a victim he was preparing to rape, raised his rifle and leveled it at the newcomer.

"That's far enough," he growled.

The rider held up both hands to show he wasn't carrying a weapon. His rifle was in his saddle scabbard, and the pistol at his hip remained in the holster.

"I'm here to see Amos," he said, naming the gang's leader.

The guard exchanged a glance with the others, and his lips curled into a sneer. "That so?"

The newcomer nodded. "I have business with him."

"What kind of business?"

"That's between me and him."

The guard spit on the ground. "We don't let just anyone into town because they wanna talk to the boss."

"If you're uncertain, send someone to tell him a representative of a powerful organization is here with a proposal. I've ridden a long way to meet with him."

"What organization?"

"One that can change the Blood Dogs from controlling a city to controlling the whole western seaboard."

The guard looked the rider over. He spoke with the certainty of an educated man. His features were lean, his beard jet black but neatly trimmed, and his trail coat was clearly an expensive one, as were his boots and saddle.

"What's in the mule's bags?"

The rider smiled. "If I told you, I'd have to kill you."

The guard's expression hardened and he took a step forward, still training his rifle on the man. "You're in no position to make threats."

"Were you ever in the service?"

The guard frowned, confused by the question. "What's that got to do with anything?"

"It's helpful to know who I'm speaking with."

"Fine. Yeah, I was in the Army for one tour."

"Excellent," the rider said with the trace of a smile. "Then you'll understand the full import of what I'm about to say. Right now there's a sniper with a Barrett who's got you in his crosshairs." The rider noted the look of recognition in the guard's eyes. "I see you know what that is and what it's capable of. So let's make this simple. If you don't lower your weapon, you'll never see your death coming. Same for your friends. If I don't give my man the all-clear signal, or if you fire at me, all three of you are already dead. Do you understand?"

The guard's frown deepened, along with the confusion in his eyes.

He was used to giving the orders, not being handed ultimatums. But the rider was absolutely calm and indifferent in spite of the AK pointed at him, and seemed utterly disinterested in the exchange beyond mild irritation that he hadn't yet been allowed to enter the city limits.

"You're bluffing," the guard spat.

The rider glanced at the two gunmen standing a few steps behind acid face. "Which one of your friends would you like to sacrifice to learn that I'm not?"

The guard on the right shuffled farther back. "Drew, man, I don't think he's bluffing."

"Sure he is. Where could a sniper be hiding?"

The rider nodded as though he'd been expecting the question. "On the roof of one of the buildings by the airport. Perfect line of sight. We got into position last night, and I waited until the shift change to approach you. And now here we are."

Drew sneered again. "That's almost a mile away. Nobody could make that shot." He looked to his companions. "I told you he was bluffing."

The rider sighed. "The Barrett M82A1 fires a .50-caliber round and has an effective firing range of 1800 yards – granted, that's usually for larger targets, like material, but the point is that it can more than reach us. But just in case you think I'm pulling your leg, the building in question is a little less than 1300 yards. The sniper who's got you in his scope's crosshairs has been known to put down smaller targets than your torsos at near the maximum range on a clear day with a light breeze, like...now. So while you're correct that it would be nearly impossible for someone without the proper skills and training, I'm afraid today isn't your lucky day."

He paused and looked over the other guards before returning to Drew. "Let's save one of your chums' lives, shall we? Send someone to alert Amos and pass along my message. Either that, or choose who has to die so you learn that while I have a number of vices, bluffing isn't one of them." He paused, his body language relaxed. "We're wasting valuable time."

"You've got a mouth on you, I'll give you that," Drew said.

"Make your choice. Of course, I can't guarantee that he won't pick you for his first kill. One in three odds, but you're also pointing a gun at me, so maybe not. I suppose there's only one way to find out, right?"

The rider sat motionless in the saddle, watching the guards as the wheels in their heads seemed to grind in slow motion. Eventually one of the other guards walked over to where the horses were tied. "I'll go."

"No," Drew snarled.

"Drew, I'm not getting shot to prove a point. The man wants to talk to Amos; seems like we should let him decide, not you."

The rider dipped his head once in acknowledgment. "A wise decision, I assure you. It's early in the day to have blood on my hands."

"Don't move a muscle," Drew threatened.

"You might want me to signal to the sniper that all's well, unless you want to take the chance he puts a bullet through your skull. Again, it's your call, but that's how I'd play it."

Drew chewed his lower lip and shook his head when a fly landed on the mass of scar tissue that passed for his left profile. "Fine. Do it."

"Certainly. Lower your weapon so he doesn't get the wrong idea, and we'll just wait for your man to return."

Drew did as instructed, but still held the gun so he could fire it in a split second if necessary. The other guard rode away, and the rider reached up and removed his hat, ran gloved fingers through his hair, and then fixed the hat back in place. "That pauses everything. Now we wait."

"It'll be a while," Drew said sullenly.

The rider shrugged. "Rome wasn't built in a day."

The pair stared each other down and then tired of it. Drew's eyes flitted to the buildings by the airport. The rider, if he had a concern in the world, didn't show it and could have been watching someone change a flat for all the emotion he displayed.

"Where you from?" Drew finally asked.

"All over."

"What the hell kind of answer's that?"

"An honest one."

Drew fell silent again, his attempt at an interrogation failed, and resumed sullenly staring at the rider.

The guard returned a half hour later with three more brawny gang members on horseback, their skin bronzed by the sun, their Hispanic heritage obvious from their black hair and features. The biggest of the bunch faced off with the rider and looked him up and down.

"You wasting Amos's time, you got a death wish," he snarled.

"I don't waste people's time."

The thug glared at the rider for several beats and then gave in. "Follow me."

They escorted the rider through a destitute residential area, all the windows broken out and the doors kicked in, and stopped at a shopping mall that was now fortified with gun turrets and hundreds of heavily armed gang members.

"Welcome to the Pleasure Dome," the big gangster said, and swung down from his horse. The rider did the same.

"Where can I tie my ride up?" he asked.

"Over there. The mule too."

The rider smiled good-naturedly and shook his head. "The mule's coming with me. She's carrying gifts for Amos."

"I gotta inspect the bags."

The rider shrugged and held out his hands by his sides. "Fine by me."

The man moved to the mule and unstrapped one of the enormous saddlebags. He opened it and his eyes widened, and then he turned to the rider. "You serious?"

A nod. "Deadly."

"Come on, then."

They entered the mall through double glass doors, and the thug guided the rider and his mule over detritus and the scattered remains of stores to a furniture outlet that boasted a dozen men with assault rifles standing in front of it. They stepped out of the way at the sight of the rider to allow him in. The big man led him to the rear of the store, where an enormous figure with a gleaming bald head and arms the size of tree trunks sat on a sofa, smoking a hand-rolled joint.

"What the hell you want with me?" he barked. "And what's that damn donkey doing in here? Thing smells like ass," he said, and laughed loudly at his joke.

The rider nodded in agreement. "Amos, I presume. My name's Brett. I've ridden from Las Vegas to see you. In those saddlebags you'll find four hundred pounds of gold maple leafs as a token of our seriousness."

Amos's eyes narrowed. "Yeah? Who's *we*?"

"A group you've no doubt heard rumors about. A group that's survived for centuries and is the power behind the throne in all epochs."

Amos took a long drag on the joint. "That so?"

"It is. And I come with a proposal. Tit for tat. The gold is to get your attention. I can offer something far more valuable than coins, though."

"Like what?"

"Victory over your most hated rivals in Stockton, for starters. And after you've vanquished that area, over the rest of the Bay Area."

Amos exhaled a cloud of pungent sweetness. "You must be smoking more of this than me. Where you get your stash? This shit's played."

"I'm serious."

Amos sat back and blew smoke at the ceiling. "How the hell we gonna do that? Stockton's got thousands of fighters. Hard cases. And weapons out the ass. We tried to take 'em three times, and they beat us back every time."

"I can give you their heads on a plate. Access to anything you'll need to win the fourth time."

Amos grinned with good humor that never reached his eyes. "Yeah? Like what, a nuke?"

Brett smiled with similar warmth. "Not quite. But almost as good.

28

The contents of the national guard armory here that was locked down during the collapse."

Amos waved a hand the size of a catcher's mitt. "We've tried everything to get in. Those doors are steel. A foot thick, at least. Maybe more. A torch wouldn't dent it. Neither would explosives."

Brett's smile widened and he nodded again. "Yes. I'm sure they had no effect. But I have the keys."

Amos sat upright, his eyes more alert. He licked his lips and considered his joint before framing his monosyllabic question. "How?"

It was Brett's turn to wave. "That's unimportant. What matters is that I do. Which means that everything inside can be yours."

Amos studied Brett like he was seeing him for the first time. He put the joint in an ashtray and watched the smoke corkscrew into the air. When he spoke, his voice was deadly earnest. "What do you want?"

"We have a problem. You can solve it for us."

Amos blinked. "What kind of problem?"

"Rumor has it that you have a working steam locomotive?"

Amos narrowed his eyes briefly before responding. "That's right. One of my boys used to work on the thing before the collapse."

"Can it haul five thousand men?"

"Where to?"

"Oregon."

"That thing can haul anything. But why? What's going on?"

"We have an enemy in Seattle. We received word from an informant that he's going to try to make it to Salem with a large force. We need him ambushed and his force destroyed. No prisoners."

"Five thousand men's almost my entire crew. It'll leave me defenseless here."

"We're aware of the strength of your group. That's why we're approaching you rather than one of the others. That, and you have the means to transport them quickly. Which makes you extremely valuable to us. As the offering of gold is intended to convey." Brett

29

paused. "Once you wipe out the Stockton gang, you aren't going to have any need for a huge defense force. So that's the priority. Then you take care of our errand, after which we'll help you move on Oakland and San Francisco – you'll be able to leave a group in the Pacific Northwest and take over as much of it as you like." Brett paused and eyed Amos knowingly. "With what's in the armory, Stockton will fall in a day."

Amos grunted. "Okay. You got my attention. Tell me more about this enemy of yours that needs killin'."

Chapter 6

Denver, Colorado

Elijah stared out over his gathered troops. His father's white robe did little to insulate him from the mountain chill, but if the cold affected him, he gave no sign. His call had gone out to all his able-bodied men, and he'd assembled a fighting force nearly two thousand strong, equipped with weaponry and sufficient ammunition to overwhelm anything in its path. Benjamin, an ex-military officer who was his top tactician, was standing by his side in front of the convention center. The plaza before them was filled with humanity, their customary white replaced with clothes more suitable for the trail, and their horses were waiting nearby.

Benjamin cleared his throat and turned to Elijah. "We should probably get moving," he said, his voice as gruff as his features were ruggedly chiseled.

"Yes. Of course. But first, a few words." Elijah stepped forward and stretched his arms to the sides, forming a human cross for effect. "Men! You have answered the call, for which you will be blessed. My father gave his life to create a better world for us, and was rewarded for his efforts by being cut down by cowardly assassins as his plan was coming to fruition. Everyone here knows the story, so no need to belabor the details. Today we embark on a journey of revenge, acting as the sword of God. His wrath will know no bounds – either you are on his side or you are on the side of evil. The cursed members of the cult in what they call Shangri-La demonstrated which side they're on. As servants of the Dark One, they must be punished, and we are the vehicle of punishment."

Elijah paused for effect before continuing.

"We will be traveling to the den where these snakes live to eradicate each and every one of them. There can be no mercy. Our mission is a holy one, a crusade of the righteous against the forces of darkness. You are all, to a man, angels of justice, with the Holy Spirit guiding your bullets home. There can be no higher calling, no more noble pursuit, and I am honored to be riding with you to put an end to this blight on humanity once and for all."

A murmur went up from the crowd, and Benjamin frowned as he leaned toward Elijah. "You're coming with us? Perhaps that isn't the wisest—"

Elijah continued speaking as though he hadn't heard the older man. "You're all making a supreme sacrifice, leaving your families, your loved ones, to bring justice to the miscreants in Shangri-La and put an end to their depraved worship of the prince of lies. Know as you ride that you are all knights destined for eternal reward for your service to the cause. As privileged survivors, it is our duty to root out Satan's toeholds in this world and to right wrongs.

"My father was murdered because these sick animals were frightened of him and all he represented. As light drives out darkness, he was expunging a pestilence that was waiting to sweep across the land, and they could have none of that. So they took his life while he was on the threshold of his greatest triumph." Another hesitation, and when Elijah resumed, his voice was louder and more confident. "That affront to all that's holy will not go unpunished. We are the instruments of the Lord's righteous wrath, and together we will eradicate the blasphemers to the last man!"

A cheer rose from the assembly, and fists thrust into the air at the prospect of the coming bloodshed. Benjamin tried again to get Elijah's attention, but the young preacher seemed entranced by his own rhetoric and was beaming at the troops, oblivious to the military man's discomfiture.

When Elijah turned to Benjamin, there was a manic gleam in his eye. "Wait for me. I need to pack a proper kit. Give me ten minutes."

"I'm not sure the trail is a fitting place for the leader of the church. You're needed here, to guide the flock during these troubled times," Benjamin tried.

"Nonsense. I ride at the head of the greatest army this country's ever seen. That's the true place for a leader, not locked away in some musty building waiting for his men to carry out his wishes."

"But the city—"

"The city will do fine in my absence for a week or two. The church is strong. Have a little faith, Benjamin."

The older man did his best not to show his disapproval, but his effort was wasted – Elijah wasn't paying any attention to him. Elijah spun and entered the church with a hand wave, leaving Benjamin to stare at his billowing white robe with his arms still outstretched, resembling a giant stork trying to take flight as he disappeared into the convention center's depths. The crowd's cheers followed him as he marched into the darkness, and Benjamin swallowed hard.

"All right," Benjamin called out when the clamor had died down. "Everyone should know who their commanding officers are. We'll organize into platoons, and you're to take your orders from the platoon leader, who in turn will report to me. This may seem like a simple exercise, given our number, but for all of you who've never been in combat, there's an old rule that summarizes what you're going to see: there's no substitute for planning, even if a plan is only good until the first shots are fired. We're going to run this operation like a real army, which means organization and discipline, which can save your life. Anyone who's got a problem with that, ride back home now – we won't allow any insubordination once we're on the move."

Benjamin stared at the men, his eyes hard gray in the sunlight, and nodded when everyone remained in place awaiting his next orders. But his stern expression couldn't completely mask his concern over Elijah accompanying them into the wilds and the possible disruption that might cause in the chain of command. The prophet's son had no experience other than orating from the pulpit, and if he chose to insert himself into the decision-making process when it came to battle, it could be disastrous. Benjamin wasn't looking forward to the discussion he'd be forced to have with his leader, but knew that he had no choice but to have it, and the knowledge soured his stomach even as he stood ramrod stiff, a model to his men.

Chapter 7

Seattle, Washington

Lucas paused at a run-down intersection clogged with wrecked cars that had been stripped of anything usable, their tires degraded to the point of disintegration by the sun, and looked around. He'd followed his instinct and made his way down a long straight street, taking his time, alert for any further ambush attempts. After an hour of dodging around the thousands of cars that filled the avenues, if he was any closer to his destination, he couldn't tell. He'd been sure at first that he was making progress, but because of the height of the surrounding buildings, he couldn't see anything to confirm he was close to his headquarters, and he'd grown increasingly frustrated at being hopelessly lost in a city he'd just helped liberate.

"What do you think?" he whispered to Tango, who snorted and shook his head at the question. The big horse had powered along tirelessly, but Lucas would need to get him some water sooner than later – not to mention his own stomach was growling.

Lucas caught movement in an upstairs window just on the periphery of his vision and pressed Tango forward as he ducked down. A shotgun blast reverberated off the gutted storefronts, and the windshield of a Chevrolet truck a few yards behind him exploded in a shower of glittering safety glass. Lucas leapt from the horse and darted into a double doorway and, when there was no more shooting, peered around the brick edge, M4 at the ready.

He scanned the building and spotted the barrel of a shotgun protruding from a second-floor window. Thumbing the firing selector to burst mode, he loosed a couple of three-round bursts at the window, tossed Tango's reins over a bannister, and then sprinted across the street to the building's dark entryway while the shooter was taking cover from his fire.

The interior of the building was dank and reeked of stale urine and rot. Mold had devoured much of the sheetrock walls, and the ceramic tile floor was littered with debris. Lucas took careful steps, avoiding the broken bottles, discarded syringes, and refuse that covered the ground. He stopped at a stairway at the rear that led to the second level, and cocked his head to listen before ascending.

When he could see over the second-floor slab, he eyed the long hall. The apartment doors that lined it had been staved in by looters and left in splinters. He continued up onto the landing with his M4 aimed down the corridor, and froze at the sound of footsteps approaching from one of the rooms. A glance around yielded no ready cover, and he knelt down in a combat crouch, ready to shoot whatever came through the doorway.

A small Asian man wearing little more than rags appeared at the threshold, clutching a cheap pump shotgun. He looked around, obviously agitated, and made for Lucas's position, blind to Lucas in the darkness.

"Drop the gun or I shoot. No second chances," Lucas said when he had the wiry man's torso in the crosshairs.

The Asian froze for an instant and then threw the gun to the side and ran in the other direction. Lucas fired off a burst at the ceiling over the man's head, and he stopped in his tracks, visibly cringing. He slowly pivoted to face Lucas, his hands in the air.

"Please. I…don't shoot."

Lucas straightened. "Anyone else in here?"

"N-no," the man stammered.

"I should return the favor and plug you," Lucas said.

"I…I'm sorry."

"Sorry doesn't cut it when you're trying to back shoot a man," Lucas replied, and walked toward him, rifle trained on his head.

"It…it wasn't personal. I'm…I'm desperate. No other choice."

"Than to shoot anyone on the street?"

The man shook his head. "No. I've been tracking you for six blocks. You're not just anyone. You're the leader of the army. Lucas. There's a price on your head."

Lucas's eyes narrowed. He stopped six feet from the man and studied him. Emaciated, probably late forties to early fifties, with a gaunt look of malnutrition that was all too familiar to Lucas. Hardly a credible threat now that the shotgun was on the floor.

"Turn around and put your hands on the wall. You try to kick me or do anything stupid, I'll put a bullet in you."

The man obliged, and Lucas performed a perfunctory frisking before stepping back.

"I don't have any other weapons," the man said.

"Tell me about this bounty. Who put it out on me?"

The man turned toward him. "I can help you."

"That's not an answer."

"My name's Yi."

Lucas's frown hardened. "Didn't ask. Last time: who put the price on my head?"

"You're in a Chinese gang's territory. Triad-affiliated. They want you dead."

"Why?"

"They're hiding some of the Chinese invasion force. Whether they want revenge for you foiling their plan, or to destroy your army's leadership…does it really matter?"

"How many invaders?"

Yi shrugged. "I don't know for sure. That's just the word on the street. But they want you badly, and they're willing to pay to get you."

"And you thought you'd play bounty hunter?"

Yi nodded again. "I haven't eaten in three days. I…I thought maybe I could get lucky. I said I was sorry."

"You're a lousy shot. And that scatter gun's the wrong tool for the job."

"I'm not an assassin."

Lucas slowly lowered the rifle. "I'll say." He regarded Yi. "So this is some gang's territory? How many more like you are on the street?"

"I'm not part of the gang."

"That's not an answer."

"They'll have watchers on some of the corners. I can help you. I know where they'll be."

"Why so helpful?"

"I need food. And…gold."

Lucas considered the desperate man. "How about I just shoot you and take my chances?"

"That would be foolish. And your army has both food and gold. It's common knowledge."

"You seem to know a lot about me. How did you know I'd be here and not downtown?"

"From a rumor that you were to meet with one of the other warlords. Word went out this morning. They want you dead. Who kills you doesn't matter."

"How much are they willing to pay?"

"Ten ounces of gold. A fortune."

Lucas gave a grim smile. "I suppose I should be flattered."

"I'll guide you to safety for…three. And as much as I can eat." Yi paused. "Please. We can help each other. It will cost you nothing but a token."

Lucas grunted. "You can eat your fill once I'm safely back at our headquarters. You're welcome to stick around if you like and join up – not that you're what I'd call prime material. That's the only offer you're going to get."

Yi's face fell. "No gold?"

"Listen, you little runt. You tried to shoot me. You really expect me to give you a bunch of gold for your trouble?"

"How about two ounces, then?"

"How about a few grams of jacketed lead? You're wearing on me."

It was Yi's turn to frown, and the skin of his face creased like a shar-pei. "Fine. I accept your offer."

"Let's get moving before the gunfire draws company."

"That's not unusual here."

"You lead. I get a whiff of any sort of double cross and you'll be the first to die."

"I won't betray you."

"Move."

Back on the sidewalk, Lucas whistled, and Tango came at a trot from around the corner. Lucas swung up into the saddle, his eyes and gun never leaving Yi. When he was seated, he motioned with the rifle. "Which way?"

"We need to get off this street. They'll have an outpost farther along on one of the rooftops."

"Lead on."

Yi walked ahead and Tango dutifully followed as he rounded a corner onto a smaller artery. They proceeded two blocks before the little man made another left, looking over his shoulder occasionally at Lucas, who was riding behind him. All of the buildings had the same dilapidated appearance, but Lucas could occasionally make out a faded sign with Chinese characters, signaling that they were still in what had once been the outlying area of the International District, now little more than abandoned ruins.

After another turn, a large sporting arena came into view. Lucas was about to ask Yi if he was sure of their direction when shots broke the silence, and divots of concrete sailed through the air to Lucas's right. Yi threw himself behind a car, and Lucas dismounted in a single fluid move and sprinted for the cover of a doorway. Tango galloped away as more gunfire echoed off the asphalt. There were at least two shooters, and they had Lucas pinned down.

Whether it was good fortune or just bad shooting, after half a minute of random volleys, the area quieted. Lucas retreated farther into the doorway, and a slab of plywood an owner had nailed into place buckled when he leaned against it. He put all of his weight on it, and it gave with a crack, and then he was in the building as the assailants wasted ammo on phantoms.

He ran to a stairway and took the steps two at a time. By the time silence had settled over the street again, he'd found an ideal vantage point deep in the recesses of what had once been an office. The window glass had long ago been broken out, offering him a good view of the street from the shadows and a protected area from which to engage his attackers.

Lucas didn't have to wait long. Two Asian men with assault rifles appeared in the entryway of a tenement on the far side of the street, and one of them beelined for where Yi was cowering behind a rusting Chevy. Lucas could hear the gunman shouting at Yi in Chinese and Yi shouting back, pointing along the avenue and motioning with his hands.

Lucas waited until the other shooter was stationary to put a round through his clavicle, and then shifted his aim and stitched three bullets through the second assassin's back before he had a chance to react. Both men dropped to the pavement, one clutching his shoulder, the other already dead. Yi stepped from behind the car, scooped up the second man's rifle, and fired point-blank into the first assailant's head. He repeated the maneuver with the other gunman and set the rifle down before calling out to Lucas.

"You can come out. Only the two of them. But more will be on their way."

Lucas was back on the street in twenty seconds and whistled for Tango again. The stallion was longer in returning this time, and Lucas strode over to where Yi was waiting, his expression unreadable. "I thought you said that you knew this area."

Yi bobbed his head insistently. "I do. They've obviously put more men on the street. We're going to have to keep going south instead of west until we're out of their territory. They'll have concentrated their firepower between here and your camp. So we'd do best to avoid the entire mess."

"I thought that's what we were doing."

"This way."

Yi took off at a run, moving surprisingly quickly for his age and malnourished frame, and Lucas urged Tango to follow him. They traversed a series of small streets, some nearly impassible from rubble and junked vehicles, until the composition of the neighborhood abruptly changed and they were in a more upscale business area, where the buildings were taller and mostly steel and glass.

"Their territory ended two blocks back," Yi explained. "The rest of the way should be safe."

"Why are the locals helping the surviving Chinese?"

"They cut a deal to be able to continue to run things when the invasion force took over."

"But we defeated them."

"True. But they'll send more from China. It's just a matter of time."

To hear Yi confirm what Lucas, Sam, and Art had been discussing sent a chill up Lucas's spine, but his face could have been carved from stone. "They might not find it as hospitable or easy to conquer as the last time now that we know they're coming."

"Maybe," Yi said, but he sounded unconvinced.

An hour passed with no ambushes, and then they were in friendly territory again as they neared a roadblock a quarter mile from Art's headquarters. The sentries waved Lucas through, and the headquarters rose up in front of them. Hundreds of men were milling about, stockpiling weapons and ammunition. Lucas slid from the saddle and handed one of the stable boys Tango's reins, and then walked Yi to the mess tent that was set up in an adjacent park and introduced him to the cooks. He left the little man loading up a plastic bowl with unimaginable quantities of fish stew and rice, and made his way to Art's building to share with him what he'd learned and to formulate a plan to deal with the rogue Chinese gang.

Chapter 8

Stockton, California

Shelling from a hundred Blood Dog mortars began before dawn, taking the Stockton gang by surprise and raining death down onto the outlying defensive positions at the main entry points. Thousands of Blood Dogs had ridden through the night in order to maximize the shock and awe of their offensive, and the first salvos had proven devastatingly effective, catching most of the Stockton warlord's men unawares.

The weapons cache that the Illuminati envoy had made available to the Blood Dogs had made them unstoppable, and between mortars and grenade launchers and anti-tank rockets and large-caliber guns, the Stockton gang was hopelessly outgunned, even if its members were as hard as they came and fought with the desperation of cornered rats. Amos's commanders shelled them relentlessly, and when the visible outposts had been flattened, they directed their squads forward into more aggressive positions within the city limits, where they continued lobbing freight cars' worth of high explosives at the section of town the gang used as its base.

After a half hour of mortar assault, the Blood Dogs switched to more strategic use of the dozens of .50-caliber machine guns they'd liberated from the armory, cutting buildings, vehicles, and gunmen to pieces with solid streams of fully jacketed rounds. The Stockton gang fought without flinching, but by the time the sun was warming the morning sky, hundreds of its members lay dead or dying, with the Blood Dogs pushing their advantage and slaughtering anyone they came into contact with.

Amos's troops were being directed by his top lieutenant, a former serial murderer and rapist named Scott who'd earned a dishonorable discharge from the Marines before embarking on a meth-fueled rampage across four states that had ended in a shoot-out in Sacramento and life behind bars. Scott had demonstrated remarkable abilities in leading his fellow gang members, and had eventually risen to his current position as Amos's second-in-command. He'd led the charge through the Stockton gang's fortifications, toting a machine gun Rambo style, his powerful muscles gleaming with sweat as he gunned down anything in his path.

Scott and fifty of his best men had driven a wedge between two flanks of adversaries and were now powering toward the Stockton gang's headquarters. Gunfire and explosions were roaring around them when their progress was stopped by a pair of machine-gun nests on the rooftops at least five hundred yards down the wide boulevard.

Scott surveyed the impossible crossfire and turned to Rand, his lieutenant. "What's the range on that grenade launcher?" he barked.

"We can't hit them from here. Too far."

"Well, we can't walk directly into their fire, so we need to do something."

As if they'd heard Scott, the enemy gunners peppered the building inside of which the men were hiding, gouging chunks of concrete and brick from the façade. A few of Scott's troops returned fire, but with little hope their small-caliber .223 rounds would do much damage against sandbags.

"We're stopped dead unless we can get them," Scott muttered, and swept the interior before turning to the other man. "Rand, take three of the grenade launchers and work your way along the back side of the buildings until you've closed the gap, and then get up to the roof. Those things will be pretty accurate to about four hundred yards, so you should be able to take the nests out if you can make it any closer."

"Pretty heavy shooting on the back side as well."

"Nothing like out in front. Just do it."

Rand still hesitated, his expression dour. "Nobody lives forever, right?"

Scott glared at him. "I'll kill you myself if you aren't moving in ten seconds."

"Roger that, boss man."

Rand trotted to where the gunners with the six-round grenade launchers were hunkered down, and explained what they'd been ordered to do. Two of the men stood, and a third handed Rand his MGL-140 and a canvas bag with twenty spare grenades. They'd discovered dozens of the lethal devices in the armory and had carted every one to Stockton, along with as many grenades as each gunner could carry. Between those weapons, the mortars, and the heavy .50-caliber Browning machine guns, Stockton was fighting a losing battle, but the Blood Dogs hadn't expected their arch enemies to go easily, and they were living up to expectation. Stockton also had some of the Brownings, although far fewer, and had positioned most of them at the town's perimeter entrances. The ones on the roof were as clear an indication as any the Blood Dogs needed that they were closing in on the Stockton gang's nucleus, which would be heavily defended.

Rand hefted the MGL-140 and moved to the rear of the building. He kicked open the rusting steel door and regarded the alley beyond, and then signaled to his men to follow him as he began making his way along the narrow strip, pausing at abandoned vehicles for cover as the sound of shooting echoed through the area. At the alley mouth, Rand halted and scanned the street before whispering instructions and darting across to another alley that ran perpendicular to the boulevard.

An assault rifle barked from a window in an office building down the block, but none of the rounds hit Rand, and he was safe in the far alley by the time the shooter's magazine ran dry. A typical rookie mistake was to fire on full auto at a moving target in the hopes that more bullets meant a greater chance of a hit, and the shooter had succumbed to the temptation. Rand's men didn't give the gunman a chance to reload, and were already bolting across the pavement by the time the first seconds of silence had passed.

They resisted the urge to waste grenades or ammo on the lone shooter and continued down the alley at a jog, their heavy boots clumping through puddles of murky water as they ran. They reached the next street, and Rand repeated his survey of the area, but this time no gunfire accompanied his zigzagging race to the next block.

When he was sure they'd closed the distance sufficiently for the grenades to be accurate, he began trying doors until one swung open. Rand stepped into the gloom and found himself in what had once been a restaurant kitchen, and he picked his way past steel pots and pans that littered the floor. He pushed through a pair of double doors while his men waited in the kitchen, and then returned with his report.

"There's a stairway by the bar that leads to the second floor. Probably an attic for roof access," he said through gritted teeth.

"No signs of shooters?" one of the men asked.

Rand's expression darkened. "Is this stupid-question day? Get your asses on the roof, and stay low or you'll give our position away. We don't know what the sniper situation is, but they'd be crazy not to have them scattered around."

The men followed Rand up the stairs and up a steel ladder to the roof. He pushed the trapdoor open and waited for shooting and, when none came, peered over the edge at a flat tarred surface with a two-foot rim, providing just enough cover so any gunmen on the other roofs wouldn't see them when they dog-crawled to the lip. He was up and on his stomach in moments, making his way to the far side, which by his reckoning would be the one facing the machine-gun nests.

Rand raised a pair of binoculars, looked over the rim, and easily spotted the targets. The shooters didn't seem to be monitoring the roofs, being too busy strafing the streets below to bother. Rand nudged the closest man and handed him the spyglasses.

"Can you get a range? I'm thinking under four hundred yards, but I suck at reckoning," Rand said.

The man took the glasses and eyed the machine-gun nests. "You don't suck that bad. I'd make it at about three seventy-five, give or take."

Rand took the glasses back and slowly scanned the surrounding roofs. When he didn't see any other nests, he returned his attention to the pair that were guarding the approach to the Stockton gang's headquarters.

"All right. Mark your ranges, and on my count, you take the one on the right, and you the one on the left. Drop a couple each on them and then adjust based on where they hit."

The gunners did as ordered, and when they'd set their sights on the maximum accurate range, Rand set down the glasses to raise his M16 and provide cover if needed.

"All right. Three...two...one...fire!"

The two men squeezed off two rounds, and the projectiles arced toward their targets before falling no more than twenty yards short. The explosions startled the machine gunners, but by the time they'd reacted and swung their guns at their attackers, Rand and his men had fired the rest of their grenades, and the roof around the gunners exploded in fireballs when the projectiles found home.

After ten seconds, the smoke cleared and they could see that the sandbags had been obliterated and the shooters' bodies were strewn across the rooftops, the machine guns ruined. Rand glanced over his shoulder at the trapdoor. "Let's get out of here and tell Scott we're in business."

They returned to where Scott and his men were hunkered down, and broke the good news. Scott offered an ugly grin that a pucker of scar tissue made even more menacing.

"Good. Let's hit them while they're trying to regroup. The loss of the machine guns is going to freak them out. Those things would have stopped us cold before we got the grenade launchers. That was probably their secret weapon on headquarters defense." He held Rand's gaze for a moment. "Send a runner back to the main group and get another couple of hundred men here now. It's time to do this for real."

Rand was gone no more than twenty minutes, and when he returned, he did so with a swarm of Blood Dogs, all equipped with new gear from the armory. Scott explained to the squad leaders how he planned to approach the Stockton headquarters, and when everyone understood his strategy, they split off to make their final push.

The blocks leading to the headquarters were heavily defended, and Scott's men used up most of their grenades and mortars pummeling the gunmen who opposed them. The fighting raged through the morning, but by the time the sun was high overhead, the headquarters was ablaze and the Stockton leadership had been slaughtered like dogs on the steps.

When it was obvious that the battle was lost, the surviving fighters surrendered with the promise that they wouldn't be killed if they joined their rivals from Sacramento and swore loyalty to the Dogs. Most chose life over summary execution, and by the day's end the town was securely under Blood Dog rule, thousands of their adversaries having died defending their stronghold in vain. The locals labored under their new masters' watch to drag the corpses to a central square, where they were stacked like cordwood in a massive funeral pyre and set ablaze in order to avoid the disease that would accompany leaving the city an open cemetery.

Amos watched the burning pile of humanity with Scott and his other lieutenants by his side, and nodded in approval as the sky filled with the nauseating stench of searing flesh.

"Smells like pork, doesn't it?" he commented to nobody in particular, and then flashed a grin. "Looks like our new friend was right. Let the men have their way with the town tonight, but tomorrow we head back home and repay our benefactor with a trip to Oregon. Leave a skeleton crew here to watch over the prisoners until we're sure which are dependable, and plan on being on the road by first light."

The men took off to relay Amos's orders to the gang. They'd lost fifteen percent of their fighters, but considering the victory, it had been a worthwhile cost. Amos was now the sole ruler in the northern central valley, still with nearly five thousand capable fighters under his command.

He watched his lieutenants leave, and the twisted grin tugged at his lips again as he inhaled the rank putrescence of burning flesh. With the Illuminati's help he was unstoppable, and soon he would count the entire Bay Area and the Pacific Northwest as his territory – a prize that would have been unimaginable a week ago now within his grasp.

Chapter 9

The hall Art had selected for the meeting with his officers to discuss the future was filled with armed men, and the testosterone and manic energy of the group was palpable. Art and Lucas were seated on a polished wooden stage where natural light was filtering through a skylight, with Sam and his Salem contingent grouped in front and the Newport fighters beside them. The hall was packed to the rafters, and Art had notified the new Seattle city council that he wanted to have a special meeting following his logistical one.

Art was fielding questions from the men, inviting them to speak up and be heard. The overwhelming message was that the Salem and Newport groups were anxious to return home now that they'd been victorious against the Chinese.

Art gestured for quiet and fixed one of the Newport contingent with a hard stare. "I'm afraid it's not as simple as we all just go home. Aside from the fact that we have an opportunity to reclaim our country from the miscreants who stole it from us, we have a very real issue with the nuclear plant that's gone Chernobyl."

"What about it? Salem isn't anywhere near it, and neither is Newport," someone called from the back.

"Good question." Art rubbed a hand over his face. "We've talked to some people with scientific backgrounds, and the news isn't good. It's melting down, and it'll continue to do so for way longer than any of us will be alive. What that means is that the river will poison the ocean, and the entire coast will eventually become uninhabitable. I won't bore everyone with the implications for the Pacific ecosystem. Let's just leave it at the future doesn't look good."

"What can we do to stop it?" another voice called.

"Nothing. We don't have the technology or the know-how. But even if we did, there's not a lot we can do. Look at that one in Japan – Fukushima. It's been dumping three hundred thousand gallons of radioactive water into the ocean a day for years, and they'd been trying forever to come up with solutions before the collapse. So the bottom line is all we can do is predict how fast the West Coast will become uninhabitable. The guys I talked to said the currents carry the radiation south, so even someplace like Newport isn't going to be safe for long."

"How about Seattle?"

"It should be okay for now, but eventually it's going to get hit too. The damage to the Pacific will mean no fish, and some of the radiation will make it north. It's all just a matter of time. It could be okay for one year, or ten, but make no mistake – it's not going to survive forever." He sighed. "Having said that, I was also told that it's impossible to predict with any accuracy how long the city has. The experts suggested regular testing of the ground water and the Sound, which seems like a good idea. That way the locals will get plenty of warning as things start to go bad." Another pause. "The bigger deal is radioactive rain. It's going to poison a lot of Oregon and Washington."

"Rain? How does it get radioactive?" someone from Sam's group called out.

"When the river water and radioactive ocean water evaporate into the atmosphere, the radiation doesn't just vanish. It's still there, and when it rains, the showers will be radioactive. The only way to avoid all this is to relocate from Newport and Salem, just like Portland did. There's no other way. I'm sorry. I wish I had better news."

"So what are we supposed to do? Move everyone to the middle of the country? That's crazy."

Art's expression softened for a moment. "That's about the only option other than dying of radiation sickness. Look, maybe Seattle will be safe for twenty more years. Or two more months. We don't have the equipment and models to know with any certainty. But the rain issue is real, and it's eventually going to affect everything within a few hundred miles of the coast. Don't shoot the messenger. I'm informing you so you know what we're dealing with, not making recommendations. All I ask is that you discuss it among yourselves and come up with some options you can live with. I would recommend moving your families to somewhere safe, but these days it's hard to say that anywhere is totally risk-free."

Art wound up the questions after patiently answering a dozen or so more, and then motioned to Lucas, who replaced him center stage.

"Got to admit, leaving sounds pretty appealing," Lucas began. "It's no secret I want to get back on the road. But we're not quite done here yet. Appears we have some Chinese stragglers who're hiding out with a gang, and word is that they're expecting another boatload – sooner than later." His gaze bored into the audience. "We can't just ride off and leave the locals to be slaughtered by the next batch. We need a plan, or all of this will have been for nothing."

Sam cleared his throat. "Sounds like the place is going to melt down anyway. Why not just leave it, like Portland? Let the gang and their buddies fry?"

"As Art made clear, that could take a generation or more. In the meantime they'll terrorize the residents and, whenever the Chinese make a reappearance, will actively work to help them take over the city. From there they'll spread east, and nobody will be safe.

"So as I see it, there are a couple of things we need to do before we can leave. The first is help the locals organize a real defense force that can drill to defend the city whenever the next invaders show up. We can work with the new city council to organize it and decide who it reports to. But we'll also need to take down this Chinese gang before they sense weakness and start guerilla attacks."

Lucas paused and regarded the front row. "Word is there's a price on my head, so this isn't an empty threat. Only reason they'd want to take me out is to hobble us. Same for Art – it's a given they've put one on him, too. That can't stand. So we're going to have to go after them."

"It's not just the Chinese," Sam agreed. "We've been hearing reports of attacks from the outlying neighborhoods."

"Right. So we have to send a clear message that we're not going to tolerate that, and we're going to stand by the council until they've got it under control. I have a feeling if we eradicate the Chinese, word will spread pretty fast, and things will settle down."

"So…we're not leaving yet?" Sam asked. "I kind of miss Salem, Lucas. Not that Seattle isn't…whatever."

"I'm with you there. But no, we have to knock out these two problems, and then we'll hit the trail. Which brings me to another point: we've now got almost six thousand troops, which is going to be hell to feed once we're on the move. That means we need to plan our route and send advance scouts to forage and pick sites to camp. A group this size is going to attract a lot of attention, and we can't depend on local help for supplies. We have to be self-sufficient or we'll bog down before we get anywhere. Art and I have been discussing it, and he's got some good ideas. Next meeting he'll go through them with you, so we can work on implementation."

Art nodded from his seat. "That's right."

Lucas drew a long breath. "If nobody's got any more questions for now, let's get the council in here and have a powwow. Everyone below the rank of captain can go. We don't need a full house for their meeting."

The majority of the men rose and filed out, talking in hushed tones as they left. Lucas knew that the news about the western seaboard becoming a toxic wasteland had shaken the group, but they needed to understand what they were dealing with, and there was no point in sugarcoating the situation, which was dire and getting worse.

The council members entered and took their seats, and Lucas's eyebrows rose when Levon strode in moments later and joined them. Levon tipped his hat to Lucas and took a seat at the end of the row, arms crossed, his expression serious.

Art rose and walked to the front of the stage. "Everyone, thanks for coming. We have a lot to discuss, so let's get to it. The main issues we need to tackle today are setting up a defense force and a functioning law enforcement arm, which will probably be the same group. And we need to alert you to the latest findings on the nuclear plant that's poisoning Oregon."

Two hours later, a tall man named Eric had been named the commander of the self-defense force, due to his armed forces background and willingness to take on the job. The first order of business would be to assemble several hundred recruits to serve as the city police and put a stop to the robberies and assaults that had been increasing since the Chinese had been defeated, and then to grow and equip a militia that would be able and willing to stave off an invasion.

When the meeting broke up, Levon approached Lucas, hands on his hips. "Heard you ran into some trouble."

"Lost a good man," Lucas said.

"If there's anything I can do to help with the Chinese, let me know. I thought about what you said, and it made sense. I appreciate your coming to talk to me. And I'm sorry your man got killed."

"What do you know about the Chinese gang?" Lucas asked.

"They keep to themselves. Our guys don't talk to theirs. You could say it's more like mutually assured destruction than any kind of cooperation. They got their territory and we got ours."

"We need intelligence on them."

Levon nodded. "I can nose around, but you'd do best to get one of their own to do it. Someone who won't stand out." He laughed humorlessly. "None of my boys can pass for Chinese."

"Don't suppose they could," Lucas agreed. "See if you can find anything out, and I'll put out some feelers. Between us we might be able to locate their headquarters."

"Yeah, might. They're smart, though, so they move it around. It won't be easy."

"Don't suppose anything is these days."

Levon nodded again and turned to go.

"You made a good call," Lucas said.

"Guess we'll find out," Levon replied, and then marched from the hall without looking back, leaving Lucas and Art standing by the stage with their entourage.

Chapter 10

Sacramento, California

Amos and Scott crossed a wide street and continued to what had once been the train station, where a swarm of men was busy loading a long row of railway cars with guns, ammunition, and provisions. Thousands of fighters were seated around the platforms or leaning against the walls, waiting as the loaders went about their work. Heavy wheeled carts packed high with crates fresh from the armory waited by the boxcars, and crews of laborers hoisted them into the boxcars, their torsos slick with sweat. Amos watched the activity with an approving gaze and turned to Steve.

"How much longer?"

"We should be ready to get underway within the hour."

"And we're sure that the engine will make it to Oregon?"

"Our engineer says it shouldn't be a problem. The coal carrier holds enough for a five-hundred-mile range, and the water tank almost two. There are rivers along the way where we can pump it full and coal-fueled power plants, so it's a done deal, assuming the tracks are intact."

"And if they aren't?"

"No reason to believe they won't be. But we're bringing tools in case someone sabotaged them. Although to what end?"

"We don't want any surprises."

"Which is why we're taking precautions."

"How long will it take to make it to Salem?"

"Depends on how hard we want to push the engine. Caution says a couple of days, tops. The slower we run, the more efficient the coal and water burn."

Amos nodded, and they walked along the platform. The working men scampered out of their way as they approached. "How many cars can the engine pull?" Amos asked.

"Between fifty and seventy if we take it easy. The thing's over a hundred years old, but the museum kept it well maintained for tourist rides, so it's in good shape."

Amos licked his lips. "Who would have believed ten years ago that the only reliable transportation would be an old steam engine?"

"I know. We're just lucky we have someone who used to work on it. Otherwise it would take weeks to make it to Salem."

The Blood Dogs had used their possession of a fully operational steam engine to expand their reach beyond the city limits, and ran it on trading trips up and down the line for a hundred miles. But that was hauling only a few cars of goods. This was a completely different trial, carrying five thousand troops and their weapons and supplies, and Amos was concerned that the weight would be too much for the locomotive.

"We're positive it can handle it?" he asked again when they arrived at the engine.

Scott called to a man who was turning a valve in the cockpit. "Clark? Get down here. Amos has some questions."

The man straightened, wiped his face with a stained bandanna, and dismounted from the engine. "What can I do for you, boss?"

Amos studied his lined, sunburned face and weathered skin. Amos had met Clark a few times, but only in the course of him issuing orders – they'd never had a discussion.

"You sure that this thing can make it north without any problems, with all the weight?"

Clark patted the black side of the engine. "Hell yes. I've kept her up. We'll have to be careful on speed and coal consumption, but she'll get 'er done."

"There are a lot of cars."

Clark shrugged. "Fifty-eight. But in the old days, this baby hauled ore, so we know she can take it. Not saying it'll be easy, but where there's a will…"

Amos squinted at him. "If you're wrong, I'll have most of my men stranded hundreds of miles in hostile territory. I don't need to tell you who I'll blame if that happens, do I?"

Clark's expression hardened. "I'm not wrong. I'd bet my life on it."

Scott cleared his throat. "Sounds like you just did."

Clark's grin was skeletal. "The engine won't let you down. Neither will I."

Amos clapped a hand on Clark's shoulder. "You pull this off and you'll have a blank check. Anything you want. But if you don't think you can do it, speak up now."

Clark studied his boots before meeting Amos's stare. "We'll make it."

Amos grunted and turned away. "Then don't let me hold you up. We've got a date we don't want to miss."

It would take three days to get to their destination, assuming all went well, and the Illuminati messenger had pushed Amos to mobilize his men as quickly as possible. After taking Stockton, the preparations had been accelerated until a force of five thousand fighters was ready for a foray into the unknown.

The loading continued, and when the innumerable weapons crates were secured in the boxcars, Scott directed a shrieking whistle at his subordinates, who began herding the fighters onto the carriages, a hundred on cars designed to comfortably accommodate fifty. When they were filled to capacity, fighters began climbing the sides and taking up position on the roofs, assault rifles slung over their shoulders. Last to go on the two ancient livestock cars at the rear of the train were sixty horses – the maximum the locomotive could safely carry.

Clark ordered one of the two men in the cab to continue shoveling coal into the furnace – a process that would repeat every fifteen seconds for the trip in order to keep the steam steady and sufficient to pull the load. He checked the pressure gauges and wiped them with his sleeve, and then jerked on a rawhide cord. The train whistle's wail pierced the air, and the old engine's steel wheels spun on the track for a moment before gripping with a tortured screech of metal on metal.

At first nothing seemed to happen in the slow-motion tug-of-war, and then, inch by inch, the long line of cars began easing forward. Black smoke belched from the locomotive's smokestack. Clark yelled at the firemen to shovel coal faster, and the string of carriages slowly moved away from the platform.

Amos watched the train trundle down the tracks until it disappeared, leaving a contrail of smoke in its wake, and made his way to the depot exit, his brow furrowed. The Illuminati man had made incredible promises, which so far he'd kept, but Amos couldn't help but wonder just how irreplaceable he was in the organization's scheme. He ran a major metro area, but being a successful local warlord hardly qualified him to run a whole swatch of the country, and he wasn't kidding himself that he wasn't merely a means to an end for them.

Which didn't bother him. Amos was pragmatic and had low expectations from the world. That he'd managed to climb to the top of a pile of corpses and plant his flag as the ruler of the Northern central valley had pleasantly surprised him, but it didn't mean that he trusted the Illuminati messenger any more than he would a venomous snake. Once his army had slaughtered the enemy force from Seattle, his usefulness to them would largely be over, and he fully expected some sort of betrayal, although he couldn't see what it would be. But years of hard-learned lessons in prison had taught him that trust, faith, and hope were useless contrivances that predators used to their advantage against the weak and vulnerable, and he had no plans to join their ranks.

His big vulnerability now was that he'd only kept a few hundred fighters to maintain order in Sacramento and Stockton, so until his men got back from Oregon, it would be laughably easy for one of the big Bay Area gangs to overthrow him. Stockton would remain in a state of uneasy flux until any of that gang's loyalists among the locals had been flushed out, but the men he'd stationed there would get the job done – he'd left some of his best in charge. He wasn't terribly worried about Sacramento's civilians rising up against him; after years of terrorizing them, they had no will to fight left.

Which left only the chore of tightening up the possible exits from the city, where a disloyal informant could slip through and make it to the Bay Area to alert his enemies there that he was virtually defenseless. He'd have to impose a curfew so nobody was on the streets at night, and devote all of his resources to patrolling to enforce it, as well as to ensuring that the roads west were impassable.

Two things that were well within his capabilities, even with a skeleton crew.

Brett had disappeared east after Amos had committed to sending his men to tackle the Seattle group; the Illuminati had received a broadcast that they were planning to leave shortly and travel to Salem. The plan was to ambush them as they approached Salem and wipe them out, although Amos would leave the actual logistics to Scott once he scouted out the lay of the land. The Illuminati man had convinced Amos that the Seattle group would be tired after the long slog from Washington, while his men would be well rested and garrisoned in Salem, so it would be an easy victory, especially considering the armaments they now had.

Amos wasn't so sure of the inevitability of the outcome, but the win in Stockton had emboldened him, and he saw no way to reject the messenger's offer. How it actually turned out was another matter. In Amos's experience, no plan was foolproof, and when dealing with an armed force of unknown size, assuming that victory was assured would be dangerously stupid.

But Scott was the best he had, and if anyone could defeat Seattle, he was the man.

Amos just hoped he'd chosen wisely. If not, his hold on the valley would come to a decisive and ugly end.

Chapter 11

Elliot sat by a smoldering campfire with his advisors, obviously tired, his face creased with fatigue. The discussion had been ongoing since Arnold and Julie had rescued Eve, but now that an enemy patrol had made it to their enclave, Elliot's sense of urgency had mounted. He'd called this meeting to decide whether to stay and defend their camp or go in search of something else.

It was obvious that nobody wanted to uproot and move if they didn't have to, but with Denver capable of raising a large army, Elliot was increasingly convinced that they had no choice.

"Look, I understand everyone's reluctance," he said. "But no matter how well defended we are, we're not going to be able to counter a sustained attack by thousands. It would be the end of us, no matter how heavy the damage we were able to inflict. And there are the women and children to consider."

Arnold spoke up from across the fire pit. "We have to assume they're going to come at us hard, which means an army. Elliot's right. It would be a massacre."

Elliot nodded. "So the question isn't whether we need to move. It's really where to go. It has to be something sustainable through the winter and hopefully hospitable and defensible enough that we can put down real roots for good. Now that we've completed our vaccine distribution, secrecy isn't as much of an issue, so it's more about the best candidate area than anything."

After another half hour, a decision was made to make an overture to the inhabitants of the most promising location: Provo, Utah.

Edwin, one of the Shangri-La scouts who had been chartered with distributing the vaccine, had traveled there recently and had nothing but heartening reports about how the survivors were thriving. He described his two weeks among the population, and his report was passionate and glowing – it sounded perfect, not the least of which was its proximity to the Provo River and Provo Lake, both of which had abundant fish, and which the scout said provided water for numerous agricultural projects the survivors had undertaken since the collapse.

While it was 350 miles from Shangri-La, the distance could be traveled in under three weeks, and the highway west was said to be in reasonable shape. The area was one of the few that hadn't been taken over by criminal warlords or fanatical despots, although it was deeply religious and what served as the government was guided by faith, although not in any destructive manner.

The problem would be gaining the population's approval to integrate into the city. The scout had been welcomed due to his precious cargo, and had been impressed by the community's tolerance and openness, but he'd also seen numerous travelers turned away and discouraged from setting up camp nearby. The city council was jealously protective of what they'd built, and didn't relish outsiders introducing problems or conflict.

"Don't get me wrong," Edwin said. "They're not aggressive or militant, but they do have a hell of a militia, and they're well trained and serious. It would be impossible to force ourselves on them – we'd have to get the council's approval to settle there. I talked to some of the members when I was with them, and they at least seemed open to the idea, if not excited about it." He hesitated and looked around the gathering. "But Provo's got a lot going for it, as I've said. Worst thing are the winters, but compared to what we've been through, it would be like a Hawaiian vacation."

Arnold suggested sending Duke along with Edwin to propose a move to the residents, and Elliot could see no negative other than the amount of time it would take to travel to Utah.

"I'm sure we'll be able to find a radio once we've reached Provo," Edwin said. "We know they've got some – there are a few operators we've spoken with, who helped coordinate the vaccine distribution."

The meeting adjourned, and Elliot made for his office cabin, where the radio transmitter was set up. He had his operator send a coded transmission every half hour on the channel Duke had been asked to monitor, and as night fell, Duke replied, speaking in veiled language and using the substitution cypher they normally employed. Elliot conveyed to him that he wanted him to travel to Provo and make an overture for relocation, and that the scout would meet him at a strategic point on the route through the mountains.

"When do you want me to go?" Duke asked.

"We had an unexpected visit a little while ago, so it would probably be best to make it a priority. Our friend will be waiting for you within two days at the coordinates." Elliot paused. "Did you move your enterprise?"

"10-4. Up the road a spell."

"Might want to warn your partner about our uninvited guests."

"You read my mind."

When Duke signed off, Elliot knew that he would unscramble the name of his destination as well as the spot where the scout would be waiting, and would be en route at first light. He was glad that Duke had taken the prudent step of relocating, as he'd indicated he'd been contemplating, but was concerned that he might be steamrollered when the Denver cult powered toward the hot springs.

Elliot exited the cabin and inhaled the crisp mountain air. He paused and looked around at the dwellings that his compatriots had created with little more than their hands and the sweat of their brow. The outpost was a remarkable achievement, and he felt no small twinge of remorse at having to ask everyone to undertake yet another dangerous and lengthy trek. But there was no other alternative he could see. Staying and making a last stand was out of the question, even though a vocal minority was in favor of it – mainly the younger men who'd survived the battle with the Crew and believed themselves to be bulletproof and invulnerable now that the horror of the rout had faded. Elliot had a more accurate memory of that engagement and remembered like yesterday how it had claimed many of their best.

Regardless of the bravado of the young bulls, his job was to herd his flock to safety, not to lead them to slaughter.

He just hoped that they would have time to make the move without leaving obvious tracks, like they'd managed on the trek from Pagosa Springs. The problem now was that their number had been radically reduced from the fight with the Crew, and some of his most capable trackers had perished – and trackers were the best at covering the signs of passage since they knew what would give them away to others.

He exhaled and stretched his arms over his head, and then set off for his modest dwelling for a simple meal of rabbit stew and spring water. Later, he wound up tossing and turning through the night, pursued by unforgiving demons of his past and the specter of an uncertain future.

Chapter 12

Galveston, Texas

Six figures skulked in the gloom near an old beachfront hotel, now partially in ruins, the area dimly aglow from faint moonlight. Wood smoke from cooking fires lingered on a light breeze as they made their way toward the antique building on foot. Their horses trailed behind them, led by the last in the group. Occasional distant gunshots interrupted the night calm, but that didn't slow the men, their hats pulled low over their brows, AK-47s carried with easy familiarity.

A voice called from the darkness. "Stop and identify yourselves."

The leader of the group, a heavyset man with swarthy skin and a thick black mustache, paused. "Julio and amigos. Here to see Wink," he said in heavily accented English.

"Lower your weapons."

The group did, and four heavily armed men in leather vests appeared from the darkness, rifles trained on the group. "No weapons inside. You can leave them with us. We'll watch your horses."

Julio exchanged a glance with the man beside him and shrugged. "Sure."

One of the gunmen approached the group and collected the assault rifles. "Pistols too."

Julio sighed and handed over a gold-plated Colt 1911. The others

64

followed suit, and when they'd tendered their guns, Julio smirked. "We done? We've ridden a long way."

"He's in there," one of the guards said, indicating the hotel with the barrel of his rifle.

The group trouped into the old building and followed the faint glow of torchlight to what had once been the hotel's main conference room.

"Grab a seat," a big man with hair close cropped to his skull said from behind a desk the size of a grand piano.

Julio did as instructed, and the others pulled up chairs around him, facing the speaker, whose face was heavily tattooed with prison ink, his left eye a sightless white orb in a puckered socket.

"Señor Wink," Julio said, "an honor to finally meet in person. Your messengers have been most efficient, but it's always better to eliminate the middleman, no?"

Wink nodded. "Likewise. So you thought over my proposal?"

Julio looked at his companions and allowed himself a small smile beneath his moustache. "We have. It is most intriguing. But we have several questions that your messengers were unable to answer satisfactorily."

"Well, now's a good time to field them," Wink said evenly.

"The most obvious is, how do we know that you have the influence and the manpower to succeed in your attempted coup?"

Wink nodded again. "Reasonable question. Look, I was one of the top dogs under Magnus. For years I ran half of Houston for him, so I know everybody. I've been talking to my former buddies for months, and they're ready to get rid of Snake. He's a loose cannon and he's way out of his depth. He's a liability to the Crew, and anyone with a brain knows it. Once this starts, most of the gang will side with me. Thousands of men are all fed up."

"Yes, we've heard this from your messengers. But how can we know it's all true? No disrespect intended."

"Check on me. Ask around. I may be stuck in Galveston now, running a nothing backwater, but my history's well known."

"We have. That's why we're here."

"You'll just have to take my word for it at the end of the day. I have at least two hundred men here who are loyal to me. I have ten times that number in Houston who would help me once it's obvious what's going down."

"You've asked us for logistical support – men and weapons. Why, if your base is so sound?"

"There will be pockets of undecided fighters. I want them to be completely overwhelmed. I don't have enough men here to accomplish that. It'll be a chain reaction. First, we make our move. Most will hold back on choosing a side, waiting to see who's likely to win. When they see the Snake loyalists being butchered, it'll make deciding to back me way easier."

The cartel leader grunted. "Assuming we do this, we have some conditions."

"As I expected you to."

"If we dedicate a thousand men to your fight, when it is over, we will have final say over major decisions. And we will take half of all profits. That will leave you at the head of the Crew, but part of a bigger group. Our cartels run Mexico, have taken El Paso, and are positioned to take over the other key border towns. Between your gang here and in Louisiana, and ours controlling everything south of the border, we'd effectively be running an area the size of a country. We have decades of experience doing so. You don't." Julio paused. "That's our condition. You become part of our group, although you continue to be the Crew to outsiders."

"Why would I give up half of everything?" Wink snapped. "That's loco."

"No, it isn't. You can't achieve this without our support. We both know it. That's why you've been trying to get us to back you for months. So let's just understand that if we help you take over the Crew, you wouldn't be there unless we got you there. Our percentage isn't negotiable. It's all or nothing."

"And if I say no?"

"We'll continue to take your territory, and if you ever manage to pull this off, we won't be giving it back. You'll be our enemy, not an associate. And we deal harshly with adversaries."

"That sounds like a threat."

"It is a statement of fact. We took El Paso, and your group has been unable to get it back. We own it now. We move around Texas as we like, and the Crew forces can do nothing to stop us. Your men lack leadership. Distrust is common, as are petty rivalries. We have no such problems. It is just a matter of time until we have a hundred percent of your territory. But we're willing to allow you to keep half in order to accelerate the process."

Wink considered the men in front of him without expression. Unlike many of the top Crew bosses, he'd gone to college and had only turned hard once behind bars after a triple homicide when one of his drug deals had gone wrong. As a cartel-affiliated importer of meth, heroin, and cocaine, he'd built up a distribution network that cleared seven figures a month, but it had all fallen apart when he'd been the victim of a sting operation by the Houston police. When he and his men had gunned down three undercover cops as the deal came apart, he'd been caught dead to rights and imprisoned on death row, where he'd turned to prison ink and bodybuilding to pass the time.

A jailhouse fight before he'd been sentenced had blinded him in one eye, and the authorities had added on the death of his attacker to his toll. He'd been fond of joking that they could only fry him once. He'd become close with Magnus while on the row, and that had carried into the new world when the collapse had resulted in the prisons emptying. Wink had been one of the most loyal of the Crew's founders...until Snake had seized power and banished him to Galveston, out of the way and far enough from the seat of power to not be a threat.

Now that idiot was destroying everything Wink and Magnus had built. That couldn't stand.

Wink weighed the option he was being presented. The Crew would be relegated to the U.S. operating arm of the cartels, effectively taking orders from them and paying tribute. But the cartel boss was right – it was just a matter of time until the more powerful and aggressive Mexicans took by force what they were offering to Wink as a concession, and paying him what amounted to a management fee for operating their domestic franchise.

While his ego hated the idea, was it really so bad? The alternative was remaining the commander of a fishing town with a limited future that was an afterthought to Houston, and which would eventually cease to be even a faint satellite of real power.

"Half is excessive," Wink replied.

Julio grinned. "You don't have to accept fifty percent. We can always take more."

Wink laughed. "How soon could you get your men into position?"

"Two days."

Wink swallowed hard and fixed the cartel chief with his good eye. "You drive a hard bargain, but I agree."

"The rumors about you are true. You are a smart man." Julio sat back. "Now we discuss your plan. Tell me, my friend, how do you plan to unseat this Snake, who from what I understand is surrounded by guards and is paranoid about his own shadow?"

"More than half his men would gladly string him up and set him on fire. We just need to create a suitable diversion, and then we can flush him out of his headquarters in the confusion. Simultaneously, your men will attack specific points throughout the city, which I'll identify for them. It'll be over before it even starts."

"This diversion. What do you have in mind?"

It was Wink's turn to smile. "Something that will stop his guard contingent in its tracks and have them chasing their own tails while we overrun the building."

They discussed Wink's plan for an hour, and by the time the Mexicans left, an agreement had been reached. Two days later Snake would cease to be, and Wink would take his rightful place as the head of the Crew – even if it had been gutted by the cartel, still a position of considerable power that would enable Wink to live a life that would have been the envy of medieval royalty.

Wink looked around the dingy conference room and exhaled heavily. His exile was almost over, and with it his humiliation. He was sick to his stomach at being in charge of a place that stank of fish and decay, whose only value was as a food source for Houston. That Wink had been relegated to a position as insulting as this spoke to Snake's lack of judgment, as well as his vindictiveness.

For Wink, vengeance would taste as sweet as honey and would be worth the stiff price the Mexicans had demanded, he was sure.

"Bart! Bring me a bottle of the good stuff!" he called through the doorway, and sat back with his eye closed, imagining Snake's charred remains hanging from the rafters of the church the Crew used as its headquarters. The vision brought a smile to his lips, which he had to muster all his willpower to erase when his assistant entered with a scratched bottle of locally brewed rum.

Chapter 13

Seattle, Washington

Lucas strode through the interior of the hospital that was being used as the medical triage area for those wounded in the battle with the Chinese invaders. He'd asked at the mess tent for Yi and been directed to the hospital, where the little man had been put to use tending to the injured.

Even with a fair number of personnel with medical backgrounds, judging by the looks of the casualties, many wouldn't make it. They'd been administered antibiotics, and those with the most grievous injuries had been given transfusions from neutral donors who'd volunteered their fluids, but there were limitations that even a reasonably well-equipped surgical suite couldn't overcome, and the rooms he moved through reeked of rotting flesh and death.

Clouds of black flies colored the air like inky smoke when he entered a large hall where the wounded lay on cots like cordwood, attended to as well as the nurses could manage. Moans and racking coughs greeted him as men drifted in delirium. He couldn't move through the area quickly enough, his gag reflex triggered by the time he made it to the far exit.

A hatchet-faced man looked up at him from where he was transferring fluid from a bottle to a large pot. Lucas nodded to him.

"Pretty grim in there," Lucas observed.

"I wish I could say you get used to it, but I'd be lying."

Lucas glanced over his shoulder at the ward and then back at the man. "I'm looking for a Chinese guy who's supposed to be helping here as an orderly. Older, smallish fellow. Name's Yi."

The man's brow furrowed. "Yeah. Sure. Little guy. Doesn't talk much. He's out in back. Just ducked out a few minutes ago."

"Much obliged."

Lucas worked his way to the rear exit, past a row of cadavers in body bags, and gratefully breathed in the fresh air as he burst through a pair of double glass doors to what had once been a loading zone. Yi was helping a muscular Hispanic man at the far end heave body bags onto a wheeled cart fashioned from the rear bed of a pickup truck, with a pair of mules tethered to it.

The little Chinese man looked up at Lucas, who waved him over. Yi said something to his companion and walked over to where Lucas was standing in the shade of the overhang.

"See you're making yourself useful," Lucas said.

"The food's good, and the work isn't hard."

"Crummy detail."

Yi shrugged. "It's what they assigned me. I've done worse." He eyed Lucas expectantly.

"Got a few questions for you," Lucas said.

"Sure."

"The Chinese gang. You said we were in their territory. But that's a big area. Where's their headquarters?"

"I told you. They move it around. Smart."

"How hard would it be for you to find out?"

"Here? Impossible."

"No, I mean if you go back to where we met. Act as an operative for me."

Yi's eyes narrowed. "You mean a spy."

"Call it whatever you want."

"What's in it for me? I could get killed."

"Seem to recall you have a taste for gold. I'm thinking you get me what I need, there's an ounce in it for you."

"One? Maybe if we were talking three or four, it would be worth it. But one? There's a good chance I'd get my head blown off if anyone's seen me working here."

Lucas sighed. "Fair enough. Two. But I need the info now."

"I'll need an advance. Some rounds and at least one ounce. I'll need to share some of the wealth to get anyone to talk."

Lucas's lips tightened into a thin line. "You screw me on this and you won't have to worry about any of your gang buddies."

"Don't you think I know that? I won't screw you. But I'm going to need to bribe some of the street hustlers to get the location, and they won't work for free."

"How many rounds you figure you'll need?"

"As many as I can carry. Couple of hundred, at least."

"Who's your supervisor?"

"Carter."

"Don't know him."

"I can introduce you."

Yi led him down a long corridor. He turned into one of the wards, Lucas on his tail, and the little man approached a gaunt giant of a man who could have modeled as a human scarecrow.

Carter's eyebrows rose as Lucas neared, indicating he recognized Lucas.

"Howdy, Carter," Lucas said. "I'm afraid I'm going to have to take Yi here off your hands for a while."

"We're pretty short on help." Carter paused. "Lucas, right?"

"That's right. Sorry, but I really need him. I'll see if I can't rustle up some more men to help. It's pretty ugly out back."

Carter frowned. "Can't it at least wait until dark? We've got a backup of cadavers and need to move them out before they really start decaying."

"I understand, but no. I need him now."

Carter nodded slowly. "You're the boss. But please send some more help. We're buried here."

"I saw. I'll do my best."

Yi accompanied Lucas to the supply tent, where Sam, Terry,

72

Henry, and thirty of his men were stacking ammo cans. Lucas told Sam what he needed, and Sam side-eyed Yi before agreeing. He counted out two hundred rounds of jacketed .223 ammunition and hefted the metal container. Yi took it, the ropy arm muscles beneath his copper skin straining from the weight, and turned to Lucas.

"Need that ounce you promised me, and I'll get moving."

Lucas fished a single gold maple leaf from his back pocket and slipped it into the breast pocket of Yi's shirt. "Remember what I told you about crossing me," he warned.

Yi grunted. "Don't worry. I want the other one more than I want to spend the rest of my life dodging you."

"Smart man."

"How will I find you when I have answers?"

"Check with Sam here. He'll know where I am."

Yi walked off with the tin of bullets, and Sam leaned into Lucas and spoke in a low voice. "Pretty shifty little weasel there."

"No argument. But sometimes that's what it takes to get the job done."

Sam smirked. "Ten rounds says you never see him again."

Lucas watched Yi disappear around a corner and shook his head. "No go. I wasn't thrilled about having to use him, but he's our best shot."

"He'll disappear into the city like a plague rat. Mark my words."

Lucas sighed. "Probably right." He paused. "Don't suppose you have a couple of spare men you could send over to the hospital, do you? Guy running it, Carter, needs a hand in a big way." Lucas described the situation, and Sam frowned.

"I'll ask, but we're all shorthanded right now."

"I know. Consider it a personal favor."

Sam shook his head. "Only for you."

Lucas managed a small grin and gazed after Yi, a sense of foreboding nagging at the core of his guts, the air suddenly almost too thick to breathe.

Chapter 14

Colorado Springs, Colorado

Elijah remained well to the rear as his army battled with the neo-Nazi holdouts who ran what had once been Colorado Springs. After two hours of running firefights, the defenders were on their last legs, and Elijah's men were mopping up the last of them. He'd sent an envoy into town with an offer for the Nazis, but it had been rejected, and his messenger returned to him with his body lashed faceup to the animal's back and gutted, his intestines dragging in the dirt as his horse neared.

The message had been a simple one: join Elijah's army and reject their evil ways or face complete destruction. That they'd chosen the latter, either convinced of their superiority because of their entrenched position or merely unwilling to bow to a new master, didn't surprise or bother Elijah. He was sure he'd be able to grow his force from the town's residents, whom the Nazis had preyed upon. Once freed, his bet was that they would find their way to the Lord, lest they suffer the same fate as their oppressors.

The boom of a detonating grenade reached him, and he twisted to where Benjamin was sitting beside him on horseback. "Sounds like it's almost over."

Benjamin sounded almost regretful when he spoke. "They had no chance."

"Yet they still chose to fight. Fools, all of them."

"They're used to running the show. I would have been surprised if they'd given in. Besides which, we're better off without them. They don't really fit the profile of our target…recruits."

"True, although the Lord works in mysterious ways. And as we've seen, they're ferocious fighters. We could have used more like that."

"The trouble they would have caused in the ranks outweighs any benefit we'd have seen. But it's a moot point now. They're obviously going to fight to the last man."

Elijah shrugged. "It doesn't matter. We'll gather the townspeople and make them an offer they can't refuse, and add more men than we lost. Everything happens for a reason."

"Still, we should seriously consider avoiding a repeat in Pueblo. Just bypass the town and continue to the hot springs."

"No. We need our force battle-hardened for what's to come. And it serves the additional purpose of ridding our southern border of scum who would have eventually caused us trouble. After we're done, we'll march on Pueblo and do the same as we've done here."

Benjamin didn't protest. He'd already spent enough time with his new master to understand that there was no talking him out of an idea once it had taken root. That Elijah would willingly sacrifice any number of his troops to prove a point didn't surprise him in the least. After all, Elijah had never been close to a battle and even now sat as far removed as possible from anything resembling real danger. So of course he could be glib about death and the process of killing.

Benjamin recognized him as a megalomaniacal sociopath, but the prophet had been cut from the same bolt of cloth, so that hardly came as a shock. Perhaps what did was how quickly Elijah had been able to step into his father's shoes and infect the entire congregation with the madness of bloodlust and a thirst for revenge that required the slaughter of an entire tribe – one that had by all accounts saved humanity from the latest iteration of the virus. Regardless of the rhetoric, Benjamin knew in his heart that was the case from speaking to newly converted travelers, who'd described their terror of the new version of the bug in unmistakable terms. Members from Shangri-La had willingly risked their lives to rescue their fellow man from a horrific end, and even if it was heresy within the Church to speak that truth, Benjamin was neither a stupid nor a naïve man. He stayed in his position with Elijah because it was the best opportunity, not because he believed every bit of superstition the father and son team could conjure up.

None of which he would ever admit, upon pain of death.

Another blast boomed from within the town, and then the steady *ack-ack* of a big machine gun – no doubt one of the Brownings they'd brought from Denver.

"Our men must be moving on their headquarters now," Benjamin observed.

Elijah nodded. "The final showdown. May the Lord have mercy on their souls."

The only glimmer of sunshine had been that Elijah had stayed out of the tactical decisions, leaving them to Benjamin's greater experience. At least for now. But he could see the young prophet's hubris strengthening and his feeling of invulnerability increasing with each conquest. They'd mowed through two encampments of settlers who had established themselves beyond the southern city limit perimeter, demanding loyalty and obedience or putting them to death as tools of the Dark One, and the ease with which Elijah had made life-or-death decisions had gone to his head even more than the power of running the most powerful organization of its kind in the west.

Delusion and ego were a dangerous combination anywhere, Benjamin knew, but on the battlefield, they could be deadly.

An hour later, the battle for Colorado Springs was over, and Benjamin had lost thirty-nine seasoned fighters. As Elijah had predicted, the bulk of the residents, many little more than skin and bones, had agreed to join the ranks of the saved – but unlike Elijah, Benjamin viewed the mass conversion as more mouths to feed, and would have happily traded the lot of them for his thirty-nine men back.

Elijah stood in front of his army with a beaming smile as the Colorado Springs inhabitants were pressed into service, and when he spoke, his voice was strong and confident.

"We have won a great victory again today, against a foe that was as evil as they come. Some of us fell in doing so, but be assured that their deaths were not in vain, and that they even now have joined my father in heaven, where they are basking in the everlasting glow of the Creator. Their reward is one of eternal bliss, as will be that for any of you who make the ultimate sacrifice." A cheer rose from the men's throats, and fists and rifles pumped in the air. Elijah soaked up the adulation for several beats and then held up his hands to silence the crowd.

"As your reward for fighting bravely and exterminating the vermin who enslaved this town for years, we'll make camp here for the night while we bury the dead. I'm sure the locals will be happy to break into their stores and prepare us a feast as thanks for ridding their city of the menace that terrorized them." He paused for a moment to let his words sink in.

"So rest easy tonight, and tomorrow we will ride on Pueblo, where the same fate awaits anyone who serves Satan. Once we've freed those who have suffered under their rule, we will make our way to Shangri-La and destroy the last refuge for true evil in our land. It is a proud moment now for me to see you triumphant, but I'm confident it is only the first in a series of victories that will be spoken of for generations. Guided by the New Spirit, we are unstoppable!"

This time the cheering was even louder, and Elijah stepped back, arms extended into the air like he was supporting the sky with his hands. Benjamin's face could have been etched from stone, his eyes revealing nothing, as his men roared approval for a killing spree without precedent in the Church's history. It wasn't lost on him that the locals appeared far less enthusiastic about having been liberated from their masters than Elijah's words indicated, and he wondered what gruel they would be able to scratch up for the hungry troops from supplies that were meager by any measure.

Not his problem, but yet another friction point to be aware of lest some take it into their heads to wage a guerilla attack during the night.

Chapter 15

Seattle, Washington

Lucas was dozing in the shade following a bout of afternoon rain when Henry called out to him from near the supply tent.

"Lucas! Your man's back."

Lucas pushed the brim of his hat from where it had been covering his eyes and glanced over at Henry and then beyond him to where Yi was beelining toward Lucas from the encampment perimeter. Lucas yawned and stood and waited for the little Chinese man.

"Well?" Lucas asked when Yi drew near.

"I found out where they're holed up. Cost me all my ammo, but I got the info."

"Where?"

"In Chinatown. A building that used to be a gym. They've been there for two days." Yi eyed Lucas expectantly. "I'll tell you exactly where when you give me the other coin."

Lucas shook his head. "That's not how it works. You take us, show us the building, and you get paid once we verify they're inside."

Yi's eyes darted to the side and then fixed on Lucas's face. "Going there again would be too dangerous for me."

"I'll bring a small army. You'll be fine. I'm not asking you to lead the charge. But there's no way in hell I'm giving you another dime until we've verified you're telling the truth."

78

"I wouldn't lie."

Lucas's mouth twisted in a tight smirk. "Right. Last honest man. But you're still not getting the coin until you show us the place."

"How do you intend to get a small army deep into Chinatown?"

"We'll wait until after dark. We should be able to sneak a hundred of my men past any sentries. Assuming there will be any at night."

Yi looked uncertain. "There…there might be. I don't know. Normally, just the usual places, but everything's upside down now…"

Lucas glanced at the fading light in the sky. "We'll leave in a couple of hours and hit them once it's dark. Go grab yourself a hot meal and be back here then."

Lucas's tone didn't leave any room for argument, so Yi slunk off, his shoulders slumped, obviously unhappy that he was going to have to venture into what was now enemy territory yet again. Lucas believed he'd found the headquarters, but he wasn't about to bet his life on it, much less the lives of his men. It was always possible Yi was playing both sides and would lead them into an ambush. But the risk would be far lower at night, with no lights or reflective material on any of the fighters. And with Yi in the thick of the group, the likelihood he would turn on them was greatly reduced.

At least that was what Lucas told himself. He'd learned the hard way to be prepared for anything, including treachery from those who were supposed to be on his side.

Lucas went in search of Art and found him in consultation with his subordinates in his temporary quarters near the hospital. He explained the situation with Yi, and Art's face clouded as he finished.

"I know you want these guys, but heading into Chinatown at night on the word of a sketchy informant…I'll give you the okay if that's what you're asking for, but I'd be lying if I said I liked it."

"That makes two of us."

Art handpicked a hundred of his best fighters and had Sam equip them with flak vests and enough ammunition and ordnance to go to war. The men ate and then sat for a briefing about their objective and the approach they would use. Lucas and Sam would direct the operation while Art held down the fort, on alert for a counterattack.

"The goal is to capture any of the invasion force we can, and then to neutralize the gang so the residents don't have to fear anyone once we leave town. The mission will depend on stealth, so no chatter once we're underway, and no mention about it before we leave. As far as anyone's concerned, this is a drill or a surprise patrol, nothing more," Art said.

Lucas took up the thread. "We have an informant who's located their den, but we should expect the area to be well guarded. He knows the locations of the guard posts, but those might have changed, so we need to be ready for anything."

"How do we play it once there?" Terry asked.

"It'll be a fortified brick building, so we'll have to figure out the best way once we're there. Maybe a roof entry. I don't know. Nobody but the informant has seen it, and he's thin on details other than it's a two-story building in a dense urban area. My hunch is we enter the adjacent buildings at the far end of the block and make our way to the target that way, but until we know if there are snipers on the roof, it's up in the air."

After the briefing, the men checked their weapons and adjusted their gear. Conversation among them was hushed. It was obvious this would be a dangerous sortie and, as with all such missions, would likely result in some of them not making it. As the light leached from the overcast sky, a quiet settled over the group, the calm of men who had killed and knew what was to come, and were prepared to take life or give their own.

Yi returned after dark, walking slowly, clearly unhappy with his circumstances. He approached Lucas and spoke in a quiet voice. "They'll have to be careful not to make any noise. No horses. Otherwise this will all be for nothing. There are hundreds of them, and if they have enough warning…" Yi eyed the assembled men skeptically. "This is all you're going to send in?"

"Don't worry about us. Just lead us to the building and keep your lips buttoned." Lucas spit to the side. "And don't forget that if you try to lead us into an ambush, my bullet in your back will be the last thing you'll ever feel."

He threw up his hands, his face a study in misery and resignation. "How could I?"

Lucas walked over to where Sam was talking to two of his fighters. "Ready to move out?"

Sam looked over at Yi. "I don't know about him, Lucas."

"Noted. Let's get this over with."

The men donned their NV goggles, and Yi led them through the perimeter and onto the dark streets. The moon hung low in the night sky, and the light from the early stars was faint. The only sound other than the rustle of the men's clothing and the thumping of their boots on the pavement was the sough of the wind off the water through the buildings, and the streets were ghostly in their stillness. Yi moved at a rapid clip, sure of the way, and they were soon clear of the downtown area and entering the outskirts of the International District.

Yi slowed at an intersection and signaled to Lucas to near. When he was beside him, the little Chinese man whispered a warning. "They'll have watchers on the rooftops every couple of blocks from here on, but at night, as you can see, it's pretty hard to make anything out."

"How far are we from their headquarters?"

"Maybe six, seven blocks."

They continued forward, the fighters shadows as they darted from building to building. Their advance was far more coordinated and military than it would have been prior to multiple battles against the Chinese. They crossed a wide thoroughfare, Yi running in a crouch as he navigated through the wreckage of abandoned vehicles that clogged the way, and Lucas followed close behind, his nerves tingling as they closed on their target. Sam and a cluster of his fighters were on Lucas's tail, scanning the surrounding buildings as they moved like wraiths through the night.

Yi slowed again and raised a hand in warning, and then pointed at an edifice eighty yards away. Lucas ducked behind a stoop and the men scattered, with some entering any building they could gain access to and making their way to the roofs.

Lucas led Yi up the crumbling stairs of a three-story tenement, and they climbed through the attic to the roof. Once on the tar-paper surface, they inched to the rim, and Lucas scoped out the headquarters building. After several moments, he turned to Yi and spoke in a low voice. "No sign of anyone guarding it. You sure that's the right place?"

Yi nodded. "Positive."

"Did you check it out before coming to tell us about it?"

"Of course. There were lookouts everywhere. They might feel there's no threat at night…" Yi said, but his tone now betrayed some clear doubt.

"Wouldn't that be the most obvious time to attack?"

"They probably believe they're invincible in their stronghold of Chinatown."

"Then why move their headquarters continually?"

Yi said nothing for several moments. "I'll go down and scout it out at street level."

Lucas shook his head. "We both will."

They retraced their steps to the building entrance, and Lucas peered through the night vision goggles Sam had equipped him with and surveyed the gym. There was no sign of life, no telltale glow of torchlight seeping from beneath a door or through a shuttered window. Lucas grabbed Yi by the shoulder and pushed him forward. "Come on. If you wasted our time for nothing, you're going to wish you'd never been born."

"I swear—"

"Move."

Yi stumbled forward, helped along by a shove from Lucas, and they worked their way down the sidewalk toward their target, Lucas with his M4 sweeping the street as he walked with measured steps. Yi stopped at a doorway fifteen yards from the building and cocked his head to listen.

"I don't understand. They were here earlier. But now…"

Lucas pushed past him and made for the entrance. He stopped at where a pair of double doors gaped open and did a cursory scan of the interior before turning to the little man in disgust. Yi padded to the door and peered inside, and then glanced over at Lucas.

"I swear they were here. Not five hours ago."

"Sure they were," Lucas growled.

Sam arrived and Lucas lowered his rifle. "Nothing. But now we have to consider that this scum led us into a trap, so warn the men that we could be attacked at any point on the return trip."

Yi took a step backward, hands raised. "I didn't…"

"We'll deal with you later," Lucas said, and pivoted away.

"They couldn't have cleared out that fast without leaving a sign they were here," Yi said, and darted into the gym.

Lucas was about to respond when a massive detonation from inside the building blew a fireball through the doors and windows, hurling Lucas and Sam backward and sending a rain of debris into the street.

Lucas lay on his back, stunned, as his troops ran toward them, and was struggling to rise when strong hands lifted him to his feet.

"Are you okay?" one of the men asked.

Lucas shook his head to clear it, his ears ringing as loud as a siren. "Where's Sam?"

"Over here," Sam called from behind him. "I'm fine. Little scorched is all." He coughed loudly. "What the hell happened?"

Lucas blinked as flames licked from every opening, sending inky smoke belching into the heavens. "They must have booby-trapped it. Probably a tripwire deep inside. Which means they knew we were coming."

Sam nodded. "Looks like your friend wasn't lying, then. He didn't strike me as suicidal."

"Someone must have spotted him and followed him back to our base." His expression darkened. "Or tipped them off."

They watched the building burn for a beat, and Lucas's expression hardened. "Let's get out of here. We're sitting ducks if this was just the opening salvo."

"Back to HQ?" Sam asked.

Lucas's frown deepened and he eyed the street with foreboding. "Assuming we can make it."

Chapter 16

Fairplay, Colorado

Duke and Edwin slowed their horses from a trot when a flock of birds rose into the air from a grove of trees ahead on the trail. Duke raised his rifle while keeping hold of the reins in one hand, and Edwin did the same.

The chatter of an assault rifle shattered the stillness, and Duke and Edwin split up, urging their steeds into the pine trees at the side of the road while bullets whistled and snapped around them. A round tugged at the sleeve of Duke's trail coat, beneath which he was wearing his plate carrier, but it didn't draw blood, and he ducked low as his horse made it to the tree line. He swung from the saddle and took cover. Edwin returned fire at the invisible assailants from horseback, and Duke covered him with methodical volleys aimed at where he thought the shooters were lurking.

Edwin dismounted from his position across the mountain road, and the two of them began moving toward their unseen assailants. Raiders were a constant threat on the main highways; though they'd hoped that the more remote mountain passages would prove too thinly traveled to merit their presence, that idea had obviously proven erroneous – an ambush from just around a bend was a classic raider technique. Fortunately the ones they were up against seemed inept, given that they'd begun shooting while Duke and Edwin had been well out of guaranteed kill range.

That small bit of luck wouldn't be much help, though. There was no other way across the mountains than this road – at least none that wouldn't take them many miles south of their desired routes, across some of the most inhospitable territory in the state. Barring climbing trails that mountain goats would be loath to try, it was the road or nothing, and obviously some group of miscreants had decided that anyone foolhardy enough to try to navigate it would be easy pickings.

Duke suspected that the shooters were rank amateurs, opportunists without any military training or useful combat skills, judging by how they were wasting ammo shooting at shadows. That was a second piece of luck – in the post-collapse world, ammunition wasn't abundant, and most were limited to what they could easily carry.

Edwin spotted Duke between two trees and gestured to him that he was going to retrace his steps to where the road curved and cross over to Duke's side. Duke readied himself and popped off a few three-round bursts at the shooters for good measure, drawing their attention as Edwin tied his horse to a low branch and jogged back.

A couple of minutes later he joined Duke, who never took his eyes off the road ahead as he leaned into the younger man. "What do you think?" he whispered.

"Bushwhackers. They should have let us get up on them more, but the birds must have spooked someone trigger-happy. Lucky for us."

They would normally have been traveling at night, but had figured that the area was so devoid of humanity they could risk moving during the daylight hours at least while still in the mountains. Once on the plains it would be a different story, but few had the temerity to try to eke out a living in the barren expanse of the Rockies, and they'd decided to speed along their travels by riding as much as possible – a decision they were now paying for.

"We need to get closer and see what we're dealing with," Duke said. "How do you want to do this?"

"I'll head off to your left and move up the gulley there. You keep plinking at them from here, edging closer when you can, and I'll see if

I can flank them."

"Sounds like a plan."

Edwin slipped away through the trees and vanished like smoke among the conifers. Duke continued to lob bursts at the sniper position, changing trees periodically. The rounds they returned slapped harmlessly into the trunks around him without doing any damage. He'd left his horse lashed out of sight to one of the trees near the road, and had advanced on the shooters to the point where the animal was in no danger of being hit by a stray.

The shooting from up the road slowed to a few desultory pops now that their quarry had disappeared, and Duke took the opportunity to move forward another fifteen yards, sticking to the trees lest one of the shooters got lucky. He estimated there were three of them, certainly no more than four, based on the number of different rifles that had been firing during the peak of the shooting frenzy. At least two were AR-15s or similar smaller caliber weapons, and there was one AK he'd heard. Perhaps a lever-action .30-30 somewhere in the mix, although he couldn't be sure.

He reached a pair of promising trees and searched the scrub ahead for any signs of life. Movement stirred in one of the bushes, and he sprayed two three-round bursts in its direction, counting the seconds until Edwin made it close enough to take out the attackers. Like the raiders, Duke and Edwin had a limited supply of ammunition; they carried as much as was practical in their saddlebags but didn't want to weigh down their animals with unnecessary weight, so they had to be sparing in their fire. Once the skirmish was over, they would retrieve all the usable rounds from the bushwhackers and replace their spent stock, and take anything that didn't fit their weapons for barter.

Assault-rifle fire exploded from near the trees. Edwin's weapon was on full auto, which emptied his magazine in little more than an instant. Screams of agony drifted from the grove, and Duke broke into a sprint, his weapon at present arms. Another shorter burst of automatic fire told him that Edwin had changed magazines, and the lack of answering fire meant that he'd put down the threat.

He reached Edwin in under a minute, approaching cautiously in case he hadn't completely taken out all the shooters – Duke knew all too well that even a wounded man could be lethal with a gun. Edwin was standing with his weapon trained on three bodies, their clothing soiled with filth and stained with blood. Only one was still breathing, each intake of breath a rasp as he bled out from a half dozen bullet wounds stitched from his abdomen to his chest.

Duke remained by Edwin until the last man died. "Good shooting," he said, and wiped the sweat from his cheek with the back of his arm.

"Damn fools were lined up like a turkey shoot. Didn't take a lot of skill to put them down."

Duke swept the surroundings with his rifle. "Sure you got them all?"

"Positive."

Duke moved over to the first man, who'd been using a grime-encrusted AR-15. He felt in the man's jacket for spare magazines and retrieved one with a look of distaste. "Idiots wasted most of their ammo. This one's full," he reported, and then snatched up the rifle and ejected its magazine. "This one's maybe a third," he said, weighing it before pocketing it.

Edwin walked to the next corpse and repeated the process. "AK. Two full mags."

"Good for trade, unless you feel like going Commie with your gun."

Edwin offered a grim smile. "Not likely."

They finished searching the dead men and secured their pistols and rifles for barter, and then walked back to where their horses waited patiently, their terror from the shooting abated. Duke loaded his saddlebags with the AK and its mags and did a quick inventory of how much ammo the skirmish had cost them. Adding back those of the dead men, he was still twenty rounds poorer than before the gun battle, but he could trade the AK rounds for more 5.56mm further down the road, he was sure.

He untied his horse and mounted up, and Edwin did the same. Duke spurred his animal forward, the deadly exchange now just another slice of the past, a not unusual part of survival in the brave new world that had emerged from the collapse. Both men had been in dozens, if not hundreds, of similar fights, and the adrenaline rush that always accompanied one quickly receded, leaving them feeling hollow and fatigued as they continued on their way, the only sound the clack of their horses' shoes on the asphalt and the occasional plaintive call of an unseen bird.

Chapter 17

The locomotive's wheels screeched as the heavily loaded column of cars rounded a gentle curve on approach to Redding, about which the Blood Dogs knew little other than what they'd heard from travelers. Clark squinted through smoke at the tracks ahead and then yelled to the fireman over his shoulder, "Hang on. Out of track ahead!"

Clark yanked on the brake and jerked the transmission out of gear, eyes wide at the sight of a section of track a quarter mile ahead where the steel beams upon which the train ran had been removed, leaving nothing but ties, like rows of decaying brown teeth. Momentum carried the train forward, even as the locomotive's wheels locked and wailed against the railings, throwing showers of sparks as the heavy procession continued inexorably toward the gap that would spell the end of the trip to Oregon.

"Clark–" the fireman shouted, but Clark was seemingly mesmerized by the empty section rushing to meet them, his jaw clenched so tight the muscles along the sides of his face looked hewn from wood. The fireman lurched forward to shake the engineer from his trance, but then Clark was in motion, leaning over the side to stare at the wheels that were doing precious little to slow the train.

"We'll make it," Clark said under his breath, counting the seconds as the forward movement gradually ebbed. "We'll make it," he said more loudly, and turned to the fireman. "But it'll be damn close."

"I don't know," the fireman muttered.

"Have a little faith," Clark countered, and then gripped the side railing in case he'd called it wrong.

The old engine groaned to a full stop fifteen feet from the missing tracks, and the fireman exhaled a tense breath he'd been holding as Clark threw him a grin. "Told you," he cackled, and then leapt from the cockpit and walked forward to the naked ties.

Scott approached from farther down the line at a jog and stopped beside Clark to consider the track.

"Sabotage?" he asked.

Clark shrugged. "Against what? We're the only thing that's run on these rails since the collapse."

"What, then?"

"Somebody probably took it for raw material for something. Beats me."

"Great. What do we do now? Can't go any farther, and we're, what, still a couple of hundred miles from Salem?"

"More than that. But don't sweat it. It'll take some elbow grease, but we can pull up some track behind us and use it on this stretch."

Scott regarded the missing rails doubtfully. "That's got to be a few hundred yards minimum."

"Yep. I didn't say it would be easy. Just that it'd work."

Men piled out of the cars, and Clark explained to them what needed to be done. He was finishing up describing how to uproot the spikes that secured the rails when a deafening volley of gunfire exploded from ahead of the locomotive, and a hail of bullets cut down dozens of the fighters where they stood.

"Take cover!" Scott screamed, and the men scrambled back into the steel railway cars or threw themselves beneath them. Those positioned on the roofs returned fire, responding with the devastating destructive punch of the .50-caliber Brownings, whose range easily exceeded the most powerful assault rifles by a factor of three.

The shooting had originated from a scattering of lopsided houses in a run-down neighborhood of shoddily built dwellings, and the jacketed rounds sawed through the plywood and stucco walls, shredding anyone inside to pieces. Clark watched from the cab of the locomotive as a shower of bullets pulverized the homes; and then the shooting stopped and Scott was yelling commands.

"Doug! Mike! Move your men and some big guns to those houses and set up a defensive perimeter so nobody can get near the train. Al, I want three thousand fighters ready to move on the town in fifteen minutes. Clark, commandeer as many men as you need to lay track while we're gone. Get moving! Now!"

Clark sprinted to where Scott was issuing orders. "I figure a few hundred should do the trick," Clark said. "We should put some of the horses to use, too. They can drag rails faster than we can carry them."

Scott shook his head. "I'd rather not risk the animals."

"There'll be more in town, right? We're losing daylight. If we have to sacrifice some of ours, we can replace them."

Scott considered Clark's words and nodded. "Fair enough. Keeping the train rolling is the most important thing."

"What are you planning to do?" Clark asked.

"We didn't ask for this fight, but we're going to finish it."

"Might have just been a few random squatters…"

"Doesn't matter. We're Blood Dogs. Nobody messes with us."

Clark went to work, and Scott strode off with his lieutenants. Soon most of the fighters on the train had been deployed to create a buffer zone against further attack or to raze the town. Those left guarding the train grumbled good-naturedly about missing out on the fun, and watched their unlucky peers laboring over the rails, prying the spikes loose and then harnessing the ends of the steel tracks to a pair of horses to be dragged to the front to replace the missing sections. It was backbreaking work in the hot sun, but Clark was a tireless taskmaster and kept up the pace so they'd be done in as few hours as possible.

When they got to Redding, the Blood Dogs' superior force easily overwhelmed the town's defenses, and Scott ordered his men to slaughter every male they found and to only spare the younger females – all others were to be killed, including any children, as was the gang's policy. The gunmen went house to house and butchered the inhabitants indiscriminately, dragging them into the street before bludgeoning them to death to save ammo.

The town only yielded two dozen women deemed worth saving for continual gang raping on the train, and every other living thing except the horses and any edible animals was executed without mercy. A search party scoured the dwellings for ammunition and weapons, but the results were paltry – Redding had largely survived by trading with travelers and by harvesting fish from Lake Shasta, and was as poor as any outpost the Blood Dogs had run across.

By the time the town was in ruins, the wooden buildings set ablaze by the gang, the air was thick with smoke. The returning fighters hurried back to the train, their day's work done, eager to celebrate on the packed railcars with their human spoils and to cook the few chickens and pigs they'd found when they made camp for the night. Clark had deemed it too dangerous to run the locomotive round the clock, given their lack of knowledge of the condition of the track, so that night would be a victory feast for the gang as they camped beneath the stars, with only the sobs and whimpers of the captive women for company.

Clark checked the newly laid track and approved it, and the firemen shoveled coal with all the speed they could muster until the engine had built a sufficient head of steam to crawl forward. It lumbered over the fresh rails until it had regained speed, and within minutes had left the destroyed husk of Redding behind as a cautionary tale for any foolish enough to dare to risk the Blood Dogs' wrath.

Chapter 18

Art and Lucas sat at a table mulling over the Chinese gang's aborted attempt to bring the building down on Lucas and his men the prior day, unsure of how to proceed. Art sat forward and poured a shot of Chinese whiskey from one of the bottles they'd scrounged from the enemy's stores, and tilted the glass to Lucas in invitation.

Lucas shook his head. "If I start now, I'll finish the bottle," he said, his expression grim.

"I wouldn't judge you," Art said, and tossed back the drink with a grimace. "You aren't missing much. Tastes like gasoline."

"You and I both know that if we don't find these bastards, they're going to wait until we're gone, and then all of this will have been for nothing."

Art shrugged. "Normally we agree, but at this point I'm not sure what more we can do. They've disappeared. Your man got played and almost took you with him. There's no trace of the gang, and nobody's talking. Did I miss anything?"

"The part where we can't get out of here until we find them."

"At the rate we're going, that's going to be a long winter. Maybe this would be a good place to start leaving local problems to the locals?"

"They're not equipped to go up against an organized group yet, and we both know it. The Chinese will have taken Seattle back before we've disappeared over the horizon."

"Look, Lucas. Some of the men are grumbling. We won some big ones, but that momentum won't last forever. They want to get back to Salem, and if we're going to go after some of the really big gangs, we need to figure out who and do it. I'm not saying they're right, but morale's about all we have right now."

Lucas eyed the bottle like it was a scorpion. "No argument. If you remember, I wanted out of this a while ago. It wasn't my bright idea to try to lead an army cross-country to tackle every scumbag that's been able to take over a city. I just want to go home."

"Like it or not, you're the point man, Lucas. That's why the decision on how to play this situation is yours. I'm just offering an old man's advice."

"That doesn't sound like the General who took on the Chinese and won. And you're not that old."

"I feel triple my age, and that's on a good day. Look, we did some good here. But we can't play cops forever. The council's been set up. We did our job. I've repeated to the men that any who feel like staying and helping out can, with our blessing." Art poured another shot. "Armies are liabilities in peacetime, Lucas. They need a purpose. We gave them one with Seattle. The vision of clearing out the vermin and taking back the country is powerful, but it won't last forever. We need to *do*, not sit on our hands."

"I'd just as soon mount up and never look back. Leave the men to you."

Art's face split with a sad grin. "You keep saying that, but you're still here."

"I blame Ruby. Woman's a damn witch." Lucas exhaled heavily. "Maybe I will have a shot of that snake oil."

Art slid a dusty glass from the center of the table, blew into it, and poured it half full. "There you go. It'll clear your head. And kill any parasites that have taken up residence in your black heart."

It was Lucas's turn to grin. "Silver-tongued devil, as usual," he said, and tossed the drink back neat. His expression didn't change, and Art snorted.

"Glad I never had to play poker across a table from you. I'd-a lost every hand."

"Don't try to sweet-talk me," Lucas said, but the corner of his mouth twitched.

A knock at the door interrupted them, and both looked to where Sam stood with a man Lucas knew; someone Sam had suggested would make a solid Seattle commander for the men who decided to stay.

"Got some news," Sam announced. "Brad here got a tip." Sam looked to Brad. "Go ahead. Tell them."

"One of the patrols down at the waterfront says there was some suspicious activity at one of the big warehouses yesterday, near one of the marinas. He heard it from one of the scavengers who works the area. A big group of men and animals loaded in after nightfall."

"Why are we only hearing about this now?" Art barked.

Brad shrugged apologetically. "It's a big city. Lot of people. I guess the patrol didn't think much of it, or their group leader didn't. I came to Sam the second I heard."

Lucas glanced out the high window. "Too dark to move on it now, even with the night vision gear – we'd never be able to spot all their snipers. But I want some men stationed around the area. We don't want to lose them again."

"I'll see to it personally," Brad said.

"I don't want them spooked. Stay out of sight. Assume they have watchers. Use NV gear, but stay far enough away so they don't spot you," Lucas instructed.

"Will do," Brad said, and brushed past Sam on his way out.

"What do you think?" Art asked.

"Got to be them. Timing's right. They cleared out of the gym after Yi spotted them, and lay low until it was dark enough to cover their tracks," Lucas said.

Sam frowned. "Wonder why they chose a warehouse on the water?"

"Maybe they're going to try to use some of the sailboats to get the invaders out of Seattle," Art said.

Lucas nodded. "Could be. Or maybe they know something about the district that we don't. They could have a weapons cache we missed. Might be anything." He looked at the whiskey bottle. "You want any of this poison, Sam?"

"No, thanks. Sounds like we're going to be up early, right?"

Lucas offered a wan smile. "Good guess. We'll want to hit them at dawn. They're not the only ones who can use the dark to get into position."

Art cleared his throat. "Probably want to go in heavy, then. No point in fooling around."

"I'd like to take as many as possible prisoner," Lucas said. "Some of the invasion force may have intel on how soon we can expect another bunch to show up from China. We don't know enough about their capabilities. For all we know, those were the only ships the Chinese had that still ran."

Art considered their options for a moment. "Fair enough. But I still say we use overwhelming force."

"No question. As many men as you think we need. My only concern is moving them into position without being seen or heard. We both know how hard that can be, especially assuming they have experienced watchers."

"It can be done."

"I know. Once Brad has his people in place, we'll assemble a strike force and get them outfitted. Give ourselves plenty of time to surround the place."

"Sounds like you don't want to hit them with everything we've got," Sam observed.

"Correct. Any survivors from the invasion force will be invaluable." The Chinese had fought to the last man when confronted; that had been one of Art and Lucas's annoyances, and the news that there had been some who had gotten away offered a glimmer of hope for their capture.

"So what's the plan, other than to rally the men?" Sam asked.

Lucas frowned. "I'll need to slip down to the warehouse tonight and scope out the area. Meet back here in a few hours?"

Art nodded. "Sure. I'm not going anywhere."

"In the meantime, I can put the word out to the men. How many you figure we'll need?" Sam asked.

Art's expression hardened. "Five hundred of your best."

"Sounds like that would do the trick," Sam agreed.

Lucas rose. "Let me go catch up to Brad so he can show me the place. See you in a couple of hours."

Art pushed the half-empty whiskey bottle away with a rueful gaze. "Deal."

Chapter 19

Houston, Texas

The night sky was overcast and the air heavy with humidity. Torches flared around the exterior of the Crew's headquarters, a former mega-church that had been converted into an impenetrable fortress. Sentries sat in machine-gun bunkers at strategic points on the roof, the stifling conditions with slim ventilation the worst part of the duty, but still better than the day shifts, which were infamous for broiling the guards in spite of shade tarps and plentiful water.

Two men watched the street from above the front entrance, though their machine gun on a tripod was pointed at the stars. One of them yawned and wiped sweat from his brow with his shirtsleeve and reached for a canteen. His partner stirred and then resumed snoring softly; the boredom of a guard routine where nothing ever happened was overwhelming even at the best of times, much less on a miserably hot South Texas night.

A tarnished Airstream trailer rolled slowly up the street from out of the shadows, pulled by a team of four mules. A thin man wearing one of the Crew's distinctive black leather vests and a pair of ragged jeans was perched on a makeshift bench seat at the front of the trailer, flicking the reins to encourage the beasts to pull harder. A marijuana cigarette dangled from one corner of his mouth beneath a raggedy mustache and barely above the filthy snarl of his unkempt beard.

The trailer inched along the street until it reached the front entrance of the headquarters, where the guard above called down to the drover.

"What the hell do you think you're doing?"

"Following orders. Snake wants this thing here by dawn. I'm early."

"He didn't say anything to us about it."

"Probably got a lot on his mind."

The drover stepped down from his seat and began unharnessing the mules. The guard frowned, perplexed, his forehead wrinkling with the effort of evaluating the situation and formulating a response. The man finished with the mules, climbed on the lead animal's back, and gave the guards a wave. "See you tomorrow. Go back to sleep."

The slumbering guard groaned and sat up, his face and eyes puffy. "What was that?"

"Something for Snake."

"What?"

"That thing," the first guard said, pointing at the trailer.

"Ha! What's he planning to do, go camp–"

The Airstream exploded in a fireball so large the foundations shook. The entire front of the building caved in, and the guards were dead before they hit the ground in a shower of flaming rubble. A section of roof farther toward the center of the structure sagged for a moment like a geriatric's chin and then crumbled downward into the cavernous interior with a roar.

Men scrambled from the nearby outposts that ringed the building, and then assault-rifle fire began stuttering from nearby, their rattle muted after the deafening blast.

Snake bolted awake, shaken by the explosion, and leapt to his feet. He pulled on a shirt, pants, and a pair of boots as pounding at his door boomed through the room.

"We're under attack," Derek, one of his lieutenants, called through the heavy slab.

"What? Who?"

"Dunno. But they destroyed half the building with the first salvo, and it looks like thousands are attacking."

"Shit." Snake knew that there was no way his few-hundred-guard contingent could hold off a sizeable assault force, so now it was going to be about saving his own skin. He strapped on a gun belt with a holstered Desert Eagle and a sheathed combat knife and ran to the door. When he threw it open, he found Derek and Nate, his two most loyal men, standing with torches in the hall.

"Let's go," Snake said, and took off at a run down the corridor just as another, smaller detonation shook the floor – a grenade, he guessed, and far too close for comfort.

The men followed him down the corridor to a maintenance doorway. Once Derek and Nate had caught up to him with their torches, Snake threw the door open and proceeded toward a stack of crates against the far wall. "Move those," he ordered.

The pair exchanged a look. Nate handed Derek his torch and began heaving the crates aside. In moments he'd cleared enough of a gap for them to see a steel door that had been hidden behind the boxes.

Snake shouldered past Nate and twisted the door handle. It groaned inward on rusting hinges, and Snake snapped his fingers at Derek.

"Torch," he barked.

Derek came forward and handed him one of the torches, and Snake stepped into the space beyond the door and called over his shoulder, "Follow me. Last one in, bolt the door."

Nate was first into the breach, and Derek followed. He slammed the heavy steel bolt into place, and then they were moving through the basement of the massive edifice. The sound of rifle fire from above was now little more than barely audible popping in the distance. Snake led the way, moving with sure steps down the familiar path. He'd always feared he'd one day have to use the secret passageway to his hidey-hole, where he'd stashed gold, weapons, different clothes, and other basics in case he had to duck out of Houston quickly.

They reached another door, also a thick steel slab, and Snake pushed it open. Once inside, he handed Nate the torch and scooped up an LED lantern with a hand crank for power generation, and spun the handle for thirty seconds before flicking it on. The room flooded with white light, and Snake looked around at his trove in satisfaction. Everything was still there exactly as he'd left it, which told him nobody had discovered the chamber.

He moved to a leather pouch that contained a hundred gold Krugerrands and bounced it in his hand, the heft reassuring that even under attack he had options. Snake wasn't kidding himself that it would be easy to get away clean, but if he could make it to safety, he'd have a chance; and more importantly, the gold would buy him influence. He didn't know who was assaulting his headquarters – an external enemy or internal – but it hardly mattered in a world where a hundred gold ounces would enable you to live like a multimillionaire.

Snake slipped the pouch into his pocket and turned to the assault rifle, an M16 with a metal can filled with rounds. He would have preferred to have loaded the magazines when he'd secreted the weapon and gold, but he knew from experience that the springs inside the mags would compress over time if he did, and wouldn't function well – which could be potentially fatal in a firefight.

"We need to figure out who's attacking us," he said, eyeing the ammo.

"All I heard before I came for you was that it looked like some of ours," Derek said.

Snake's face twisted with rage. "I'll kill everyone involved. They'll pay with the worst kind of death."

"Right now we need to get out of here," Derek emphasized.

Snake shrugged out of his leather vest and donned a long-sleeved black T-shirt and a flak jacket. "Right. Help me load the magazines, and we will."

Nate and Derek each took a pair of thirty-round magazines and began feeding 5.56mm cartridges into them; Snake did the same. When they were done, Snake slipped the full mags into the compartments in his flak jacket, sweat coursing down his face from the additional layer of clothing. He looked around the room, lifted a black nylon backpack from the floor, and walked to a metal hatch on the far side that resembled a pressure door on a submarine.

"This connects to an old sewage system that lets out a quarter mile away. Once we're clear of the fighting, we'll figure out what to do," he said, and twisted the oversized handle to open it.

The distinctive sound of a pistol cocking stopped him in his tracks, and he slowly turned to find Nate pointing a Colt 1911 .45 at him.

"You're not going any farther," Nate snarled.

Snake's eyebrows rose, and his mouth twitched with cold fury. "You're part of this?" He looked to Derek, behind Nate. "You too?"

A gunshot rang out, and Nate jerked like a marionette. Snake threw himself to the side and drew his pistol. Nate coughed as his gun fell to the ground, and a stream of crimson spewed from his mouth before he crumpled to the floor. Derek stood behind him with his gun leveled at the dying man, his expression cold.

"I suspected he might be involved. But I wanted to wait for him to make a move," Derek said, and holstered the weapon. "Let's get moving. We can leave him for the ants."

Snake rose and walked to where Nate was gasping like a beached smelt. He stared down at him with hatred and then drew his combat knife and stabbed him in the stomach. He twisted and gored the dying man with a sneer, and finished by wiping the blade clean and kicking Nate in the head.

"Shame to let a nice gun like that go to waste," he said, and retrieved Nate's 1911 and stuck it into his belt. "Be worth something in trade."

Derek straightened. "Lead the way. It'll take them a while to get through all the doors, assuming they bother."

"You have any idea who's behind this?" Snake asked.

"No, but I can guess. Doesn't matter right now. They timed it so we couldn't mount a decent defense, so they're going to win. All we can do is get clear and see if we can pick up the pieces."

Snake spit on Nate. "Bastards."

Derek grunted and tossed the torch on the floor. He grabbed the lantern and cranked the handle again. The light increased in intensity, and he handed it to Snake, who took it and faced the open hatch.

"Okay. Let's go," Snake said and ducked through the opening, lantern in one hand and rifle in the other, the light's glare blazing down the length of the concrete chute as he considered how close he'd come to bleeding out on the cold, hard floor.

Chapter 20

Amber Hot Springs, Colorado

Elliot walked slowly along the central path that led through Shangri-La, deep in thought. A cold wind was blowing through the trees, wrinkling their tops and making the starlight seem even more frigid.

A voice called from behind him. "Elliot! Wait up."

Arnold emerged from the darkness and walked toward him.

"You're up late," Elliot observed.

"Same can be said for you."

"Guilty conscience won't let me sleep."

Arnold smiled. "Mine's nothing so dramatic. More a bathroom trip."

Elliot chuckled. "Just wait till you're my age." He paused, studying Arnold's expression. "How are you and Julie getting along?"

Arnold's smile faded. "Women are a mystery to me."

"Don't worry. They get easier to figure out as you get older." Elliot paused. "I'm lying, of course."

"That's reassuring."

Elliot gave him a concerned look. "Anything serious?"

"Mmm, no, not really. Just…never mind."

"It's okay if you don't want to talk about it."

"There's no point."

Elliot began walking again, and Arnold joined him. "Why are you really up?"

"We got a transmission a few hours ago from Duke's partner, Luis. Apparently both Colorado Springs and Pueblo have been destroyed and ransacked by Elijah's army. Which means we're out of time. They know we're here, and they're on their way."

"Crap. So…what do we do?"

"I've made a command decision. We're going to pull up stakes tomorrow morning and hit the trail. There's no other rational choice. There's no way we can withstand that kind of attack, no matter how committed we are."

"Lot of folks are going to hate having to do that."

"They'll feel better about it when they're still alive in a week."

"Good point." Arnold cleared his throat and shifted the shoulder sling of his assault rifle. "Doesn't give everyone a lot of time."

"We've been talking about this for days. They knew there was a good chance we'd have to leave. It won't come as any surprise. Besides, there shouldn't be much that can't be ready within a few hours. It's not like we've been here for years."

"True. But it doesn't sound like we've got much of a head start."

"Maybe three, four days? It'll be enough. It'll have to be."

"Where are we headed?"

Elliot slowed. "Provo, Utah. We'll just have to hope that Duke's able to convince them to take us in. If not, maybe we can establish a new home somewhere nearby. If we're careful, we should be able to cover our tracks, and Elijah will never be able to find us."

Arnold looked doubtful. "We were pretty careful about our tracks when we left Denver, and it didn't do much good. We might be underestimating them. A group as big as ours is going to leave some kind of trail."

"Should start raining again soon. That would erase anything obvious."

"Maybe," Arnold said, but he sounded skeptical.

"In any case, I'm not sure we have a choice. You see any other way out of this?"

Arnold thought for a moment and then shook his head. "Not really. Although the one thing we have going for us is, from what I saw, they don't really have a fighting force. More like a bunch of untrained civilians with guns. Which is bad enough, I know, but it means they won't have any discipline, and they may lack the stomach to track us halfway across the west. Although we did kill their glorious leader…"

"It'll take us the better part of two weeks to get there."

"With a group numbering in the thousands, it's sure to take longer. Not sure a lot of people would sign up for that duty."

"They may not have much choice. From what Luis said, they're recruiting the hard way. Anyone who says no gets shot."

"Which means they won't be loyal or very motivated. We both know that."

"We have to assume the worst."

"Oh, yeah. Believe me, I am. But we may get lucky on this one."

Elliot gave him a pained grin. "Never had much faith in luck for anything important."

"That makes two of us." Arnold yawned. "Guess I'd better get back to Julie and give her the word."

"She's a good woman."

"I know. I'm just not sure I'm a good enough man for her, and I'm afraid she might be catching on."

"She might surprise you."

"I hope so."

Arnold trudged back to his cabin, leaving Elliot to appreciate the stars alone. Down the path, he knew his night team of four guards was keeping watch, but still a knot of anxiety twisted in his stomach. Mobilizing the entire town wouldn't be easy, and masking their passage would be harder still, but it could be done. And there was always the wild card of the weather that could help, as he'd considered.

He just hoped they hadn't delayed too long. His instinct had been to leave when they'd first intercepted the patrol and failed to catch the man who'd gotten away, but he'd allowed himself to be talked out of it. Now that hesitation might wind up costing them everything. He hoped not, but as he always said, hope, like luck, was a lousy way to run a railroad, and he didn't put much stake in it.

"I'll leave the optimism to others," he muttered, and smiled as he caught himself. It wouldn't do for the legendary leader of Shangri-La to be found talking to himself in the dark. Bad for morale to believe your decision maker might be coming apart in real time.

His thoughts shifted to the Illuminati. If everyone managed to make it to Provo safely and lose Elijah's force, that group would still be out there, and Elliot knew from experience that they wouldn't just give up. They had the resources and the horsepower to track them to the ends of the earth, and likely would.

He sighed in resignation. One problem at a time. In the strange, new world they'd found themselves in, there was always a threat to worry about, and it could drive a man mad to consider how slim the odds were of making it to a new year. Better to tackle the hurdles as they came than to project into the future and fear uncertainty.

For now, he had to lead his people to the Promised Land. Or at least, Utah.

Which he hoped would be close enough.

Chapter 21

Houston, Texas

Snake and Derek made their way along Houston's darkened streets. The sound of gunfire from the Crew headquarters wasn't much more than the distant snapping of twigs now that they'd been on the move for hours. That anyone was still putting up a fight encouraged Snake only slightly – the conclusion he'd come to was that it was an internal coup, not an attack by an external enemy, which meant that whoever was behind it had done their homework and concluded they could succeed. If they'd been recruiting the support they would need to not only win but dominate the Crew as its leaders, then victory was all but assured, and Snake could flush any notions of mounting a counter-coup to take back what was rightfully his.

"There it is," Derek said, pointing at a darkened building. "We can use that as a safe house during the day and keep moving tomorrow night."

"What is it?"

"Used to be a meth lab. But they weren't paying us our cut, so we took all the gear and killed the operators. It was the only thing in the area that was worth anything. Nobody lives around here – if you stay for very long, you wind up sick or dead. Probably a chemical spill from the plant, or a leak," he said, pointing to a line of huge tanks jutting into the night sky a few hundred yards away. "Whatever. It's perfect for one night."

"They'll be looking for me when they don't find my body."

"Maybe. But right now they've got their hands full taking over."

"By tomorrow they'll have figured it out."

"Sure. But where do they start looking? Houston's huge. And we're on the outskirts."

"Okay. I'll follow your lead," Snake said.

Derek grabbed his arm. "Shhh," he hissed, and cocked his head to listen. A clank reverberated from near the building, and he flipped his rifle's safety off and brought it to bear. Snake did the same, and they waited to see what had disturbed the night's stillness, weapons at the ready.

A mangy dog appeared from behind a debris pile with a rat in its jaws. It glared at them with red eyes and slunk away, reluctant to share its meal with anyone. Snake chuckled and lowered his rifle, and Derek exhaled nervously.

"Come on," he said, and walked toward the decimated building entry.

They stopped on the stoop and listened for sounds of life, but only heard the rhythmic dripping of water somewhere deep in the structure's bowels. Snake snuck a look at Derek, whose face was taut with concentration, and then peered into the pitch-black interior.

"Why don't we keep moving?" he asked. "The farther we are from Houston once it's light out, the better."

"We'll need to rest eventually. Neither of us knows what's going to be available outside the city. Better something known than an ugly surprise."

"This is plenty ugly," Snake said.

"True, but it should be safe, and–"

The sound of hooves clopping on asphalt stopped him, and they spun to face the noise. Three riders were approaching from down the street, rifles in hand. Derek grabbed Snake's shirt and pulled him into the shadows. "They couldn't have seen us," he whispered.

They watched as the patrol neared, and heard one of the men cough – a phlegm-filled excretion that terminated in loud spitting.

One of the riders laughed, and a baritone voice drifted to them. "Gotta stop the loco weed, dude. It's killing you."

"You kiddin'? It's the only thing keeps me goin'."

Snake leaned into Derek and whispered, "We could use horses."

"Too dangerous," Derek cautioned.

"You take the one on the right. I'll take the two on the left," Snake said, and he stepped from the doorway with his rifle leveled at the riders and began firing bursts.

Snake didn't hear Derek's curse behind him, but saw the man Snake had singled out for him buck in the saddle and tumble backward onto the street. The two that Snake had picked barely had time to raise their guns before his rounds stitched through them, and they fell from their animals, guns clattering on the pavement.

One of the horses bolted away, dragging its dead rider by one leg. The other two froze, unsure of what to do, and Snake ran to the nearest and grabbed the reins.

Derek joined him moments later, snared the other stallion, and glared at Snake. "They'll be missed."

"Not tonight they won't. Any other night, sure. But not tonight." He eyed Derek. "Mount up. Let's put some miles between us and Houston."

"Their weapons. We can use them for trade," Derek said, and went to collect the dead men's guns and ammo. Snake soothed his horse while his lieutenant gathered the weapons and searched the corpses, and by the time Derek returned, the skittish animal had calmed down. Snake knew that the patrols pulled horses from a common stable, so the horse wouldn't have any particular affinity for its deceased rider – the dead man had been just another weight on its back.

"Toss those in the saddlebags and let's get moving," Snake ordered. Derek did as instructed and then swung up onto his horse's back. Snake followed suit, and then they were cantering down the street, the sticky air hot on their faces.

An hour passed, and they reached the city's outskirts. Derek looked to Snake for a decision on how to proceed, since he hadn't taken any of his counsel. Snake eyed the stars and turned in the saddle to take a final look at the skyline behind him before nodding as though having made a momentous decision.

"We probably have another hour of night left. Let's keep riding and then find someplace quiet to lie low during the day."

"Which way?"

"North. To Dallas. There may be some loyalists left there."

Derek shook his head. "They'll have radioed the news. I'm the only loyalist you've got."

"We need a direction, and there's nothing the other way, so north's it."

"We'll have to stay off the roads."

"Of course. We can do that. We'll travel at night, like you said."

"Dallas is over two hundred miles. It'll take us at least a week to get there."

"You got any better ideas?"

"Let's ride. I'll tell you later."

Derek spurred his horse forward, leaving Snake frowning at his back, wondering what had gotten into his man. He'd been loyal so far, but could he be having second thoughts? Snake wouldn't have blamed him – it was the smart position to take – but he needed to continue asserting his authority, even if it was a fiction at this point. Otherwise he would lose control and Derek would view him as an equal and, as such, might start wondering why he'd risked his neck for him.

Just before dawn, they came across an abandoned low-income neighborhood whose homes were well on their way to being reclaimed by nature. They picked a suitable clapboard house with a separate garage, led the horses into the empty building, and then lay down on the hard floor by the door.

"What were you talking about back there?" Snake asked. "You were going to tell me later?"

"Let's see your guns," Derek said, his pistol in his hand, not pointing at Snake, but still gripped like it could be in a nanosecond.

Snake's mouth dropped open. "What? Have you lost your–"

"Now. Butts first. Nice and slow."

"You're in on this?"

"No." He motioned with his pistol. "The guns, Snake."

Snake was trembling with fury as he slid his pistol to Derek, and then Nate's 1911. His rifle came last, and his face was a death mask when he snarled at Derek, "You're robbing me?"

"You've got it all wrong. But I can't afford for you to overreact. So no guns until you've heard me out."

"You work for me—"

Derek shook his head. "Wrong. I work for myself. Just like you do. And now, without the Crew to back you, you're out of a job. So I have a proposal."

"What the hell are you talking about?"

"I've been working with the Illuminati for months. Watching your empire crumble. They know you killed their messenger, which means you owe them big. And they plan to collect. Which is where the proposal comes in."

Snake tensed, ready to lunge at Derek, and his hand moved to the sheathed knife in his belt.

Derek shook his head as though disappointed. "You'd be dead before you could reach me. Now stop acting like a fool and listen to what I have to say."

"You can't talk to me like—"

"I can and I will. Now shut up and pay attention," Derek said, cocking the hammer on his pistol.

That stopped Snake, and his jaw clenched and unclenched as he sat in silence.

"That's better," Derek continued. "Here's what they want you to do. They have a line on the whereabouts of Shangri-La. They need you to find it and kill its leader – Elliot Barnes. Some doctor. He's thrown a wrench into their plans too many times, and they want him dead."

"Me? Why me?"

"You've got cunning, and you're a survivor. Maybe one who enjoys his chemicals a little too much, but you're sneaky and vicious, and you'll do what's best for you. If you find him and kill him, bygones will be bygones, and they'll help restore you to heading up the Crew again."

Snake's eyes widened. "You know who's behind this, don't you?"

Derek nodded. "Of course. They know everything." He paused. "Remember Wink?"

"That one-eyed piece of shit? You're joking. He wouldn't have the balls."

"He partnered up with the Mexicans. They helped him out, and now the Crew works for them. Which will be a problem for Wink over time, but he's not smart enough to realize how big of one until it's too late. Your men aren't going to be excited about handing over most of what they earn, and that'll backfire. But it'll take time. Time you can use to find Shangri-La and put a bullet or a knife in Elliot. They don't really care how you do it. Just that it gets done."

Snake absorbed Derek's words. "Where is it?"

"Up in the mountains of Colorado. Place called Amber Hot Springs."

"If they know where it is, why haven't they sent someone else?"

"They just learned a few days ago. The Illuminati aren't the only ones with a bone to pick with Elliot. Besides, you're available, and you've got nothing else to do." He grinned, sending a shiver up Snake's spine. "They know about your little stash of gold. Gold they gave you. So it's really theirs. They want you to hire mercenaries and ride for Shangri-La. Make it your life's mission. You do as they ask and you'll get everything back. But you even think about betraying them and they'll find you and see that you die in the most excruciating way possible."

"And you're in on this. So what do you do now?"

"I disappear into the sunset. Or I follow you at a safe distance and make sure you don't get any bright ideas. All the same to me."

"How much are they paying you? I'll pay more. We can vanish together and they'll never find us."

"You have no idea who you're playing against. That was always part of the problem. They can do anything, Snake. Anything. There's no place that's safe from them. So forget about the double cross. You'd never live to spend the gold."

Snake eyed Derek, who was completely calm, and thought through the offer. He could get back command of the Crew and punish those who'd dared to overthrow him. All he had to do was kill one man and he got everything back and then some – revenge being the best part.

Snake exhaled sharply. "Fine. You have a deal. Where are they?"

"There's no changing your mind on this, Snake. Understand?"

"I said you have a deal. Now answer the question so I can get some sleep, or shoot me. At this point, I don't really care which."

Chapter 22

Salem, Oregon

Ruby made her way up a crooked trail in the hills outside town. The glow of the dawn in the eastern sky did little to warm her even with the exertion of the climb. Peter, a friendly older man who'd taken a liking to her, followed her like a faithful hound, the backpack with his shortwave radio set and the solar battery he used to power it bouncing against his shoulder blades with every step.

Reception in town had been terrible the last few times she'd communicated with Shangri-La, and for whatever environmental reasons, she'd been unable to reach Seattle when she tried the prior day. Their method of communication was fraught with uncertainty at the best of times, but it was her lifeline to home and to Lucas, who'd last told her that they'd won the battle for Seattle and would be underway to Salem shortly – without defining exactly what "shortly" meant.

They reached a plateau at the top of a hill that Peter had assured her would be perfect for improving reception, and he laid out a blanket on the moist grass before removing the battery and radio and setting up the transmitter. He plugged an old-fashioned microphone and two pairs of headphones into a splitter he'd engineered, and then powered on the system and turned the dial to the frequency Ruby had given him.

"You ready to do this?" he asked, with all the eagerness of the teenage geek that he still resembled so many years later.

"Absolutely," she said, and took the headphones from him and slipped them over her head.

Peter cleared his throat, depressed the transmit button, and spoke in what Ruby thought of as his radio-disk-jockey voice.

"Gabriel 820. Gabriel 820. This is Ladybug. Do you read?"

He released the transmit button, and they listened to static for a full minute before he tried again.

"Gabriel 820. This is Ladybug. Do you copy? Over."

Nothing but the slow oscillation of white noise greeted them, and Ruby exchanged a look with Peter, who felt the side of the radio and shook his head.

"I have no idea why this damn thing keeps heating up like this," he said. "It shouldn't. No shorts I can find."

A burst of white noise interrupted him, and a male voice spoke. "Go ahead, Ladybug. This is Gabriel 820. Over."

Peter handed Ruby the mic and removed his headphones to give her privacy. Ruby waited until he'd walked a discreet distance away before speaking. "Checking in as asked, Gabriel. Any way you can put the pilot on?" she asked, using Elliot's alias.

"10-4. Stand by."

Ruby knew the best time to reach Elliot was at dawn. He would be preparing for the day in his cabin at the early hour rather than prowling the grounds, thus easier to hunt down, especially when limited battery power made transmission time precious.

A minute later Elliot's voice answered. "Greetings, Ladybug. Hope all's well on your end."

"Not much new to report. Playing the waiting game for our friend."

"I wish it was as calm here. We've run into a little situation, though, and are getting ready to go walkabout."

Ruby digested that. "Oh. All of you?"

"The whole family."

"When?"

"We're packing up the tent now."

"Weather related?" she asked, using the code for danger.

"Storm's approaching. Seems prudent to try calmer surroundings."

"Any idea where you're headed?"

"Do you have a pencil handy?"

"Sure," she said, feeling in her jacket for the pen and pad she always had at the ready when speaking with Shangri-La. She withdrew them and toggled the transmit button. "Ready."

"Headed to SURXR."

"Stand by."

The code was a simple substitution cipher, where she simply had to replace each letter with the one three before to come up with the true message. She quickly did the work and tapped the word she'd written. Provo.

"Oh my. That's a jog, isn't it?"

"Nothing worth doing's ever easy."

"When do you expect to get there?"

"Couple of weeks, assuming the river don't rise and the gods cooperate."

"Anything you need from my end?"

"Pass the info on to our friend."

"He's been dark lately."

"Probably busy. You suspect otherwise?"

"No. I'm sure you're right."

A burst of white noise garbled Elliot's response, and Ruby touched the side of the radio and then pulled her hand away like she'd touched a hot stove. The metal casing was frying hot.

"Repeat," she said, and waited, cursing the jury-rigged radio's penchant for thermal unpredictability. When no response came, she called over to Peter, "This thing's on fire."

He came at a trot and knelt by the device. "Damn. You're right. I honestly have no idea why it's doing that."

"It cut off in the middle of a transmission," she said, pocketing the pen and notepad before he could see what she'd written.

"We'll have to wait until it cools off."

"That could be a while."

His right eyebrow cocked. "Are we in a hurry?"

"There's some urgency to this one, Peter."

He sighed and powered the system off. "Well, there's not much we can do but wait."

An explosion from Salem echoed off the hills, followed by gunfire. Ruby bolted to her feet and stared down at the buildings. "What the hell–"

Peter joined her and they watched in horror as a swarm of men descended on the town and easily overcame the guard outposts, the number of attackers in the thousands to a few hundred defenders. Assault-rifle chatter filled the morning air as battles waged hot, and Ruby grabbed Peter's arm. "We have to do something."

"What can we do? Look at that. It's…an army."

The color drained from her face. "But why? Why Salem? And who are they?"

"Wish I had my binoculars. Maybe we could make something out."

"They're butchering everyone," she whispered. "Listen to that." She hesitated. "Oh, God. It could be the Crew…"

"Who?"

Ruby had forgotten that Peter had been born and raised in Oregon and hadn't heard of the Texas gang, which had not reach that far west or north.

"They're animals from Texas. Jailbirds. Worst of the worst."

"There are a few like that here, too, but not with that many men. I've never seen anything like it. I mean…how did they get here? That's a ton of mouths to feed. And why come here? It's not like we have much to take."

Ruby shook her head. "I don't know, Peter."

They watched in grim silence as the shooting continued, the sun's ascension into the sky bringing with it the sound of mass murder from below. After an hour of fighting, the shooting slowed and eventually stopped, leaving them watching as the invaders overran the town.

"Oh God, Peter," she whispered.

"He's not around today," he replied grimly, and then his breath caught in his throat and he pointed at the outskirts of the town. "Look."

Six figures, tiny as insects from their vantage point, ran into the woods from the last of the buildings just as dozens of gunmen came around a corner behind them. Apparently they'd disappeared before the attackers had seen them, because no shooting followed their escape.

"At least a few people are getting away," he said.

Ruby's jaw clenched with resolve. "We need to help them, Peter."

"How? We only have our rifles and this damn radio."

"I don't know. But we have to do something. There may be more."

Peter appeared unsure. "I mean, sure – but then what?"

"We can hide in the woods. You know this area like the back of your hand. Whoever that is isn't from around here. That's an advantage."

"A few locals up against that…look how that just turned out."

Ruby's lips tightened to a thin line. "I'm not saying we attack them, you damn fool. I'm saying we see who made it out and figure out what our options are."

Peter responded to the harsh vernacular like he'd been slapped, and Ruby's expression softened.

"I'm sorry, Peter. That was uncalled for. It's just…"

He looked away. "I know. Forget about it. You're right. It's either that or we're out here on our own. Maybe there's some strength in numbers. We can take turns guarding wherever we make camp, and share hunting and fishing duties."

"Of course. But for now, we should probably steer well clear and see what happens next. If they come into the woods and start searching for survivors, we're better off a few miles away."

"No argument there. Later on we can look for the others. For now, we'll watch and wait." She looked at the radio and frowned, her concerns over Elliot's announcement that Shangri-La was again in jeopardy suddenly distant compared to the ransacking of the town, including the murder of many of those she'd grown close to over the past weeks. Even after years of hardship in the aftermath of the collapse, it still chilled her blood how destructive and brutal her fellow humans could be, and she shivered involuntarily in spite of the sun's warmth.

"Animals," she spat, her tone disgusted as she watched the aftermath. She had no doubt that had she been in town that morning, she would have been killed without hesitation, too old to rape or force into slave labor. Her younger counterparts wouldn't have been so lucky, she knew, and it was all she could do to keep the sour bile that rose in her throat from choking her at the thought of what would come next. "Animals," she repeated, and walked away from Peter, her chest heaving, shocked to her core at what she'd just witnessed.

"Ruby…" Peter tried, but she waved him away.

"I'll be fine. Just give me a minute."

"Sure thing," he said, obviously shaken as well. Peter was single, all of his relatives long dead from the virus or post-collapse hardship, but every friend he had on earth had been in Salem, and the chances of any having made it out alive were practically nil. He sat on the blanket, face slack and eyes blank, and watched as Ruby sobbed quietly at the tree line, clutching her rifle in white-knuckled hands.

Chapter 23

Seattle, Washington

Plum and tangerine streaked the predawn sky as Lucas studied the waterfront warehouse from the staging point for the planned attack. Occupying most of a long block, the building was a single-story structure with weathered, graffiti-covered walls, windows largely broken out, and a corrugated metal roof. On his late night reconnaissance, Lucas had spotted multiple guards skulking behind the roof rim, as well as several in nearby buildings facing the water; now from his vantage point on the third floor of a tenement three blocks from the wharf, he could make out a few more at each corner.

He lowered his binoculars and looked over at Brad, who'd spent the night there.

"Take your men over to the other office building before it gets light out," he instructed. Brad moved to the door, and Lucas's eyes followed him until he melted into the gloom. He'd told Brad that he wanted to try to take some prisoners, but wasn't sure that the man understood the importance, even after he'd explained it. Brad clearly relished a fight and was chomping at the bit to unleash hell on the Chinese in a replay of the battle for Seattle, in which he'd played a significant part.

They'd scouted out the area earlier and agreed that his men, who were equipped with mortars and grenade launchers, would shell the building when Lucas gave the signal, which would be line of sight from the office building where they were headed and Lucas's spotter position. Lucas wanted to keep Brad in reserve, though, because Lucas could better control the intensity of the attack from the fighters in the staging-area building, instructing them to increase or decrease the bombardment as necessary.

Sam had equipped five hundred gunmen, who were lying in wait two blocks away and who would only engage after the explosives had done their job. Lucas had made clear that he wanted prisoners taken on this assault, and that was the mission priority over the complete annihilation of the Chinese – which Art had argued for before capitulating.

"They put a price on our heads and would have gladly blown us all to hell," he'd said. "Why you want to spare these scum is beyond me. Even if we manage to take some of the invasion force prisoner, it's unlikely they'll tell us anything of value."

"Art, you know I was a lawman. Killing everyone indiscriminately doesn't sit well. That's not the way to do things."

"It is if you want to win."

"We're not in a war. These are criminals, not an enemy army. The rules of engagement need to be different. At least we should give them a chance to surrender."

Art had reluctantly agreed. "And then kill 'em all."

"Assuming they won't give up, then they signed up to meet their makers today," Lucas had agreed. "But I don't want to go in heavy and lose the chance to capture some of the invaders."

Art had grimaced and then shrugged. "You're the boss on this one. But I'd just put them out of their misery. Blow 'em sky high and have done with it. That sets the tone for how things will be handled once we're gone, too. No latitude for treachery."

Lucas had nodded. "Noted. But let's try it my way first."

"Sure."

The cry of a lone seagull wheeling over the sound reached Lucas, and he raised the glasses again to scan the wharf – nobody in sight, the area still as a cemetery. He hoped he hadn't missed some critical sign, or he was about to put his men in jeopardy, or – as with the earlier foray at the gym – waste everyone's time. The presence of the Chinese sentries was the convincing factor for him – unlike that near miss, the gang had deployed watchers, which told him that the intel upon which he was basing his planning was good.

The celestial glow increased over the next fifteen minutes, and he swung around to look at the office building in which Brad was positioned. A green piece of fabric was hanging out of the top window, indicating he was there and ready. Lucas lowered the binoculars, walked across the floor to the stairs, and climbed to the roof, where Sam was waiting with Henry and two dozen men, half equipped with mortars and grenade launchers, the other half serving as loaders. Crates of projectiles sat at the ready near the ad hoc artillery, and six sharpshooters lay near the roof edge, awaiting Lucas's signal to pick off the Chinese snipers when the shelling started.

Lucas crept at a crouch to Sam and Henry and spoke in a low voice. "You ready here?"

"Never more. Say the word and we'll start this party, boss."

Lucas swung the spyglasses up, took a final glance at the warehouse, and stilled. "On my count. Three…two…one…go!"

The whump of eight mortars launching simultaneously filled the air, and the crack of the sniper rifles from the roof edge told him that there was no going back. He checked the warehouse through the glasses and was reassured to see the bodies of the sentries sprawled where they'd fallen, killed without knowing what had hit them.

The warehouse roof exploded in fireballs as the first volley of mortars detonated, sending chunks of steel into the sky. Another series of whumps from behind him followed, with a second series of blasts ensuing moments later – and then the grenade launchers came into play, and the area that had been the front entrance of the long building disappeared in a shower of rubble.

The percussive bark of a heavy machine gun began from the second floor of the tenement as the gunners strafed the warehouse façade, and the armor-piercing rounds peppered the walls with awe-inspiring destructive power. Divots of cinderblock bounced off the sidewalk from where the bullets were cutting through the structure. The gunner adjusted his aim and sent several hundred rounds through a high row of windows, now dark gaps through which, because of the firing angle, they would ricochet inside the warehouse.

Bullets snapped past Lucas's head, and he yelled to his snipers, "Someone's got a fix on us. See if you can pin them down."

The shooters obliged, and after several long seconds of incoming assault-rifle fire that killed two of Lucas's snipers, the enemy gunmen were neutralized by a barrage of gunfire.

"Crap," Sam said, surveying the dead men, their blood already coagulating on the tar paper.

"I'm going below. Hold your fire until I get back."

Lucas ran to the roof entrance, down the stairs, and into the room where Terry was methodically stitching the warehouse. He yelled over the deafening roar, but Terry didn't hear him and jumped in surprise when Lucas reached him and tapped his shoulder to signal for him to stop.

Lucas's ears were ringing like church bells when the room fell silent. Motes of dust floated lazily in a narrow sunbeam that filtered through what had once been the window, and he shook his head to clear it before speaking.

"Hold until I get back, understand? Don't shoot any more unless I give the word."

Terry and his partner nodded, and Lucas returned to the roof, where Sam was watching the building with a pair of binoculars of his own.

"Anything?" Lucas asked.

"No."

"Let's give them a few minutes to figure it out."

"They might not."

"Then we'll help."

"10-4."

After a long wait, Lucas cupped his hands and called out over the roof. "You're surrounded. There's no way you'll make it out alive. This is your one chance to surrender. If you don't, we'll destroy your building and everything in it."

Farther down the street, another man repeated Lucas's words through a cone-shaped megaphone, the resonance of his voice ringing off the water as he finished.

More time passed, and then a white shirt tied to a broom handle waved from the gutted entrance, which was now a cavernous rent in the side of the building. Lucas exhaled. "Bingo. We have contact. Everyone hold your fire."

After a long beat, a Chinese man in dusty black cargo pants and a flak jacket stepped from the opening and looked around. Lucas glanced at Sam. "This is it. I'll signal from down at the street. If they don't surrender, wipe them off the face of the earth."

"You got it."

Lucas descended the stairs and ran out of the tenement to where a score of his men were holed up on the ground floor of another building. He took the megaphone from their squad leader and raised the bullhorn.

"Tell your men to come out without their weapons, or you're all dead," he warned. "You have one minute."

"We want to negotiate," the Chinese man yelled.

"There's nothing to negotiate," Lucas said. "Either surrender or die."

"We have ten of the invasion army with us. They'll never surrender."

"Convince them. You have two minutes. Anyone who doesn't want to die needs to be on the street with their hands in the air, because the building's going to disintegrate when we hit it with our artillery. This was just a taste."

"That isn't enough time."

"It's all you've got. Clock starts now. Make it happen or you'll be in hell within three."

The man turned and ducked into the building. Lucas lowered the megaphone and checked the time on his mechanical watch, and looked over at the waiting gunmen. "Now we'll see if they're suicidal."

Seconds ticked by, and Lucas handed the bullhorn back to the squad leader and retraced his steps to the staging building. He was back on the roof before the two minutes expired, and frowned at Sam.

"I'll give them another minute. They may not have a watch," Lucas said.

Sam nodded, but his expression said he thought it was a waste of time and that the attack's conclusion had been foreordained.

They waited in tense silence, and when nobody reappeared, Lucas sighed and called to Sam, "All right. Hit them with everything. I'll signal Brad."

The bombardment resumed, and Lucas raced to the far side of the roof and waved to the office building. In an instant another twenty mortars soared through the air in lazy arcs, and the warehouse transformed into an inferno, with most of the roof destroyed by the incendiary projectiles after the first volley.

Lucas raised the glasses and studied the warehouse, and then shifted his focus to the water beyond it, where he could make out a few dark shapes dimpling the surface. He shouted to Sam to stop shelling and signaled to Brad to cease fire. The explosions stopped, and Lucas called to Sam.

"Send a runner to the men. We've got some swimmers in the water. Commandeer a boat and see if you can save any of them, and have the rest of the men rush the warehouse after the next round of shelling."

Sam barked orders to one of the snipers, who rose with his rifle and sprinted for the roof-access doorway. He was gone in a blink, and Lucas shook his head.

"Hit them again. I don't want to see anything left but a smoking crater."

A score of enemy gunmen emerged from the warehouse and began spreading out, firing indiscriminately at the buildings in front of them. "Fire at will," he told Sam, and then made for the second-floor machine-gun nest to tell them to cut down the resisters.

Terry didn't hesitate, and moments later all twenty Chinese were dead in lakes of their own blood, their gesture futile. Lucas signaled to him to stop, and they waited as volley after volley of mortars pummeled the building, sending clouds of dust and smoke skyward.

"We're done here," Lucas said, and Terry nodded. Lucas climbed back up to the roof. Sam stopped the shelling, and they waited for the coming wave of their infantry to make its way to the warehouse to finish the job.

Lucas shook his head in frustration. "Damn fools."

"You did everything you could," Sam replied.

"I suppose," Lucas said. He took in the pair of dead snipers near Sam and his brow creased. He pushed the brim of his hat up an inch and turned to the mortar operators. "Good shooting."

Gunfire rattled from the street below as Lucas's main force ran toward the warehouse while a few straggler Chinese snipers futilely shot at them before being silenced by overwhelming return fire. Lucas watched the surge of men without expression, and when the first reached the waterfront and began to pour through the smoldering ruins of the warehouse walls, he turned from the scene with a stony countenance.

Chapter 24

Lucas trod along the street that fronted Art's headquarters, his boots making a steady tattoo on the asphalt and his M4 slung over his shoulder. The assault on the warehouse had ended, and a column of smoke spiraled into the air from the site, which was now little more than a pile of rubble. Two sailboats had been deployed from the nearby marina, but by the time they made it to the waters off the wharf, most of the swimmers had succumbed to hypothermia in the cold, unforgiving tide. A few had been rescued, but none were part of the invasion force as far as Lucas's men could tell, and they'd been locked up in a chain-link area that had served as a warehouse security cage in pre-collapse times, and were awaiting a medic's attention.

Two guards waved a greeting to Lucas as he entered the headquarters, and he handed one of them his rifle and pistol.

"He in?" Lucas asked.

"Yep. Getting ready for the council meeting in a half hour."

Lucas walked down the hall to Art's office and knocked on the jamb. Art looked up and offered a smile. "Ah, the returning conqueror! Come on in. I'm just finishing up."

"Not sure I'd frame it that way," Lucas said as he entered and pulled up a seat. He sat down heavily. "Pretty much went as I was afraid it would."

"I heard. Wiped them off the face of the earth. Good riddance. You may just make it as a military commander yet."

"We wanted to capture some of the invasion force. We failed."

"Your primary goal was to eradicate a treasonous group of murderers. So you succeeded. You're just not willing to admit it."

"Wasn't a very fair fight."

"The best ones aren't supposed to be. Would you feel better if you'd lost a hundred men?"

"We lost two."

Art sighed. "Which is never easy, as we both know. But it is what it is." He sat back. "While you were off on your adventure, we've been trying to reach Salem to let them know we're on our way soon. But they've gone dark. Nobody home."

"Dark?"

"They have four radios, and none of the channels they monitor are answering. That's all we know."

"What do you think's going on?"

Art's expression darkened. "Nothing good."

"Could it be a transmission problem? Sunspots or something?"

"Anything's possible. We'll certainly keep trying. But my instinct is that we should plan on moving out sooner than later. They're hopelessly under-defended there with their skeleton crew. Most of their fighters are with us, and when word gets out Salem's off the air, the guys are going to want to ride hard for home. A lot have families they left behind."

"I'm ready to leave whenever you are."

"I figured. That's why I called the council meeting. I'm going to break the news that we're moving out tomorrow morning, so they're on their own."

"Going to seem abrupt."

"They're big boys. Time to ride without training wheels. We've got things to do. We can't play cops for them forever."

"I'll be glad to hit the road."

"That's no secret." Art smiled. "You should sit in on the meeting in case it gets contentious. I could use the backup."

Lucas returned the smile. "Like you need it."

"You've got a certain moral authority that comes with your reputation."

"You really need me there? I'm beat. No sleep last night, remember?"

"It wouldn't be the end of the world if you skipped it, but I'd prefer if you didn't."

"Did you just passive-aggressive me into going?"

"Depends. Did it work?"

The council entered the meeting hall, with Levon trailing behind the rest. He and Lucas nodded briefly to each other, and everyone took seats. Art sat on the edge of the stage and surveyed the council members while Lucas stood by his side.

"Thanks for coming. As you probably heard, we tackled the Chinese gang problem this morning...and now there's no more problem."

"I really wish you'd consulted us about that," Eric said. "As the head of the defense force, I'd have thought I'd have the right to know."

"We needed to move quickly, and you were nowhere to be found. So it wasn't intended as any sort of slight." Art hesitated. "What's the status of the force, anyway? Haven't heard much about it."

Eric sighed. "We're recruiting. But it's hard to get people who've spent years watching their own backs to step up and do something for the rest. They're naturally distrustful."

"As they should be. But you need to assemble a credible militia or Seattle will fall. We all know that."

"Same for the police force, Eric," Lucas said. "Time's run out."

"That's a little easier. We have about fifty men who signed up to do it. Which is a start."

"We're going to leave you about two hundred of ours who can do double duty. Between them and your men, you should be able to keep the peace. Especially when word spreads about the Chinese and how bucking the council's authority went for them."

Art resumed his exposition. "Now that we've solved that problem for you, we're going to pull out tomorrow and head south. So you're going to be on your own from then on. I'd step up your recruiting for the defense group. There's no telling when the Chinese will show up again, and when they do, if you haven't got an army to fend them off, you're toast."

Levon's eyebrows rose. "Tomorrow? Just like that?"

Lucas smiled. "We've got things to do. You're more than capable of running the place. You just need to come up with incentives for your people to participate in their own defense. Starting with wanting to avoid being slaves for whoever invades."

Eric nodded. "I'm making my pitch to everyone who'll listen. Maybe once you're gone, it will increase their urgency."

Art waved a hand. "Whatever. Not to be harsh, but it's not our problem anymore. Whoever chooses to stay in Seattle has a stake in seeing that it's safe. The idea that someone else is going to do all the heavy lifting to keep it that way isn't going to fly, so best to point out that the only thing standing between you and the bad guys is each other. People don't want to play, that's fine – come up with a system that excludes them from protection. Probably easiest to start with the police force. If someone able-bodied isn't willing to pitch in to protect their turf, make it clear that when something bad happens to them, they're on their own. That might convince some who're on the fence to join up."

"Good idea," said Greg, one of the members. "That could work."

Lucas cut in. "Think of it as paying taxes. You want cops to show up when it gets ugly, you need to pay them. Requiring involvement in the defense force is a good way of doing that."

The meeting meandered for about an hour; the logistics of the handoff were covered as well as a discussion of basic housekeeping issues, and when it broke up, Lucas and Art headed back to his office.

Lucas yawned and stretched his arms over his head. "I'm beat. Going for some shut-eye. Let me know if you hear anything from Salem."

"You've earned your rest. I'll let Sam know we're mobilizing, so he can get everything ready. He's got a lot of prep to still do, even though we've all known this was coming."

"Good deal. I'll be up and around within a few hours, and I'll stop back in."

"Perfect. You know where to find me." Art paused. "Thanks for everything, Lucas."

"Same right back at you…General."

Chapter 25

Amber Hot Springs, Colorado

Elijah's advance scouts returned to where the army had made camp a few miles from the hot springs, and Benjamin and Elijah went to meet them. The three scouts dismounted and lashed their animals to a tree.

"Well?" Elijah demanded.

"No signs of life."

"What?" Elijah blurted.

"That's right. We didn't go into the springs, but from a distance it looks deserted. No fires, most of the cabins burned to the ground, nobody to be seen."

"Burned to the ground?" Benjamin asked.

"Looked that way. Hard to say for certain till we're there, but that's my bet."

Elijah paced in frustration. "Someone must have warned them."

Benjamin tried to keep his tone agreeably neutral. "Obviously." He didn't point out that Elijah's strategy of razing everything he came across practically guaranteed that word would travel faster than his army could, and if anyone was in communication with Shangri-La, they'd have let them know. He'd tried to reason with the man over his policy, but he couldn't tell Elijah anything – Elijah did as Elijah pleased. Benjamin had suspected they might come up empty when they arrived for that very reason, but not wanting to incur Elijah's wrath, he'd kept his mouth shut after their initial discussions.

"Tell the men we're moving out," Elijah said. "I want to be at the springs by nightfall."

Benjamin winced at Elijah's high-handed tone but tilted his head in assent. "We'll move out within the hour."

The column of thousands of men worked its way along the trail like a giant centipede, led by Benjamin and Elijah, who'd insisted on riding point in spite of the risk of sniper fire if the scouts had misread the situation. As with most of his decisions, this one had been impulsive and designed to assuage his ego more than anything – Elijah, at the head of his army, bringing God's wrath to the heathens.

The procession rounded the final bend and found the hot springs completely deserted, just as the scouts had reported. The inhabitants had burned the structures they'd built, presumably to deprive Elijah's men of shelter in the event of inclement weather, and there was little to glean from what was left.

Elijah swung down from his horse, and Benjamin did the same. Elijah handed his reins to one of his subordinates and strode to where the large central fire pit sat, and glowered at it like it had insulted him. Benjamin joined him, and Elijah cursed under his breath before speaking.

"How long have they been gone?"

"I'll ask our trackers to sort through the wreckage and see if they can figure that out. But judging by the condition, at least a few days. Maybe a lot more."

"Do it."

Benjamin looked up at the sky, which was beginning to darken. "First we should make camp. It's doubtful we'll be able to do much in terms of finding a trail until daybreak."

"No. I want them working until nightfall."

"They might miss important clues, Elijah. It's self-defeating. And they need to pitch their tents, tend to their horses…"

"We didn't bring them all the way here to loaf. Do as I say."

"Of course."

Dusk intruded in the hunt for clues, just as Benjamin had warned, and the group spent a restive night under the stars. The following dawn Elijah was up with first light, ordering the scouts to be quick about picking up the trail.

"They'll have left signs of their passage," he said with the conviction of an expert. "No way around it. That many people will leave a trail to follow."

"Possibly," Benjamin agreed. "But if they're smart, they'll have created several false trails to slow us down. And it's not impossible to go long distances without anything obvious, depending on how skilled their trackers are."

"What do you mean, trackers? We're tracking them, not the other way around."

"They'll use theirs to cover the evidence of their passage. Because they'll know what to conceal and how best to do so," Benjamin explained.

Elijah's troubled frown deepened. "I don't like how negative you've become. I sense you're not happy with our quest. Say so, and I'll relieve you of your command, so you can return to Denver with your tail between your legs while I lead the men to victory."

"It's not that. I'm trying to explain what you're…what we're up against. These people have remained hidden for years. They're experts at it. We have to expect this is going to be complicated and not get our hopes up for an easy victory. Their survival depends on their success, and if they were warned, as seems likely, they know the stakes."

"I don't want to hear anything else but solutions, Benjamin. No more problems. Am I clear?"

"Of course. I'll see to it that the scouts get to work."

The day stretched on, and by twilight the trackers still hadn't found anything definitive. As Benjamin had surmised, there were several trails to follow, which had eaten considerable time, and all of which had dead-ended into rocky terrain where the group's passage would leave no trace. It wasn't until the following day that one of the men reported that he'd found evidence of a genuine path north, and Elijah had insisted on mobilizing immediately in spite of the afternoon being more than half gone.

As the men made camp that night in a windy valley with no shelter to fend off the cold, Benjamin watched them go about their preparations with misgivings. Elijah had proclaimed that they would follow his father's murderers to the ends of the earth, that they were on a holy mission, divinely guided, and would never give up. Benjamin suspected that Elijah had begun to believe his own rhetoric of his greatness and the righteousness of his crusade, which could only lead to misery if he refused to be reasonable. Thousands of men forced to forage for sustenance as they moved would slow them considerably, and a few days of the weather turning against them could eradicate any trail, leaving them in the middle of nowhere with no place to turn, far from home and with nothing to eat.

Not circumstances Benjamin wanted to court, but Elijah seemed hell-bent on driving his men to the brink, no matter the damage to them. It baffled Benjamin that the charismatic leader could be so blind to the danger he was inviting, but he'd learned on this trip that Elijah's narcissism knew no bounds and was driving his decisions. He truly believed that he was the Lord's instrument on earth, not the son of a traveling preacher who'd struck pay dirt in the collapse, which made his leadership as dangerous as any Benjamin could imagine.

The question being what, if anything, Benjamin could do about it other than follow along obediently and do his best to avert disaster.

Chapter 26

Salem, Oregon

Scott stood with his hands on his hips as he watched Clark labor over his beloved locomotive with a welding torch they'd scrounged in one of the shops. During the fight for Salem, one of the defenders had hit the engine with multiple grenades, damaging the boiler as well as the shaft that drove the wheels. Clark had spent most of the night trying to jury-rig the contraption, but his assessment hadn't been positive that morning when Scott had asked whether it was fixable.

"Sure, I can patch it up, but it isn't going to be as stable as it was on the run up here," Clark had reported. "Even with the welds, those spots won't be as strong as the rest, and the shaft...I can cobble something together, but there's no way it's going to be able to pull fifty loaded cars. The strain would wreck it before we got a mile. At least that's my guess. Too early to tell until I really dig into it."

Now, with almost two days of work invested in the project, Clark was tentative in his prediction when Scott asked whether it could be trusted to transport the men to ambush Lucas's group before it reached Salem.

"You can see I was able to fix the shaft, so it'll run. The question is how much weight it'll take before busting for good."

"What do you think?"

"I wouldn't want to try more than...fifteen cars."

"That's impossible. We need at least double that, assuming half the men stayed on the roof."

"You have the same problem with the boiler. The patches will hold, but I wouldn't take her up past the halfway point or one's likely to blow. And when that happens, or the shaft breaks, nobody's going anywhere."

"You can't use some other material to create a new shaft?"

"That's high-tension steel. So no, any old hunk of metal won't do the job. Plus, in case you haven't noticed, I'm not a machinist and there aren't any specialty metal fabrication shops open for business, not to mention any electricity."

"How the hell am I supposed to transport five thousand men on fifteen cars?"

"Maybe we can do three trips. Assuming it doesn't blow up on one of them."

"This is a disaster."

"Not really. I mean, why not just wait for them to come to Salem and hit them once they're in town?"

Scott shook his head. "Stick to repairs and running the train. We need to ambush them on the road or our numbers are way too close to be able to be sure of winning."

Clark shrugged. "Well, you're the commander, so I'll take your word for it. I'm just telling you that she won't haul nearly the load as on the way here. That's just fact. How you work around it's up to you."

Scott glared at the old engine as though it were responsible for the predicament, and then began to pace, thinking furiously. Maybe Clark's solution wasn't so stupid after all. If they could get a couple of thousand men per run, they'd only need two trips to ferry most of the force north to what, after studying the map, was clearly the most favorable spot for an ambush.

"How do we test it so we know it'll hold?"

"There's no way other than to load up as much as you dare and see what happens. Not very scientific, but we're making this up as we go along."

"You don't think it'll handle twenty cars?"

"Maybe. Maybe not. But I'd be conservative, because once something breaks in the middle of nowhere, that's all she wrote."

"Let's split the difference and try eighteen. Fifteen passenger cars, and three equipment and horse cars."

"You're the boss. But don't blame me if she gives up on you. I'd do more like ten to be safe, and run more trips."

"We don't have that luxury. How soon before you're finished?"

"Got to deal with two more iffy seams, and then we can run up a head of steam and see how she does."

"In English, Clark."

"Maybe by tomorrow morning unless you want to run in the dark. I don't recommend that. You saw how easy it is to pull up track. No way of knowing that the rails run all the way where we need."

"You're just a font of optimism, aren't you?"

"Look, I've had maybe three hours of sleep in almost two days. I'm not sugarcoating anything for you. It may or may not make it. That's as good as I can commit to."

Scott nodded. "I'll let the men know the first bunch will be moving out at sunrise."

"Sure. Now can I get back to work while I'm still conscious?"

Scott left Clark to his job, scowling as he walked to what had been the state capitol building and was now Blood Dogs headquarters. According to what the Illuminati had shared with them, Lucas could arrive at any moment, and Scott was deeply uncomfortable taking on an army about the same size that was fresh off beating the Chinese army and had proven itself against more than a few random civilians. The Blood Dogs were meaner than striped snakes and would fight like they meant it, but depending on what kind of leadership Lucas's had, they might be outclassed, even with the latest equipment.

He didn't intend to learn the hard way in the city when he could choose the time and place to sneak attack. No, he'd have to take the risk of doing multiple runs, and hope that the engine made it. Getting home was another matter, but one challenge at a time. For now, he needed to figure out how to ship five thousand men north with all their gear as expediently as possible using a locomotive that should have been put out to scrap a century before.

The following day Clark hesitantly announced that the train was ready, and attached eighteen cars to the engine. While the first group of men clambered aboard, others loaded the cargo and animals under Scott's watchful eye. When nothing more could be fit onto the train, the two firemen began stoking the furnace, shoveling coal into it as fast as they could. Clark studied the pressure gauge with the attention of a surgeon, and when the boiler was up to three-quarters pressure, waved at Scott and put the locomotive in gear.

The engine groaned in protest as the wheels bit into the rails, and then the train inched forward. Clark moved to the side of the cab and looked over the edge at the repaired shaft. He was pleased to see it holding, the weld showing no signs of buckling. He was turning back to the firemen to urge them to shovel faster when two of the patches on the boiler gave, and jets of scalding steam shot from the rents with hypersonic velocity, catching one of the firemen in the face and upper body.

He screamed in agony as his skin was seared from his bones, and Clark ducked beneath the jets and groped for the lever to disengage the transmission. He succeeded and dropped to the steel floor as the injured fireman's agonized cries flooded the cockpit.

Scott came at a run as the train slowed and stopped, and Clark and the other fireman crawled to the side of the cockpit and pulled themselves clear of the locomotive with the help of Scott and three of his men. Once standing on the side of the tracks, Clark straightened and watched as Scott's helpers dragged the dying fireman from the floor, leaving a skid of broiled flesh and seared skin on the cockpit base.

The fireman was still screaming in tortured pain when they set him on the ground, and Scott's face hardened at the sight of what had moments before been a strapping young man, now almost unrecognizable as human, face pressure-blasted from his skull, blinded, and with only tendons and sinews remaining, most of his upper body a steaming mass of cooked hamburger. Scott withdrew his pistol, stepped to the man's side, and fired two rounds into his skull, ending his misery.

Clark stumbled three yards away and spewed up his breakfast, his body racked with spasms of nausea as he continued until he was bent over, dry heaving. Scott waited for the spell to end, and then walked over to him, his pistol now holstered.

"You were right," he said tersely.

"Hell of a way to find out."

"How long to fix it?"

"Depends on how bad the damage is. Maybe a few hours. Maybe more. I have to wait until it cools down and I can see what the problem is."

"All right. Go to work."

Clark straightened and spit bile at his feet. He coughed and grimaced and then regarded Scott with a dark expression. "Probably a good idea to unhook at least five or six of the cars."

"Yeah. I got that. We'll make it happen."

"Gonna need another fireman, too."

"I'll find someone. Anything else?"

"Have your men bring the welder and all my tools. We'll need to keep them on the train in case it happens again when we're underway."

"Check." He looked at the dead fireman without emotion. "I'll send a crew for the remains." He hesitated. "There was nothing we could do for him but end it quickly."

Clark swallowed hard and looked away. "I know."

Scott seemed like he wanted to say something else, but after a long moment he headed back to the station with his men, walking along the tracks and occasionally glancing at the train, where gunmen were dropping from the cars with puzzled expressions, leaving Clark to the hiss of steam escaping from the boiler through cracked seams and the barely audible crackle of the dead fireman's cooking flesh.

Chapter 27

North of Salem, Oregon

Over a week had passed since Lucas and Art had led their men out of Seattle, and they'd encountered no insurmountable obstacles on the road south. Because of their sheer numbers, they didn't have to fear attack by any of the usual raiders or scavengers, who had been giving the army a wide berth. They traveled from late afternoon through the night and slept during the day to avoid dehydration and unnecessary wear and tear on the animals, who could rest during the worst of the heat and make better time in the cool of darkness.

The lead riders guided the rest by torchlight when the sky was overcast, which it was much of the time, sticking to the highway for ease of passage since safety wasn't a concern.

They'd been underway for three hours and the light was going out of the sky when Lucas slowed Tango and raised his M4 to peer through the scope at the road ahead. A collection of tents stretched along both shoulders, and Lucas called to Sam to join him as the column came to a stop.

"What do you make of that?" he asked. "Trouble?"

Sam looked through his binoculars for a moment, scanned the encampment, and lowered them slowly. "Looks like a bunch of scavengers. Only a few hundred, tops. We'll be fine. They won't try anything."

"We don't want anyone taking potshots at us as we go by."

"I'll send an advance party to check it out."

"I'll go with them," Lucas said.

"Then I will too. Pretty boring lately. I could use some excitement."

"Be careful what you wish for," Lucas muttered as Sam rode off to collect several dozen of his most capable men.

They rode toward the camp and slowed as they neared when it became obvious that few of the inhabitants were moving. They were greeted by the wafting stench of rotting flesh rising from bloated corpses that had been tossed in a heap and left to decay without any regard for burial. Lucas pulled his bandanna over his mouth and nose, and Sam did the same, though the cloth did little to cloak the stink of death.

"Bad," Sam said.

Lucas didn't respond and goaded Tango forward, anxious to be past the dead.

The camp was in disarray, mostly men sitting outside their tents, gaunt and listless, their skin blistered and sickly. Lucas swung down from his horse and walked toward a group gathered around a fire, and tipped his hat at them. One of the men looked up at him with dead eyes in a skeletal face and then resumed staring at the fire. "What do you want?" he croaked, his voice hoarse.

"Just passing through. What happened here?"

The man coughed, the sound wet and unhealthy. "Portland happened. We're all refugees from there. Thought we'd made it out before the radiation got us, but we were kidding ourselves." He coughed again. "We're all dead. Been dropping for weeks. Some worse than others, but nobody's going to make it."

"How many?" Lucas asked softly.

"We started off with around five hundred. Managed to slip past the bikers and make our way north. We were mostly okay, but then we started dying. No rhyme or reason to it. Eventually we just camped out here and buried our dead best we could. But now nobody's got the energy, so we're just waiting to die. Best move through fast and stay away from the river. And don't eat anything you catch or find – radiation's getting everything."

Lucas didn't bother explaining to the man that the groundwater they had been drinking was also likely contaminated and was responsible for poisoning them, not the river. It was clear none of them was long for this world, and there was no point to explaining the fatal error they'd made.

Lucas walked back to Sam, and the men retraced their steps to the main column, where Art was waiting with Terry and Gary by his side. "Well?" he asked.

"Portland survivors on their last legs. All dying of radiation sickness. Nothing we can do for them except leave them to die in peace."

"God…"

"Seems to be out to lunch in these parts," Lucas finished for him. "Best we can do is move by quickly and turn off the road before we get too close to the river. Pass the word to the men that they're going to have to make their water last – the river's poisoned the water table, so it'll be a while before we can refill."

"You're sure we can't help them?" Gary asked. "What a horrible way to go."

"They've got weapons and ammo. I saw a few pistols and rifles. I suspect most of them aren't waiting till the bitter end after watching their companions drop."

The procession got underway again, and the men moved past the dying encampment with averted eyes, the reality of death as thick and heavy in the air as cooking smoke. Once they were well past, they turned off the highway north of Longview, using a map that had survived the collapse to guide them. They'd have to cross the river at Portland and would be exposed to radiation when doing so, but the toxicity level wasn't so high that an hour on the bridge would be grossly dangerous – at least no more so than most of the other threats that lurked around every turn of the road. And that was a problem that was at least two days' ride away. In the meantime, they just had to make the best time they could while safeguarding their water, living off their provisions rather than hoping to hunt down deer and rabbit for food.

Art rode forward to where Lucas was following the point riders and leaned into him. "Makes you wonder why the Chinese would even want to try to take this over. It's only going to get worse from here."

"Maybe nobody told them that it's going to be a toxic wasteland in a few years."

"Better to rule in hell than serve in heaven."

Lucas smiled. "Didn't fancy you for a Milton reader."

"They forced me to read *Paradise Lost* in high school. The brain remembers the strangest things."

They rode together in silence for several minutes. Lucas frowned and looked to the older man. "Got a bad feeling about where we're headed. Ruby's in Salem. If anything happened to her…"

"Let's cross that bridge when we get there. All we know is they weren't answering our calls. Nothing more. No point in making it more than it is."

"I know that. But I'm still worried. Can't think of too many things that would make four radios all go dark at the same time. Those I can…none of them are good."

"We'll know soon enough. Let's just get through this part, and then we can tackle the rest."

When the column left Seattle, it had been almost six thousand strong, with many of the local men deciding that a life on the road in the Freedom Army, as they'd taken to calling it, was preferable to waiting for the water to grow toxic at home. The troops were in good spirits, with the exception of the Salem contingent, among whom word of the lack of communication from home had spread like wildfire.

"Good advice," Lucas acknowledged. "No reason to make this more difficult than it is."

"Ruby's a tough one. If anyone can make it through rough weather, it's her."

"Eventually every cat runs out of lives."

"Let's hope this one's got a few more in her."

"Amen."

Chapter 28

South of Wilsonville, Oregon

A rider raced along the road to where two thousand Blood Dogs were waiting north of Salem, watching the highways leading from Portland for Lucas's force. The rider slowed when he neared the spot they'd chosen for the ambush and leapt from his horse. He ran to where Danny, the group's commander, stood.

"They're coming. Maybe three miles out."

"How many?"

"A lot. At least five thousand. Maybe more."

"Shit." Danny considered the odds of his two thousand men being able to take on five successfully. While the new weapons were a considerable edge, sheer numbers couldn't always be trumped by technology, and the odds didn't favor him. He figured the locomotive must have failed after the second trip or somewhere on the third, because the next thousand men had never shown, leaving the Dogs seriously shorthanded for the ambush. Less than half the full attack force facing a seasoned fighting contingent didn't appeal to Danny, but Scott had made it clear that he didn't want Lucas reaching Salem, so he didn't have much choice. Then again, he had the element of surprise, and if he could attack when Lucas's men were vulnerable, he might be able to halve their number before they knew what hit them.

"Breakdown?"

"A lot on horseback. I'd guess at least…a thousand, maybe more. The rest on foot."

"All armed?"

"Of course. The usual stuff, but they've got a bunch of wagons and carts, so there's no telling what they're hauling."

"Could be supplies."

"Or weapons."

Danny nodded slowly. "Guess there's only one way to find out."

"Maybe we should let them pass us by, and I can ride ahead and warn Salem? Bracket them from the front and back?"

Danny considered the idea and shook his head. "That isn't what they sent us here to do. And we'd lose our advantage. No, we need to get into position and take them on here."

"Not too much light left."

"That'll work in our favor."

The scout left Danny to his planning. He'd been instrumental in beating the Stockton gang, but aside from that, his combat experience had been as a sergeant in the army stationed in the Middle East before a dishonorable discharge and a long prison sentence for killing a man in a bar fight. He'd only seen active duty three times as part of patrol duty, and all had been skirmishes with terrorist factions that had been over almost before they'd started due to the army's superior firepower.

He knew he was ill-equipped to take on an army over twice his size, but he had no choice – a bad situation by any measure.

"Damn," he muttered, but the curse did little to curb the anxiety that was creeping up his throat. They had an hour, maybe less, and then they'd be in the swamp whether they were ready or not.

Lucas held up a hand to stop the march, and cocked his head while he studied the surroundings. After several long beats, he called over his shoulder, "Take a break. Fifteen minutes."

Sam and Art rode up to him with puzzled expressions. "What's going on? We just took one an hour or so ago."

"Something's off. I want some time to figure out what."

"What does that mean, off?" Art asked.

"I don't know. But I plan to find out."

Lucas drove Tango forward and disappeared into the trees, leaving Sam and Art to watch his departure in confusion. He picked his way through the conifers until he came to a game trail that roughly paralleled the road, and Tango obligingly followed it as though reading Lucas's mind.

Lucas couldn't be sure what had triggered the faint sense of unease that had descended over him as they'd approached the pass with hills running along both sides of the road, but he'd learned to trust his instinct, and it was clamoring a warning. Tango slowed as they pushed deeper into the forest, and Lucas leaned forward and patted the big stallion's neck.

"What is it?" he whispered in Tango's ear.

Tango stopped, and Lucas dropped from the saddle with his M4 and continued along the track on foot until he arrived at a gap in the trees. He lay flat in the tall grass and eased his rifle into position and eyed the far side of the valley through the scope.

At first there was nothing out of sync, but then movement drew his attention to the hillside. He studied the terrain and spotted what had drawn his eye – a pair of men in a poorly camouflaged machine-gun nest with what looked like a big-bore machine gun. He continued to scan the area and picked out another three with grenade launchers and a mortar.

Five minutes of careful perusal and he'd counted several hundred nests, many with serious weaponry. He switched to the other hill and found much the same.

Whoever was lying in wait had taken great pains to conceal their positions and were equipped like a strike force.

The men lying in wait were obviously expecting Lucas's force, which meant that they'd had advance spotters who'd notified them of their approach. Who it was didn't matter to Lucas; right now the question was what to do.

Lucas retreated to where he'd left Tango and made his way back to where Art and the men were resting. He swung down from his horse and motioned to Art and Sam to join him, and quickly explained the situation.

"They didn't see you?" Art asked.

"No."

"And you think there's over a thousand of them?"

"Looks that way."

"Then we have two choices," Art said. "We can circle around and find a different route, or we can ambush them while they're waiting to ambush us."

"How many hours of light you figure we have?" Lucas asked. "Three? Four?"

"About that," said Sam.

"Seems to me that if we could sneak up on them, we could hit them hard before they were sure what was happening and take out their positions." Lucas inhaled deeply. "The portable solar's got our NV gear charged. That could be a major advantage if they don't have access to night vision equipment."

"Even if they do, if we hit them simultaneously after dark, we might be able to neutralize most of their heavy artillery before they can put it to use," Art said. "They're expecting us to approach the valley using the highway, so they're not expecting an attack from the hills. Want to bet everything's ranged for the valley floor? They couldn't retarget their mortars in a matter of seconds. That might be their Achilles' heel."

"Let's say we did that," Sam said. "If they're expecting us, won't they get suspicious if we don't show up within an hour?"

"Fair point," Art said. "But nobody said we have to stick to some schedule. Maybe we like it here and decided to break camp early. In which case they'll let down their guard some, figuring we'll be moving again at dawn." He paused and looked back at the thousands of fighters who were lounging where they could. "Way I see it, we can either send a few thousand marching toward the valley while we sneak into position, or we pretend we're doing repairs on the carts here and make them wait – and hit them right before dawn, when they'll have gotten back into their nests. Better would be if they were forced to stay in them all night. Either way, that sounds like the win to me. And it would give us time to get our own machine guns and grenade launchers into the field, and range our mortars on their hillside positions."

Lucas nodded. "Then that's the plan."

Danny checked and rechecked his mechanical watch every ten minutes and, when Lucas's force failed to appear, called his scouts to the area he was using as his command post and instructed them to reconnoiter the valley and figure out what had gone wrong. They took off and, when they returned an hour later, reported that they'd spotted tents being pitched, and that it appeared that the army was staying put for the night. Danny did his best to control his irritation, fueled by sustained adrenaline in anticipation of battle, and instructed the scouts to return to their vantage points to watch until nightfall.

When the sky darkened with nothing having changed, he sent runners to the hills to instruct his men to stay in position. They ran too much risk if they tried to leave their nests and return to them in the dark before dawn, so it would mean a seriously uncomfortable night in the rough. He knew the decision wouldn't be popular, but he didn't see any way around it. They couldn't afford to make an error now, with the enemy only a couple of miles away around a single bend.

Chapter 29

Lucas crept through the brush on foot, NV goggles in place. He'd left Tango safely back at the encampment along with the rest of the animals. Six of Art's best fighters accompanied Lucas, all with night vision goggles enabled, to search for advance scouts any sane tactician would have put into place to alert the enemy of his force's approach.

Lucas stopped, made a hand signal, and pointed through the trees to his right. One of the fighters, all of whom were equipped with crossbows, inched past Lucas and made his way forward until he was within twenty yards of an unsuspecting enemy scout, who was watching the camp and not his back.

The bowstring discharged with an audible *thwack*, but before the scout could react, he was skewered through the small of his back with a razor-tipped hunting arrow. He dropped his gun and pawed unbelievingly at the bolt, slashing his hands to ribbons in the process, and was attempting to stand when Lucas's man reached him and slit his throat with a single swipe.

Blood spurted from his carotid artery and he crumpled to the ground, and the fighter made his way back to where Lucas and the squad were waiting in silence.

"How loud was that?" the fighter whispered.

"Pretty quiet," Lucas murmured. "But there'll be more."

They continued their search and dispatched three other watchers over the course of an hour. When they were sure there were no more heat signatures on the infrared screens of their NV goggles, they returned to where Sam, Art, Henry, and Terry were stationed with their most seasoned men – all veterans of the Seattle battle, with many having participated in Newport as well.

"We got them all. At least I'm pretty sure we did," Lucas said.

"Good news," Art said. "How many?"

"Four."

"Weapons?"

"All military-issued M16s," Lucas said, gesturing to his squad, who were carrying the retrieved rifles.

"Sounds like somebody got into an armory," Henry observed.

"They didn't look like regular army. All tatted up," Lucas said. "Looks like a gang."

"Why would some gang want to bushwhack us with military-level gear?" Sam asked.

"That's the question, isn't it?" Art replied. "If we take some prisoners, we'll find out. But the emphasis should be on eliminating their positions first. Survivors can be handled in the mop-up."

Lucas squared his shoulders. "We should get underway. It'll be dawn in a couple of hours."

Art turned to the assembled squad leaders. "All right. We'll be at the target in about forty-five minutes, maybe a little less. You've all been briefed on what we're up against. If anyone has any questions, ask them now, because I want complete silence until we're in position and ready to rock and roll."

A few of the leaders asked for clarification on the layout, and Lucas took them through the paces again, aware of time slipping away. When he was finished, he looked over the faces of the men and cleared his throat. "Remember: hold your fire until I give the signal, which will be the first mortar round going off. Then rain hell down on them. I want all of the nests wiped out before they know what hit them. Don't bother with conserving ammo. The priority is to eliminate the threats. Clear?"

The men nodded, and Lucas glanced at Art and Sam. "All right. How many mortars do we have?"

"Thirty, with enough shells to take on a small city."

"Brownings?"

"A dozen. We need more?"

"Shouldn't, but couldn't hurt to round up another three or four. Grenade launchers?"

"Twenty. About half the Chinese ones we captured," Sam said.

"They're pretty accurate. Although I like ours better."

"We can switch them out if you want."

Lucas considered. "Probably won't matter. We're losing time. Grab three more Brownings and let's do this. Safeties on until you're ready to fire."

The group set off five minutes later, taking care to avoid making any noise, Lucas and Sam on point. An hour later they were spread across the rise facing the ambush point, the nests lit large in their infrared NV goggles.

Lucas moved quietly through the brush to each of the mortar crews and pointed out which of their enemy counterparts to target. He understood it might take a few shells to zero in with any precision, but with an effective ten to twenty rounds per minute firing capability, it wouldn't take long to blanket the target areas. When he had completed his task, he crept back to where Sam and Henry were in position with a mortar pointed at the sky and fifteen rounds laid out, ready for loading.

"I make them to be about four hundred yards," Henry said. "More or less."

Lucas glanced at his watch. "It'll be light in under an hour. We need to do this." He took a deep breath and flicked the firing selector of his M4 from safe to three-round burst. "Fire when ready."

Sam steadied himself, and Henry dropped the first round into the mortar tube, where it exploded skyward with a whump. Several seconds later the projectile exploded thirty yards shy of the target, and Henry made a small adjustment to the mortar and nodded to Sam, who handed him another round.

This time the nest took a direct hit, and then the entire hillside was lit by scores of explosions as the rest of the mortars delivered their payloads. Lucas's grenade launchers opened fire on their counterparts in the enemy positions, and in less than a minute the slopes were ablaze from hundreds of blasts.

If the enemy shooters had NV gear, they hadn't put it to use, because there was no return fire, which made sense. As Lucas had hoped, the surviving gunners had no idea what or where to shoot, and were probably scrambling to get to safety rather than sticking it out and being slaughtered by the relentless grenade and mortar salvos.

Ten minutes later, the enemy area had been turned into an inferno, the nests engulfed in thick smoke and flames. Lucas rose and crossed to the nearest Browning, where Terry was waiting patiently, his loader beside him.

"If you see anything move, shoot it," he said.

"You got it, boss," Terry said, and swept the area with the big barrel, seeking a target.

Lucas didn't wait for him to find one but ran along their line to pass the word to the rest of the machine gunners, and by the time Terry's weapon began to bark death at the hillside, he was on his way back to where Sam and Henry were waiting.

"What do you think?" Sam shouted over the roar of the nearby Browning.

Lucas spit to the side. "I think a whole lot of gangbangers just learned the hard way what a real fight's all about."

The shooting continued sporadically until dawn lit the valley, at which point Lucas and the infantry swept down and took the fight to the surviving attackers. In another half hour they'd taken nine prisoners, and the machine guns had cut down hundreds of ambushers once they showed themselves, their assault rifles no match against the .50-caliber onslaught.

When the fighting was finally over, Lucas and Art faced off against their captives and began questioning them. All were covered in prison ink and overtly hostile, with the jailhouse thousand-yard stare of hard timers who'd grown up on the street shooting each other, and who seemed surprised they'd made it this far. Several were wounded, and the medics bandaged their arms and legs while they were questioned.

After an hour, it became obvious none would talk when they were together. Lucas ordered them to be separated, and they tried again. The first three Lucas interrogated refused to do anything but curse him and tell him he was a dead man. But the fourth, a not particularly bright example of the street scum who invariably terrorized the civilian population post-collapse, offered up that they were from Sacramento and had come to fight Lucas's army on behalf of their leader, Amos.

"Sacramento?" Lucas repeated.

"That's right. Sacto," the man said. "S-Town. We come hard there."

"Who's we?"

"Blood Dogs, man. BD." The man made a face and gnashed his teeth. "Woof."

"Why? We haven't done anything to you. I've never even heard of the Blood Dogs," Lucas said. "I've never been near California, much less Sacramento."

The man's eyes darted away before returning to settle on Lucas with a malevolent gleam. "Word is you pissed off the wrong dudes."

"Who? The Crew? Is that what this is all about?"

The man's expression registered genuine confusion. "The Crew? Shit, no."

"Then who?"

"You got an early expiration date on you, you know?"

"Who says so?"

He looked away. "I'm not saying any more."

Lucas decided to switch to something that genuinely puzzled him. "How did you get here? Sacramento's a long way off. Hundreds of miles, isn't it? You walk all the way here, or ride?"

The man's lips curled in a sneer. "We rigged a train."

Lucas couldn't hide his surprise. "A train?"

"That's right, *esse*. First class." He spit blood and grinned at Lucas like a demon, teeth stained with crimson. "And we would have killed your stinking ass if it hadn't broken down."

Lucas nodded as though he knew all about it. "Left you stranded, did it?"

"Not for long. Best watch yourself, homey. Blood Dogs got long memories and a mean bite."

Lucas laughed dryly. "You mean the rest of you back in Salem? You think they're going to bail you out?" Lucas asked, venturing a guess that would explain why Salem had gone dark. "Sorry to break the news, but it ain't gonna happen."

"Some bad dudes. You may have gotten over on us here, but when they…"

The gangbanger's mouth clamped shut when he realized he'd given too much away. Lucas nodded again. "Don't worry. We won't kill you. Not sure what we're going to do with you, but that's not how we roll. Even if you're an obvious lowlife, we captured you fair and square, and I don't allow my men to execute prisoners of war, even if there are no written rules."

"You think that makes you better than us?"

Lucas looked the man up and down, taking in the scars and tats and close-cropped hair and skittish meth eyes, and had to grin in spite of the bleak news that Salem had fallen to miscreants.

"Definitely not that."

Chapter 30

Green River, Utah

Shots rang out from the bridge ahead, and the horse beneath Arnold stumbled and fell, taking him down with it. One of the slugs thumped into his plate carrier, but the ceramic slab protected him, although the impact hurt. He threw himself to the side just before the animal's weight could crush his leg, and was already bringing his rifle to bear as he rolled in the beige dust that coated the highway.

The rest of the members of Shangri-La took what cover they could behind their carts while the group's forward gunmen engaged the shooters, buying time for the others to protect themselves however they could. Arnold adjusted his rifle's scope, squinted through it to see who was shooting at them, and spied a trio of scavengers, their occupation obvious from their matted hair, filthy clothes, and poor condition lever-action rifles.

"Scavengers," he cried to the gunmen, and steadied his M16 before squeezing off a single shot aimed at the center of the nearest scavenger's forehead. The man's skull fountained a spray of blood and bone, and the other scavengers ducked out of sight behind a beam. "Got one. But there's two more," he warned.

"How do you want to handle this?" one of the gunmen asked.

"Craig, you and Jim and I can push one of the carts close enough that we can take them out with a grenade," Arnold said. "No reason to let them pick us off."

159

"Done. Which cart?" Craig asked.

Arnold twisted to where the column was stalled. "That one," he said, pointing to one of the provision carts fashioned from four motorcycle tires and two metal axles. "Crawl over to it and disconnect the team while Jim and I keep them pinned down. Doesn't look like either have scopes. And you never know. We might get lucky."

Craig grunted and began dog-crawling toward the cart, which six people were huddled behind, the four men with their rifles pointed at the bridge. Craig reached it and explained what he intended to do.

"Sorry to take your cover, but there's no other way," he finished.

"What do we do in the meantime?" one of the women asked.

"Lie flat on the ground. They won't be able to hit you at this range."

"How do you know?" a man asked.

"No scopes. It's why they took out the horse. Poor accuracy."

"What if you're wrong?"

Shots boomed from Arnold's and Jim's rifles when one of the scavengers showed himself, deciding the matter. "Do as I say or we're all going to suffer," Craig said.

"You need any help with the cart?" asked Ernie, the largest of the men.

"How heavy is it?"

"Heavy."

"Damn. Think the two of us can push it to where Arnold and Jim are?"

"Maybe."

"I'll cover for you. Unfasten the horses."

"Why don't you while I cover you?" Ernie growled.

"My rifle's way better than yours. Now stop bickering and do it."

Ernie didn't look happy at being ordered around, but he said nothing more and slid his rifle into the back of the cart, and then worked his way around to the front and slid the harness free, allowing the horses to trot off. He sprinted back to the rear of the cart, where Craig had his rifle trained on the bridge, and retrieved his weapon.

"All right. Ready?" Craig asked. He glanced at the others. "Lie flat facing the bridge and keep your heads down. You'll be fine."

They obeyed, and he and Ernie heaved at the cart. The wheels grudgingly began turning, and then they were slowly pushing it to where Arnold and Jim were firing occasional shots at the bridge. When they drew near, Craig called out to them, "Now what?"

Arnold loosed three shots and crawled to the cart. Together they pushed it to Jim, and then it was blocking them all from the scavengers at the bridge.

"Okay. Let's do this," Arnold said, and together they trundled the cart toward the span as other members of Shangri-La laid down covering fire. They neared the bridge, and a few shots from the scavengers smacked into the heavy wooden sides of the cart, but didn't make it all the way through.

"How long you figure the overpass is?" Craig asked.

"Maybe hundred and fifty yards. But they're on this end, so we don't need to get much closer."

As if they'd heard him, the scavengers increased their fire at the cart, but to no effect.

Arnold freed a hand grenade from his vest and looked to Craig. "Another few feet would narrow the odds. Hate to waste more than one grenade on road parasites like these."

"You got it," Craig said, and they shouldered the cart forward another dozen yards before stopping.

Arnold pulled the pin on the grenade and lobbed it over the top of the cart, and had his rifle back at the ready by the time the orb detonated at the base of the bridge on the riverbank. He was already around the cart and running hard as clumps of rock and dirt geysered into the air from the explosion. Craig and Jim followed close behind, spreading out as they ran.

They reached the bridge and swept the area over the bank with their rifles, and spotted three corpses, two of which were nearly unrecognizable as such from the impact of the grenade. Arnold raised his weapon to scan the entire span and, when he saw no other threats, raced across to the far side to confirm there were no more miscreants lying in wait.

He was back a minute later and waved at his fellows back at the highway. Several of the men retrieved the horses that had drawn the cart, and everyone regrouped. Arnold strode back to the column with Craig, Jim, and Ernie in tow.

Once the team of horses was reattached to the cart, Elliot approached and admired the nine bullet holes in the conveyance's side. "Good work."

Arnold shrugged. They'd had a dozen similar skirmishes on the road to Utah and had overcome all their adversaries, with only one man wounded in the frays. Being attacked by road vermin had become so routine it barely registered and, if anything, broke up the boredom of the long trek west.

"Let's get across before more of their buddies show up," Arnold replied, regarding the bridge. "Although the whole place looks deserted."

"Must have been desperate or crazy to attack an armed group like us," Elliot observed.

"Scavengers aren't the brightest."

"Doesn't take a rocket scientist to do the math of hundreds against three."

"Probably weren't paying attention in school. Good riddance."

They crossed the river and continued through the town, which was ghostly quiet as night approached. Abandoned homes lined the plain to the north, and even at a distance it was obvious that the town had been looted and stripped of anything useful and now served as a waylay point for scumbags and nothing more. An arid wind blew from the buildings, carrying with it dust and the scent of muddy water, but other than the trio of scavengers, they didn't see another soul.

Once they were past the town, Elliot called a break and went to sit with Arnold and Julie, who'd joined him moments earlier. Sierra saw them and approached with Tim and Eve in hand.

"Please," he said. "Sit."

"Thanks," Sierra said, and took a seat on the rim of the cart with Eve in her lap.

"Shouldn't be much farther," Elliot said.

"Maybe, what, a hundred miles or so?"

"Or so." Elliot smiled at Julie. "How are you holding up?"

"I've had better months."

"We all have."

"What are we going to do once we get to Provo?" Sierra asked.

"Hopefully join their community and do our level best to blend in."

"What if they don't want us? Aren't they all Mormons or something?"

Elliot nodded. "It's true that they're religious. But they're honorable. There are worse things than believing in a creator."

"The point is that some of us don't."

"Maybe you'll decide you prefer their company to endless miles on the road."

"Do you think we'd have to convert?" Julie asked.

"I honestly have no idea. But I'd advise you to think long and hard about everything we've done to survive so far. Would taking on a new religion really be the worst thing in the world?"

"So the plan is to try to blend in with a bunch of zealots?" Sierra demanded. "Nobody mentioned that when we were talking about what to do."

Elliot's gaze hardened and he fixed her with a cold stare. "Sierra, if you were still back at the hot springs, the chances are overwhelming that you'd be long dead. So would your daughter and son. Instead, you're here to ask me impertinent questions. I'd suggest you consider whether your family dead is better than this alternative. If it isn't, keep your doubts to yourself. Am I being clear?"

Sierra stepped back like she'd been slapped, and managed a single nod. Eve looked at Elliot with her startlingly lucid blue eyes and smiled. "There's nothing wrong with believing in God."

"That's right, darling," Elliot said. "Nothing at all." He looked at

Julie and Arnold. "We've saved a large chunk of the human race through our efforts. I have to believe that wasn't by accident. Call it whatever you will, but there's something bigger at play here than random chance. We achieved the impossible, and we've escaped our enemies more times than I can count. If you believe that's all just chaos and entropy at work, I won't try to talk you out of it, but I'll just say this: if you don't believe in ultimate good, then at least have the brains to understand that ultimate evil not only exists but has been winning for some time now. Look at the state of the world. It's a disaster and getting worse. Gangs running the country, good people slaughtered like sheep, pestilence and violence everywhere… That's reality. You can choose to believe it's just our nature to be evil, or you can subscribe, as I do, to the idea that we're all playing our parts in a bigger play than daily survival. Doesn't really matter to me which you believe. But it will to the folks in Provo." He sighed. "Look, all I'm saying is that if you have doubts about them, keep them to yourselves." He switched his attention back to Eve and then raised his eyes to Sierra. "If not for you, then for your children. They deserve better than to be hunted down by wolves as their future."

He stood and walked away, leaving them to mull over his words, the gentle soughing of the wind across the high desert a monotone melody for their thoughts.

Chapter 31

Snake rode through the city limits and pointed his horse toward the downtown area, where Abilene, a minor trading hub, had several watering holes. While technically under Crew control, the town had been abandoned by the gang as Snake had been forced to consolidate power closer to Houston. Now it was wide open, with competitive small gangs vying for supremacy in a bloody ongoing killing spree.

That didn't stop traders and the braver of the miscreants from frequenting the bars, where virtually anything could be had for a price: drugs, alcohol, sex, weapons, murder for hire. Snake had decided that because it was now a frontier town with no contact with the Crew, it would be an ideal spot to see what quality of recruits he could source. He'd been out of the field for a long while and understood things could change depending on who was running from what to where, but one thing that never varied was that killers could be found for a pittance in most trading towns.

His horse had proved surprisingly hardy, and they'd covered on average thirty miles a day, which after the first week he'd grown accustomed to, riding at night in the cooler air and sleeping during the day. No patrols or search parties had come after him that he could tell, and he hadn't spotted Derek or anyone else following him, so he figured he'd gotten away clean. Of course he'd debated screwing the Illuminati over and living large on his gold someplace like Mexico, but in the end his desire to exact vengeance from those who'd driven him from his throne trumped his instinct to hide out with a meth pipe in one hand and a teenage prostitute in the other.

Snake sidled up to a hitching post in front of a water trough that stood outside a torchlit bar, and tied his horse to it before slipping his rifle's sling over his shoulder and patting his pocket full of gold. He eyed the interior through a pair of open doors and saw the usual collection of trail bums and hucksters and misanthropes seated at round wooden tables, nursing glasses of hard liquor. Snake walked into the place, looked around, and took a seat near the back of the room. A young woman with a face like a cobra and several dozen amateur tattoos coloring her bare shoulders and midriff approached and offered a crooked-toothed smile.

"What'll it be, traveler?"

"What's everybody drinking?"

"Home squeeze," she said, using the slang for local rotgut sour mash or whiskey made in home stills.

"Glass of that, I guess."

"You betcha. Three rounds. Pay in advance."

Snake fished three bullets from one of his vest pockets and slapped them on the table. The waitress grabbed them and walked away, her bony hips wiggling enticingly. Snake watched her move to the bar and considered how long it had been since he'd slept with a woman, but decided that he needed to keep his mind on his task and not get sidetracked by some roadhouse skank. She reappeared a minute later with a glass of cloudy amber liquor and set it down in front of him with another smile. "Three rounds doesn't include the tip. How big you go could mean you get lucky," she said, winking.

"Good to know. Shame I'm on a budget."

Her smile faded and she stalked away, her femme fatale act having failed, and he took a cautious sip of the whiskey while his eyes roved over the room. They settled on a pair of hard-looking men at a nearby table who were staring at him like he was dinner. Snake lifted his glass to them and took another sip of the foul concoction, and the larger of the pair stood and carried his half-full glass to Snake's table and sat down.

"You're new here," the man said flatly.

"If you know that, then you must be a regular," Snake fired back.

The man shrugged. "Regular as any, I suppose," he said, and took a pull on his drink. "Looking for anything in particular?"

"Depends on what's being offered."

The man nodded. "Name's Eddy. I can get whatever you want. Anything."

"That's good to know. How about crank?" Snake asked.

"Some of the best meth around these parts."

"That a fact? How much for a hit?"

"Five rounds."

"Steep."

"Not for the quality and this location, it isn't."

"How about mercs?"

Eddy's eyes darted to the side before settling back on Snake. "Mercenaries for what?"

"A job."

"What kind?"

"The kind that needs mercs."

The two men stared at each other in silence for a few moments, and Eddy seemed to come to a decision. "Me and my brother been known to do that kind of work. What's it pay?"

"Half ounce of gold per month. Job shouldn't take more'n two," Snake said, quoting a high price.

"Not a lot," Eddy fired back.

"Half an ounce buys, what, five thousand rounds and a half dozen quality rifles now? You get more than that here? Maybe I'll stick around and get rich."

"Didn't say it wasn't interesting. Just that it ain't a great offer."

"Mostly riding, so you're being paid to get a tan."

"One way to look at it, I suppose," Eddy conceded. "Where we going?"

"Colorado ways."

"What's up there?"

"Somebody needs killing."

"There a bonus for the man who tags him?"

Snake liked the question. "Sure. Another ounce."

"You got it on you?"

Snake snorted and took a sip from his glass. "I look like an idiot?"

"How do we know you aren't full of it?"

Snake leaned forward and his eyes bored into Eddy's. "You want a job or wanna play twenty questions?"

Eddy didn't look away immediately. When he did, he drummed his fingers absently against his leg. "Gotta ask my bro what he thinks."

"No negotiation. That's what the job pays."

"How many men you looking for?"

"Just a few of the right ones."

"Be right back."

"See if you can bring some crank for the ride. I'll pay the going rate."

"You got it."

Three minutes later Eddy and his brother Clint were accompanying Snake outside, where a scavenger was watching their horses for whatever he could get. Snake tossed the man a round and climbed into the saddle, and the siblings followed suit and followed Snake down the darkened street, in search of one of Eddy's contacts to load up on meth before riding out of town, the deal cinched and the down-on-their-luck brothers without a better deal in the offing. Everything the pair owned was on their backs, so the drugs were the only stop they had to make before hitting the trail.

Snake smiled to himself at how easy that had been. He still had the commanding presence, he figured, and they'd sensed the leadership in him and responded unconsciously. He'd have to keep his eye on them, of course, and might have to kill both if they tried anything, but it told him that he could raise a small army if he had to, which was reassuring given his mission.

As for the drugs, he could justify them because he was riding all night and needed chemical fortification to keep alert. He'd be careful about how much he smoked each day, though, because there was no guarantee that once they were out of former Crew territory they'd find anything more than tumbleweeds and scrub. The thought of the substance hitting his lungs like an atomic blast and sending a freezing surge through his entire body until his brain felt like it was going to explode made him smile in the dark, and he turned away from the pair so they wouldn't think he was nuts.

They'd learn he was dead serious on the road north, but for now he needed them to be compliant and willing, and if he had to share some of his stash to achieve his ends, so be it.

"Up on the right. I'll be out in a minute. Give me the rounds," Eddy said, and Snake nodded.

"Hope you're on the up and up, because otherwise your brother's history," Snake said, his eyes hard.

Eddy swallowed, swung down from his horse, and held out a gloved hand, his gaze landing on Snake's pistol for only a moment before returning to the former warlord's face, his expression showing that he understood the threat and wasn't going to risk his brother's life.

"I got it. We're on your clock now. Don't sweat it."

"If you say so," Snake said, tossing a pair of full magazines to him. "Only the rounds. Need the mags back."

"Will do," Eddy said, and then he was gone, vanishing into the shadows like a phantom, the only trace of his passing the sound of his boots ascending the building stoop and the faint tang of sour sweat on the hot breeze.

Chapter 32

Salem, Oregon

Lucas crouched at the window of an abandoned two-story home in the urban sprawl of the outlying Salem metro area, watching the activity in town through his binoculars. It had taken his group two days to travel there from the ambush point, and they'd turned off the highway ten miles short so they wouldn't be spotted by any enemy outposts. After reaching the farthest suburb, they'd doglegged to the east in order to approach from that direction. He'd been eyeing the city for the better part of three hours, since dawn, but the only activity he'd seen had been Blood Dogs – it was as though the entire local population had been eliminated, which he prayed wasn't the case.

Henry had accompanied him into the suburb, and they'd spent dawn looking for a decent vantage point where they could survey the enemy from a safe distance. They'd bet that the gang had followed the lead of the locals and avoided the rotting outer neighborhoods, preferring the city center where they could consolidate and which they could more easily defend.

Henry twisted toward Lucas from his window. "What do you think?"

"We don't have a lot of time before they smell a rat, so we're going to have to hit them tonight. Looks like they're sticking to downtown, so it should be a straightforward replay of Seattle." Lucas paused. "Only question is how close we can get before they're alerted."

"We going to soften them up with shelling?"

Lucas adjusted his hat and lowered the glasses. "Hate to hurt anyone they're holding prisoner, but I don't see a lot of ways around it. We'll want to knock out as much of their power center as we can before we start the building-by-building sweep."

"We could forego the mortars and stick to grenade launchers. Line of sight."

Lucas nodded. "But we'll incur heavier casualties. No, I think what we need to do is get closer and try to figure out where they bunk, and attack while they're sleeping. The fewer that survive that first attack, the fewer that can inflict damage on us."

"I have family here. Not close, but a cousin."

"That's rough. I know a lot of the men do. But if these animals work anything like the Crew, they either butchered or enslaved everyone they found. It's going to be next to impossible to differentiate our people from theirs in a fight, so we'll have to concentrate on minimizing the fighting to areas we know have to be gang members."

"So what do you want to do?"

"I haven't spotted a lot of guards. Let's work our way closer and see what we can learn."

Lucas led the way on foot, and they covered the ground fast, the surroundings devoid of life. Lucas remembered the last time Salem had been overtaken by enemies, and recalled the bikers like it was yesterday. He also recalled the layout as he neared the Central Area, passing several large shopping centers now in disarray, and gave a wide berth to the rust-colored state hospital, where he'd seen at least two dozen gang members from his earlier perch.

Lucas made for the gates of the penitentiary, which was a little over a mile from the state capitol building and had the benefit of being a fortress, complete with high towers from which he could scan the town. Henry followed close behind, and they crept through the open gates, long abandoned by some of the worst offenders Oregon had to offer, and headed for the nearest watchtower. Lucas paused at the base of a tall steel ladder, where two skeletons in guard uniforms lay where they'd been killed, their skulls staved in by blunt force. Henry shook his head.

"Kind of creepy to think about it, even this long after," he said.

"Yeah. Poor bastards. Just doing their jobs, right up to the bitter end."

They climbed the rungs and settled in, Henry watching the hospital, Lucas the city, and spent most of the afternoon noting the gang's movements. Unlike the Crew, there were few patrols that could be identified as such, more groups of men wandering the streets with guns like members of a lynch mob. The sight gave Lucas optimism – the Blood Dogs had little discipline he could see, which would translate into an easier time retaking the town. In a late night firefight, gunmen with no discipline or training would panic or make stupid errors. Lucas's more seasoned troops wouldn't, and he had the additional edge of hundreds of his best being Salem natives, who were intimately familiar with the city's layout.

"What do you think?" Henry asked as the sun sank behind the foothills across the river.

"Looks like they're using the capitol building as headquarters, which is a natural and helps us. I still remember it from the bikers. So will many of the others. And it looks like they're using the hospital and some of the official buildings by the capitol building as their bunkhouses, which makes sense – why spread themselves thin? Easier to defend. Although it doesn't look like they've made any preparations for an attack."

"How do we do this?"

"We bracket them from the public utility building north of the capitol and from the residential area east of the hospital and capitol. Shell them to soften them up, and then go in for the kill and do it the hard way – street by street. The good news is we've got more men than they do, and with a lot of us using NV gear, they're going to be in serious trouble in no time."

"When do we move into position?"

"Same as the valley. Only we'll want to start this attack at least a couple of hours before dawn, so we can use our NV scopes for close-in combat, too."

Once it was dark, they descended from the tower and jogged the two miles to where the troops were waiting on the edge of Hayesville, and Lucas gave Art and his lieutenants a full briefing. Sam was visibly upset at his report and, when Lucas was done, stood to confront him.

"You didn't see any of the townspeople?" he asked.

Lucas shook his head. "I'm afraid not. Wherever they're keeping them, it's not near downtown."

"Shouldn't finding them be a priority? What if the gang decides to kill them or use them as human shields?"

"We don't have time to do a thorough reconnaissance, Sam. That could take a week, and we both know it. Our advantage is the same as a few days ago: surprise. I'd suggest we do what worked and limit our risk."

"Those aren't your friends and family you're talking about."

"Wrong. Ruby, one of my only friends in the world, is in Salem." He hesitated. "So I've got plenty of skin in the game, too."

"But what you're proposing doesn't do anything to protect them."

"It protects us. That's the priority. If we win the battle, then we can help whoever survived. If we lose…"

Art stood. "Look. I know this is going to be tough for some of you, and I understand why. Some of us aren't going to make it to tomorrow. But we have to think with our brains and maintain a coherent strategy. I can't afford a bunch of you running off to try to find your kin. Sorry. We've got to be soldiers first and civilians second, or we're no better than the gang, and there's no guarantee we'll win. Our discipline and the element of surprise is our edge. They're well equipped. We know that. But just like in the valley, if we do this right, they don't stand a chance. Do it wrong, and this may be our last stand. At the very least we could suffer impossibly high casualties. So our tactics have to emphasize minimizing our risk and moving like lightning, not trying to find loved ones."

Sam sat back down, his expression clearly unhappy; but Art's words were unassailable in their logic. He'd been through enough battles to know the General was speaking the truth, even if he didn't like it. Art looked out over the group for a moment and then began describing how he wanted the men distributed.

"We'll lead with the mortars and grenade crews, just like we did in the valley. I want all gunners to be equipped with NV gear. Two groups, flanking the capitol, just like Lucas said. The main body of troops we'll hold back until we can send in a first wave. Those men will also have NV goggles. Once it's sunup, we'll send in the rest and go house to house until we've wiped them out." Art paused. "Make no mistake, this is not about taking prisoners. These men came to kill us. It's us or them. We're not in the mercy business with murderous scum, and that's what this gang is. You're to wipe them from the face of the earth, and sleep well after."

He continued, next issuing instructions on where to station the medics and field hospital, working from a half-rotted map of the city they'd come across at one of the abandoned truck stops on the way south. When he finished, he fixed the men with a steel gaze.

"Get some shut-eye. We'll move in five hours. Shouldn't take over an hour to get everyone in position once we're close to the capitol. Thank you, gentlemen, and good luck to us all."

"Not that we're going to need it," Lucas said. A flutter of nervous laughter greeted his comment.

When the men had departed, Art sat on the edge of one of the equipment carts. "Think Sam will pull his load?"

"He's a good man. I think so."

"I don't know. Even if he does, you have to know that a lot of his group won't want to maintain ranks if they think their families are in danger."

"We both know that there's only a slim chance they're alive."

"I've watched men march into hellfire on slimmer odds than that. People are strange."

"It'll be a good test. Not that we need any more of those." Lucas yawned. "It's going to be a long one. I'll be up in four hours. You should get some sleep too."

"I can sleep when I'm dead."

Chapter 33

Salem, Oregon

Lucas, Terry, and Henry worked their way west with their NV goggles on, twenty-five men hoisting 60 mm mortars with them and another fifty toting ammo crates loaded with rounds, three Browning gunner crews, and a hundred fighters armed with assault rifles. The moon was barely visible through a high overcast, and the ambient light from the stars was blocked by the clouds.

The group moved carefully to avoid drawing attention to themselves, sticking to back streets as Lucas led the way. When they could see the hospital and capitol building clearly, Lucas signaled for the group to halt. They looked around until they found a promising collection of buildings to establish themselves in – an elementary school that according to the map was a third of a mile from the hospital and a hundred yards farther to the capitol building.

One of the gunmen threw a grappling hook with a knotted rope onto the roof and quickly scaled the wall, and then the rest were doing the same with their hooks and lines, mortars strapped to their backs. After all but the Browning crews and the loaders with the ammo cans were up top, they tied the ends of the ropes to the cans and weapons, and the men above heaved them onto the roof.

Lucas surveyed the hospital grounds with his M4 NV scope and then slowly swept the tallest building's roof. He motioned to Henry and Terry, and they joined him at the lip.

"They've got some men on the hospital roof," he said. "Looks like a machine gun on each corner."

"I see 'em," Henry said.

Terry nodded. "Me too."

"Makes sense. Those are the highest buildings around here. They're going to pose a problem if they zero in on us, so focus your first shells on that building."

"I can lob a few thousand .50-cal rounds their way for good measure," Terry said.

"Muzzle flash might give us away. Let's see if we can get it done with just the mortars."

"Too far for the grenade launchers," Henry said. "Good call on leaving them with Art and the main body."

"But perfect for mortars," Lucas said. "Which is why we're here." He looked to Terry. "If we start taking incoming fire from those guns, feel free to give them everything you've got. Otherwise hold your fire until we have live targets on the grounds. My hunch is once the fireworks start, any surviving enemies will bail out of the buildings, at which point they're all yours."

"Like fish in a barrel. Got it," Terry said.

"All right. I synched watches with Art. We have fifteen minutes before it's showtime. Everyone keep your eyes open in case someone spots us. If they do, take them out."

The fifteen minutes crawled by as the men sat wordlessly staring at the hospital grounds. No lights were on, but in their goggles the building was neon green, with the machine-gun nests glowing hot with heat signals in the infrared. When it was time, Lucas called out softly to the mortar operators.

"Fire at will."

Explosions at the courthouse and the surrounding government buildings boomed from their right, and then the familiar whump of the mortars firing from the roof began, the loaders dropping in a new round every four or five seconds. They'd already calculated the range from the map and had the bearings, so most of the shells hit their targets, with only a few overshooting or falling short.

The hospital lit up with starbursts of flame, and the closest section of the roof of the building with the machine-gun nests flared as three rounds detonated, destroying two of the nests instantly. Henry adjusted the mortar a hair as his loader continued dropping rounds in, and he directed the fire with the precision of a neurosurgeon. All but the last nest succumbed to the barrage, and then the enemy gunner opened up, and the roof around Lucas shredded from the high-velocity slugs tearing into it.

"Terry!" Lucas called, throwing himself down and lying flat.

Terry returned fire, and the other pair of Brownings followed suit. A thousand jacketed rounds peppered the corner of the building that wasn't engulfed in flames, and the nest vaporized before their eyes, cut to pieces by the relentless fire.

"Hold your fire!" Lucas yelled, and the gunners stopped shooting while the mortars went back to work. Once the multistory buildings in the hospital complex were largely destroyed, Lucas ran to Henry and pointed at the hospital entrance. "They're making a break for it!"

Hundreds of men were scurrying from the buildings like ants, and Terry leveled his weapon at them and began firing methodical bursts, twenty rounds each, cutting the gang members apart as they ran from a threat they couldn't see. The other gunners did the same, and soon the grounds were littered with dead as more mortar rounds exploded by the entrance.

Rifle fire barked from the university campus in front of the capitol building, but the school was out of accurate range of the assault rifles. Lucas pointed out a group of forty or fifty gang members who'd taken to the roofs of the brick buildings, and Terry swiveled his machine gun toward them and made short work of the shooters.

"Now what?" Henry yelled when Terry finished with the gunmen.

"Turn the mortars on the capitol building," Lucas instructed. "Might as well help out Art while we're here. But only a few salvos. No reason to waste rounds now that the hospital's toast."

"Okay. Let me get a range."

Henry shifted the mortar and eyeballed the distance and, after making an adjustment to the elevation, motioned for his loader to drop a projectile into the tube and watched for the resultant explosion. A building on the university grounds flared, and he made another tweak and nodded to Lucas.

"About two hundred yards farther. How many you want me to put in their front yard?"

"Five or six, and then let's clear out of here. It's going to be light soon, and we'll be out in the open if they've got any decent marksmen with sniper rifles, or bring mortars of their own to bear."

Henry lobbed a series of rounds at the building, and then the teams gathered their weapons and remaining ammo and quit the roof, leaving one of the machine-gun squads there to deal with any targets of opportunity that presented themselves.

When they reached the main body of troops, Sam approached him. "How many you figure you took out?"

"Hundreds. No way of knowing till it's light out and we search the hospital, but a lot."

"No casualties?"

"None on our end so far. Although I have no idea what Art's doing," Lucas said as the shelling from the capitol building area continued.

"Then you were right about how to deal with this. If you were able to knock out hundreds of them without a scratch on any of our boys, that's a win."

"I'm not declaring victory just yet. But it's a promising start." Lucas turned to the advance fighters who were equipped with NV goggles or rifle scopes. "All right. Let's make our way forward, but steer clear of the campus and capitol building area. Don't want to get hit by any friendly fire, and it sounds like Art's still at work. We'll skirt it and start at the hospital, and then work our way around the west side. Shoot anything that moves. The rest of you, Art will be done when the sun comes up, and then you'll sweep in to clean up whatever mess is left after an hour of shelling. Don't take any stupid chances. Between the hospital and the rest, we've probably eliminated half of them, but we could still get badly hurt if we're not careful. We'll do a grid search after the battle and mop up anyone hiding out. Everyone clear? Sam will be in command of the daytime group."

Sam stood tall. "I know what we need to do."

"Good. No distractions," Lucas warned.

"Roger that."

Lucas led his small army of gunmen west, and the street fighting began in earnest as they neared the hospital grounds. Pockets of gang members plinked at them from the windows of the nearby buildings, but with no NV equipment, they were shooting at shadows, and Lucas's men easily overcame them. At the hospital, the stench of death was like that of a slaughterhouse; hundreds of corpses lay strewn around the grounds, many dismembered from the mortars or blown into scattered chunks.

By the time first light glimmered on the eastern horizon, Lucas's advance fighters had sustained some wounded and dead, but had pressed on and taken the western section of town from scattered collections of gang members who didn't seem to have much stomach for the fight. Once their NV gear was no longer an advantage, they slowed their advance and held their ground as the bulk of the Freedom Army swept through the now largely destroyed capitol building area, fighting in brutal skirmishes as the Blood Dogs defended every foot of their conquest.

When the shooting finally ended, the sun was high in the sky, which was filled with smoke from burning structures. Sam, Art, and Lucas gathered in front of the destroyed capitol building, now a gutted ruin, and took stock.

"We lost forty-four men, with another sixty wounded," Sam reported. "Some of whom won't make it."

"Not unreasonable, considering we took on thousands of these scum. How many captives have we taken?" Art asked.

"Thirty or so."

Sam grunted. "We need to interrogate them and find out what they did with the townspeople."

"Agreed. In the meantime we'll start a search. I'm sure there's a good number of these cowards still hiding out," Art said.

"That's a fair assumption," Lucas granted. He turned to Sam. "You're the man to lead the search. Take as many troops as you want and start a block-by-block sweep. In the meantime we'll see what we can learn from the prisoners. I wouldn't hold my breath, though."

Sam nodded. "I hear you. Shouldn't have any trouble getting hundreds of men to help. Lots of us locals in the ranks."

"Good. And let's start collecting weapons and ammo. We burned through a fair amount of our inventory on this offensive, and we'll need to replenish."

"I'll assemble an equipment detail. One thing I can say – they may not have been much in the way of fighters, but their gear was first class."

Lucas wiped the grime from his chin. "Which is now ours. Make it happen."

"Will do."

When Sam left, Art sat on one of the capitol building steps and invited Lucas to join him. "Another well-fought battle. You're getting pretty good at this for a broken-down lawman."

That forced a grin from Lucas. "Not bad yourself for a bartender."

"You know what the odds are that many of the locals were spared."

Lucas spoke after a beat. "Probably mostly the women."

"Who'll never be the same."

"No, they won't. Seems like throughout history we've done this, though, so we'll survive. Somehow." He spit and frowned. "Although what does that say about us as a species?"

"I'll leave the big questions to philosophical minds like yours. I'm just a soldier. All that's above my pay grade."

Lucas sighed and rose. "Let's go question the scum. Maybe we can learn something useful."

"Ever the optimist."

The corner of Lucas's mouth twitched. "Hope. The opiate of the unwashed."

"Let's go wring something out of them and turn that into something actionable."

"You're on."

Chapter 34

Provo, Utah

Duke and Edwin rode toward one of the barriers the Provo militia had erected across the highways leading into town, keeping their hands clearly visible and their rifles in their saddle scabbards. The journey had been arduous; they were both exhausted from weeks sleeping exposed to the elements, and they looked like shadows of the men who'd set off on the trek, their already low weight further down from surviving on whatever they'd been able to snare or shoot.

Four men stood behind sandbagged outposts on either side of the barrier, their machine guns trained on the newcomers.

"That's far enough," one of them called when Duke and Edwin were ten yards from them. "Best turn around and go back to wherever you came from. There's nothing here for you."

"We've traveled a long way. My name's Duke, and this here's Edwin. We're from Shangri-La. Edwin was here about six months ago. He brought the vaccine that saved you all, so maybe a little hospitality's a fair request?"

The guards exchanged glances. "I heard of you and about Shangri-La. What brings you here? You're a long way from home, aren't you?"

"That we are," allowed Duke. "We're here to talk to your council. Got some important business to discuss."

More looks, and the speaker nodded. "Fair enough. Come on over here and give me your weapons. We don't allow any in the city limits unless there's a threat."

"Been many of those?"

"Not once word spread that we don't roll over easy."

They guided their horses forward and handed the guards their rifles and pistols, and two of the men hauled a steel plate in the center of the barrier to the side, creating a five-foot opening the animals could just squeeze through. Once inside, the main guard walked over to where four horses were standing in the shade beneath a tarp, and led one from the rest and mounted up.

"I'll take you into town and show you to the council."

"Could use a decent meal and some rest, too."

The guard took in Duke's and Edwin's dusty clothes and scraggly beards and nodded almost to himself. "I could probably find something that'll suit you. Come on."

They rode past a scattering of homes nestled at the base of beige bluffs that towered over them, and passed an industrial park whose buildings were in reasonable shape compared to many Duke had seen. As they proceeded to the downtown area, they saw more and more people, many of whom stopped what they were doing as they went by and stared at them in curiosity.

"I guess you don't see a lot of newcomers," Duke said.

"True enough. We're careful about who we let into our midst."

"Edwin tells me you've got a good thing going here."

"Right. And we plan to keep it that way."

Duke knew that Provo had been attacked by several would-be conquering gangs after the collapse, but the citizenry had gathered together and defended themselves successfully. Subsequently the militia had formed, and now boasted thousands of men – virtually the entire town's population of fighting-age men were active, making them a formidable defending force to contend with.

"Everything pretty calm since I left?" Edwin asked.

"There hasn't been any trouble to speak of. Thanks for the vaccine, by the way. I hear it probably saved a lot of lives."

"I was just the messenger. It's Shangri-La you owe, not me."

"You risked life and limb to bring it to us, though. Not a lot would do that for strangers."

Edwin gave a rueful shake of his head. "I must have a screw loose."

"I can vouch for that," Duke said, and all three men smiled.

After passing a collection of multistory buildings, the guard slowed and pointed at a large theater. "Edwin, you might remember that's where the council meets. But there's nobody there now. We'll get you settled first, and I'll put out the word that you're in town and want to see them."

"A hot bath wouldn't hurt," Duke said. "We can pay."

"I'm pretty sure your credit's good with the town."

They reached a big Victorian house, and the guard indicated a sign out in front that announced they'd reached Glenda's Boardinghouse.

"I remember this place," Edwin said. "The food was delicious!"

"Go on in and tell Glenda your stay's on the council. She'll fix you up with whatever you need."

"Will do. Thanks for everything."

"You can reclaim your weapons when you leave at the same checkpoint. Nobody will mess with them."

"I'm sure that's true."

They tied their horses under an overhang near a watering trough, and Edwin escorted Duke into the house, where a prim woman wearing a handmade dress that reached her ankles beamed at him.

"Why, you're back! And you brought company!"

Edwin removed his hat and Duke did the same. "That's right. Couldn't stay away from your cooking."

Glenda blushed and looked away. "Why, you always did have a way with words. I remember that." She paused. "What brings you to Provo again?" she asked, and her expression grew serious. "Not another virus...?"

"No, nothing like that. Don't worry. We just have to speak to the council. Which, by the way, the guard said to tell you that our stay's on them, so break out the good fixings, not the cheap stuff."

Glenda set her hands on her hips. "Oh, you! You know it's nothing but the best for my guests, no matter who's on the hook for it."

"That's why we wouldn't stay anywhere else. Provided you have room, that is."

"Of course. We're empty right now. It'll be a real pleasure." Her nose crinkled. "You probably want to get cleaned up before you eat. I'll heat up some pails of water and have one of the boys bring them up to you."

"You read my mind." Duke sniffed the air. "What's for lunch?"

"Rabbit stew over rice and fresh-baked bread with berries and some homemade butter. Looks like you could use something that will stick to your ribs."

"It was a tough ride," Duke allowed.

"Well, go to rooms one and two and make yourselves at home. You want the boys to bring your saddlebags up and tend to your animals?"

"That would be perfect."

"Then consider it done."

Lunch was a welcome feast, and by the time they were done eating, both Duke and Edwin were ready to burst. They retreated to their rooms and drew the curtains, and were asleep within seconds of hitting the bed.

Rapping at Duke's door woke him after what felt like a few minutes, but the fading light outside told him that he'd slept for hours. He padded to the door and called through it.

"Yes?"

"There are two men downstairs from the council. They want you to accompany them," Glenda said.

"Okay. No need to wake Edwin. I'm the one who needs to talk to them. Let him rest."

"Sure thing."

"I'll be down shortly. Let me just get decent."

"I'll tell them."

Duke donned his least filthy shirt and was down in the lobby a few minutes later. A pair of men sitting on a well-padded antique sofa rose and smiled at him.

"Well, hello, Duke, right? It's a real pleasure," one of them said. "Thomas. Nice to meet you."

"Pleasure's all mine," Duke said. "And this is...?"

The other man extended his hand. "Glenn Roberts."

Duke shook, and studied the men. "So you want to see me now?"

Thomas spoke. "The council's in session in twenty minutes. We called a special meeting to see you."

"Appreciate it."

They walked together to the theater, nodding and smiling acknowledgments to passersby, and entered the building to find a skylight providing natural light and a pair of oil-burning lanterns hanging from the sides of the stage, ready for nightfall. The nine members of the council welcomed Duke warmly and invited him to sit in front of a long table, and then Thomas, the chairman, sat forward.

"All right. You have our complete attention. What brings you to see us?"

Duke cleared his throat and explained the situation with Elijah in a few terse minutes. When he was done, the council members sat in silence, waiting for him to continue.

"So here's the situation. We can't stay in Colorado, and Edwin suggested we move camp to Provo. Elliot, our leader, agreed and sent us as envoys." Duke paused. "We're all good people with values, and we basically saved the world with our vaccine, so we thought we might be welcome with your group."

Thomas looked like he'd been gut punched, as did most of the council members. Duke had anticipated the request would come as a shock, so he plowed on with his pitch.

"Look, we know that you're a religious bunch. Most of us are as well. Any differences we might have are probably small. What's important is that we've sacrificed most of what we have to keep the country safe, and that includes you. We didn't have to develop the vaccine, and we certainly didn't have to distribute it so everyone would stay healthy. But we did. I know it's hard to tell right from left these days, but surely that counts as good in anyone's book."

Thomas nodded slowly. "No question. But there are some ideological concerns, and some logistical ones as well. How many of you are there?"

"Not many. Maybe…a couple of hundred or so? Women, children, and adult men who don't mind a hard day's work to earn their keep. They're all good, capable people. Salt of the earth, just like yours. It would be a good fit."

"I'm not debating that it wouldn't be." Thomas looked to Glenn. "This is obviously a surprise, and we're going to have to talk it over. And it's not the kind of thing that we'll be able to decide in a single meeting. There are a lot of aspects to consider." His smile was smaller than before when he offered one. "Make yourself comfortable at the rooming house. We'll get back to you when we've had some time to think things through."

"We wouldn't have ridden all the way here if we had any other options. We need to clear out of Colorado, and we want somewhere safe, where we're among like-minded folks who are building a better future. We're not asking for charity, just consideration – and you have to admit, we've more than paid it forward."

"Nobody's denying that. Give us some breathing room, Duke. You make an eloquent case, but it's up to us to figure out how to proceed. Eat some of Glenda's excellent cooking, catch up on some rest, and we'll get back to you," Glenn said, his final words ending any further discussion.

Duke nodded and rose. "Thanks for hearing me out. And you're more than right about Glenda. There's worse duty than a day or two at her place. All I ask is that you understand the urgency of the request. We don't have a lot of time left on our end, and we need to do something."

Thomas sighed. "We get it, Duke. Now leave us to our discussion, and we'll try to come up with an answer as quickly as we're able."

"That's all we can ask."

LEGION

Edwin was awake when Duke returned, munching on some leftover bread in the lobby. He looked up as Duke entered, eyebrows raised. "How'd it go?"

"Hard to read. I made my case."

"They didn't give you an answer?"

"No. They need to parlay among themselves. That's expected. It's a big deal to them. They're not going to rush into anything."

"Then there's a chance they could say no?"

"There's always that risk."

"But they owe us! We saved their skin with the vaccine."

"They didn't ask us to. We chose to. If you choose to make a charitable act, I'm not sure the receiving party owes you anything – it was your choice."

"But that should still count for something, right?"

"Of course. Let's just settle down and wait for their decision. It's theirs to make, not ours."

"If the tables were turned, we'd take them in."

"That may or may not be, but it doesn't have anything to do with what's right for them. I understand their concerns. They're a tight-knit group, and they've built something special here. It's going to take a lot for them to risk upsetting that by inviting a big unknown in. So cool your jets and we'll see what happens." Duke raised his arm and sniffed his shirt with a look of disgust. "River water didn't do much for these clothes. Maybe we can talk Glenda into scrubbing them with some real soap? I feel like I rolled in hog slop even after my bath."

"This is so frustrating after all we've done."

Duke shrugged. "Welcome to the real world. Sometimes things work out, and sometimes life punches you in the face." He looked over at the dining area through a wide doorway. "Smells like Glenda's fixing up another feast for us. We could do worse."

"The food is amazing. I'd almost forgotten what a real meal tastes like."

Duke's expression grew more serious and he studied his boots before looking up at Edwin with a sad smile. "Well, enjoy it, youngblood. Nothing in this life lasts longer than a blink."

"Can't argue with that."

Chapter 35

Salem, Oregon

Ruby watched the attack on Salem with Peter and twenty-two other survivors from their hidden vantage point in the hills across the river, west of town. They'd found the others by following their trails, which Peter had been surprisingly good at. The group was evenly mixed female to male – most of the survivors had been young and fit and thus able to outrun the Blood Dogs, unlike their older counterparts. There were only five weapons among them all, and precious little ammo, but they'd been able to night fish and live off berries and roots, so while constantly hungry, they hadn't starved.

"Good God," Peter exclaimed when the first wave of gunmen overran the Blood Dogs' positions with the break of dawn. "Who is that?"

They'd been awakened by the boom of mortar rounds exploding and had watched in stunned silence as much of Salem's historic district was decimated by blasts. Ruby hadn't dared to hope that the assault might be being carried out by Lucas's men, but as she watched the methodical tactics and the seemingly endless barrage, she became convinced that he'd arrived with his Seattle force and was taking the gang out to the woodshed.

"Might be a friend of mine. We'll have to wait until the dust settles to know for sure, but it's probably him."

191

Ruby had told the rest that Lucas was likely en route, partially to build optimism as well as to give them a reason to stay put. There had been forceful discussion by the younger folks about leaving the area and heading out to the coast, which Ruby had quashed with her stories of Lucas and his unbeatable rebel army.

Now it appeared that her tales had been accurate – by afternoon the battle was clearly over, and the only sound was that of occasional shooting as the last of the enemy holdouts fought skirmishes against the conquering force.

"What do we do now?" asked Erica, a plain girl of seventeen.

"We don't do anything. Stay put. I'll go into town and see if my suspicions are correct. If it's Lucas, I'll return. If it's someone else…well…all I can say is listen to Peter and don't do anything rash."

Peter shook his head. "I'm going with you."

Ruby scowled at him. "No. You're needed here, Peter. Somebody has to mind the store while I'm gone."

"It's not up for discussion," he said obstinately.

"You're right. I'm going down there alone." Ruby's tone softened. "Please. Don't fight me on this. They need you more than I need a well-dressed friend to walk with," she teased, alluding to his camouflage fatigues.

He regarded her with a hurt expression and then relented. "If it was anybody else…"

Ruby touched his arm in gratitude. "Thank you, Peter. I'll be fine. And hopefully I'll be back." She handed him her rifle. "Watch that for me, will you? It won't do me any good against that lot if they're not friendlies."

"Ruby…"

She spun and made for the game trail that led down to the flatlands and the road into town, never looking back, her thick mop of gray hair floating behind her like a cloud.

Lucas was hunkered down, using an abandoned car for cover, along with fifty of his fighters in the buildings behind him. Their objective was a warehouse that was being used to imprison the surviving Salem locals, if two of their Blood Dog prisoners' accounts could be believed. Sam was crouched behind another vehicle – a tow truck that was barely more than rust – and they were exchanging fire with an unknown number of gang members holed up in the warehouse.

"What now?" Sam asked.

Lucas and Sam's fear was that eventually one of the Blood Dogs might figure out that they had a bargaining chip with the survivors, and would inevitably try to use that to their advantage.

"We wait for them to slip up," Lucas said, echoing the refrain he'd been repeating since they'd gotten there. "Eventually they'll run out of ammo."

"They could kill everyone first."

"Why would they use up their bullets on unarmed civilians when there's an army out here? Think, Sam. It isn't logical."

"They're ex-cons and murderers. They might not behave logically."

"They're cornered rats, but even rats have a survival instinct. We just need to make the right argument."

"What are you talking about?"

Lucas looked over his shoulder and yelled to his troops, "Hold your fire!"

The shooting stopped, leaving him with ringing ears and a throbbing headache. Lucas cupped his hands and called out to the warehouse, "You've lost the fight. You're the last of the Blood Dogs here. Now you have two choices. Surrender, in which case we'll treat you fairly, or keep fighting, in which case the grenade launchers are next, and nobody will walk out of there alive."

Sam grabbed Lucas's arm. "What the hell are you doing? They'll kill them!"

Lucas shrugged off Sam's grip. "Cut this out and use your brain, Sam, or you're of no use to anyone, yourself included."

Sixty seconds went by, and then a voice called from one of the broken windows, "We've got two hundred hostages in here. We'll kill them all if you don't let us walk."

Lucas waited a moment and then called out again, "Go ahead. You'll be joining them in hell within minutes."

Sam's expression was pained. "Lucas!"

"Shut up, Sam," Lucas hissed.

The voice yelled again. "We mean it. They're all dead unless you let us go."

Lucas's laugh was loud. "Go where? You're surrounded, and we're about to nuke you and your hostages. Either you surrender or die. What you do with your hostages doesn't matter to me – I'll kill them if you don't. So you want to die or live? I'm getting impatient. Choose one."

Realization washed over Sam's face. "If they think you don't care, they have no value…"

"You get the gold star," said Lucas.

"What if they kill them anyway?"

"They won't. No reason to now."

Sam glared at him and then looked away. "I sure hope you're right. You're playing fast and loose with our loved ones. People's families."

"And Ruby. If you have a better idea, I'm all ears."

The voice called out from the warehouse, "How do we know you won't gun us down?"

Lucas yelled back, "Got no reason to. If I want to kill you now, I'll just blow the place up. What's it going to be? Live to see tomorrow, or meet your maker today? All the same to me. I'm out of patience. Make the call."

Less than thirty seconds later, the front doors opened and a stream of gang members exited with their hands in the air.

"Stand over by the wall until the place is empty," Lucas instructed. The men complied, and when no more came out, Lucas's men emerged from their cover and began binding the men's wrists. Lucas and Sam entered the warehouse, leading with their weapons, and found what remained of Salem's townspeople caged like animals in holding areas, the women sobbing in relief, the few men silent and impassive.

"That's everyone?" Sam demanded.

One of the caged men spoke up. "They butchered most of us when they took over. We're it. They used us for slave labor...and the women...as..."

"Has anyone seen an older woman named Ruby? Is she in here?" Lucas asked.

"No."

Lucas's shoulders slumped at the news, and then he took a deep breath and squared them. "All right. We've taken Salem back. You're free. Sam here will unlock the pens, and you can return to your homes."

"I want to kill them," the prisoner snarled.

"We'll set up a tribunal where you can say your piece. Any of the gang who abused you, you can accuse, and we'll mete out justice. Nobody's going to get away with anything. You have my word."

"I can save you a lot of time. Kill them all."

"Maybe. But we'll do things my way. Name's Lucas, by the way. We drove the Portland bikers out of town for you, and now these scum. I won't break my word, but I won't allow a lynching, either."

Lucas strode from the warehouse, lost in thought, and made for the area near the courthouse and jail that Art was setting up shop as headquarters, with the prisoners behind bars and under heavy guard. When he arrived, a voice called out from behind him.

"Lucas!"

Lucas spun to find Ruby running toward him. He swept her up in his arms and hugged her tight, and then released her. She looked up into his eyes, hers brimming.

"I see you finally decided to make it," she said.

He gave a half shrug. "Ran out of things to do in Seattle."

"Took your time, didn't you?"

"Got here fast as I could." He paused. "You all right? Where were you?"

"I've been better, but yes. I'm fine. I was with a handful of folks who escaped, hiding up in the hills. I'll go back and bring them down."

"Might want to wait a few more hours till we've cleaned up downtown. Could be more of the gang hiding out."

"Okay. I'm in no rush. Still got plenty of light. Although I could use a horse."

"You can probably go find your own. The gang kept all the animals in a stable they set up over by Waldo Park. You know where that is?"

"Of course. I've been here for weeks."

"Good. That area's already been cleared by Art's troops. It's safe to head over there."

"Art's with you?"

"He's around here somewhere."

Ruby blinked twice and cleared her throat. "What are you going to do?"

Rifle shots from west of them echoed like fireworks, and Lucas exhaled heavily. "Sounds like there are still a few things to tidy up."

"I'll let you get to it, then."

Lucas hesitated. "Good to see you again, Ruby. I knew you wouldn't let them get you."

"It takes more than an invasion by a tide of human filth to keep me down."

He studied her face and smiled. "I never doubted it."

Ruby went in search of a horse, and Art approached him. "Got an interesting tidbit of how the gang made it this far north."

"Yeah?"

"Railroad."

Lucas's eyebrows rose. "You're kidding. How?"

"An old steam locomotive. They had one in Sacramento, but the thing crapped out hauling men to ambush us."

"Lucky for us."

"The luckiest part is that the engineer is one of the men we captured. He was hiding in the coal bin."

"Smart. He all ganged up?"

"Doesn't look like it. He claims he was forced into duty. From what we've seen of how the gangs play, that sounds feasible."

"But the train's dead now?"

"That's the most interesting part. He says he was doing more repairs on it, and that he can get it running again. Maybe not a hundred percent, but good enough to be serviceable."

Lucas looked thoughtful. "That could come in handy transporting troops. Lot faster than a horse."

"I was thinking the same thing. I wonder if there's a railroad map anywhere in town."

"Could cut our time to Shangri-La by weeks, depending on how fast it'll go." Lucas rubbed the scruff on his face. "I want to talk to this guy."

"I figured you might. We separated him from the rest. He's the only one who isn't covered in prison tats." Art smiled. "Glad to see Ruby made it."

"Definitely a relief."

"I told you she's tough."

"She's definitely been through a lot. Let's go see the engineer."

Chapter 36

Salem, Oregon

Lucas, Ruby, and Peter stood by the shortwave transmitter as Lucas's operator listened through headphones on the channel Shangri-La monitored. They'd rigged an antenna to a water tower, which the operator had assured them would work, but after forty-five minutes of trying, they'd been rewarded with nothing for their efforts but silence.

"Maybe they're busy," Peter said.

"Elliot always has someone at the radio," Ruby said. "Always."

"Could be a hardware problem."

Ruby shook her head. "No. They must already be on the trail and aren't monitoring anymore. He said they were packing up last I talked to him."

Upon her return, Ruby had informed Lucas that Shangri-La was relocating to Provo, and she thought they were en route. Lucas had insisted they try communicating anyway – there was always the possibility that they were using the radio while on the road as well, given that they had solar.

"Crap. I really wanted to talk to Sierra," Lucas said.

"Looks like a minor destination change," Ruby said.

"The good news is that it's not as far as Colorado, I suppose," Lucas allowed. He looked away. "I wonder if there are any railroad tracks to Utah from here?"

"What?" Peter asked.

"Nothing. Just thinking out loud."

Lucas left them and went to where Clark was being held captive. He entered the cell and sat across from the man. "You told Art the engine's busted, but you're repairing it. How long would it take to finish the repairs?"

"Maybe another day or two. Why?"

"How dependable would it be?"

"Depends on how much weight it's carrying and how fast it has to go. A bunch of factors. There's no easy answer until I see how they hold."

"Let's say you kept it to a steady twenty miles per hour. But over mountains."

"That gets complicated. Obviously gravity increases the strain on the engine, so you can't haul as much."

"I figured."

Clark's eyes narrowed. "What mountains are we talking about?"

"How well do you know the rail system between here and Salt Lake?"

Clark whistled softly. "Pretty well. It used to be my hobby. That's a hell of a grade between here and Reno."

"That's why I'm asking. Is there rail all the way?"

"Sure. We might have to switch some tracks a few times, but it's doable."

"So back to my question. How many cars could you reliably pull without blowing the engine up?"

"Depends on how well the repairs hold. I was rushed by the gang on the last ones. If I really take my time, I don't know, maybe seven or eight fully loaded?"

"So if we had one with the horses and equipment, we could carry how many men?"

"Comfortably?"

"Not necessarily. How many from a weight perspective?"

"Maybe…six or seven hundred. Eight might be pushing it."

"How confident are you that it would hold up for the trip?"

"Like I said – depends on how much time I have to make sure the welds are perfect. The shaft shouldn't be a problem. It held up under double that much weight. It's the boiler that's the issue. But I'm thinking if I can find some steel plates and weld those on the inside rather than patching the holes from the outside, that would hold better. Hell, you may even be able to get ten cars on it with no problem if I'm right."

"Why didn't you do that before?"

"They were in a hurry."

"We are too. But not so big a one that we want it jury-rigged. Better to get it done right the first time." Lucas stood and held Clark's stare. "I'll pay you four ounces of gold and release you as a free man once we're in Utah if you'll do this – provided nobody comes forward and accuses you of murder or rape. So my question to you is, are you clean, or do you have something to hide?"

"I'm not one of them, if that's what you're asking. I told you – they held a gun to my head."

"Then you're in the clear. How many days you figure you need?"

"Depends. If I can find something I can cut apart with my torch and use for patch material, the actual welding shouldn't take more than a day. Although I want to patch all the holes, not just the ones that gave."

"Fine. I'll assign two men to help you with whatever you need."

"Then I'm free to go?"

"Unless you want to stay in this hole."

"And you're serious about the gold?"

"Completely. We don't blackmail people. We pay them for what they earn. Otherwise we'd be as bad as the ones we're fighting." Lucas thought for a moment. "What would it take to get the engine back to full running condition so it could haul most of the men?"

"I wouldn't trust the shaft. We'd need a new one."

"Any other locomotives like this we could reach in a day or two?"

Clark scratched his head. "There's a couple of old ones in Redding. Don't run, though. Probably rusting apart. Damn shame."

"But could you remove this shaft and replace it with one of theirs?"

"Probably. I think one of them's the same make."

"If you patched the boiler from the inside, would it be as good as new?"

"I wouldn't go that far, but it would be as good as any."

"Then it would make more sense to get it up to speed and head to Redding with enough men to defend ourselves while you do the repair."

Clark looked away. "No need to worry about Redding. We came through there. There's nothing left."

Lucas didn't say anything for ten seconds. When he did, his voice was barely more than a growl. "That the gang's MO? Kill everyone in their path?"

"Pretty much. Isn't that how most of them operate?"

"I suppose."

Clark remained seated. "What's your deal? Why Utah?"

"It's a first stop."

"On the road to what?"

"Good question. The idea is to clear out all the bad guys who've taken over the country."

Clark didn't say anything for a moment. "Big idea."

"It is. And not mine. But we have over six thousand men who've signed up, and I suspect more to follow, so we have the firepower to do it."

"And then what?"

"One thing at a time. Hand over the cities to the residents and help them set up their own governments. There's no reason that the worst of the bunch should be allowed to terrorize the rest and turn the country into hell on earth."

"Just the way it seems it worked out. They're the most vicious."

"Maybe. But the collapse is over. It's time to rebuild now."

Clark studied Lucas and then rose. "I can see why your men would be willing to die for you."

"You've got it wrong. They're willing to die for their freedom, not for me."

"Maybe. Or maybe after years of barely surviving, they want to be part of something bigger than themselves, and they're willing to do anything to make that real."

"Sure. That's probably a big part. And a lot of them are tired of running scared. We beat a Chinese army invasion force back into the sea. We cleared a gang out of Salem before, and we've done it again. It feels good to win. So they want to be on the winning side. Human nature." Lucas paused. "The question is, how about you?"

"I'll work for the gold."

Lucas nodded. "An honest answer. Nothing wrong with that."

"I'm not ready for flag waving and parades just yet."

"Nobody's going to ask you to. Just fix the engine and get us to Salt Lake with as many men and their gear as possible."

"It's a tall order, but it can be done."

"Then do it."

Lucas's next order of business was to send riders to Newport to let them know of their success in Seattle, and relay to them that they needed to pack up and come to Salem immediately. The combination of the inevitable radiation threat and the likelihood that the Chinese would return made setting down roots there pointless, and they would be better served to join with the Salem survivors and brave the trek to Utah with the main force.

Ruby offered to join the riders in order to overcome any objections, but Lucas was opposed. She confronted him with her hands on her hips once he'd given the six scouts their marching orders.

"They can't sell it like I can, Lucas. You know that."

"You've been through enough, haven't you?"

"Trail's no place for a woman? Is that it?"

"Not at all. It's…look, why put yourself at more risk? Let them do the job."

"You want Rosemary and her family to decide they prefer to stay in Newport? You've seen how stubborn Jet and Mary can be. And the rest of them are as bullheaded as…mules."

"Which reminds me. Did you find your horse?"

Her eyes lit up. "I did! She looks fine. Like she wants to go on a trip. Raring for it."

"I'll bet." He ran his fingers through his hair. "How about your mule? Jax?"

"He was there too. One big happy family. At least they didn't cook him and eat him."

"I imagine he was relieved."

"He looked angry I'd abandoned him."

"Kids these days."

Ruby pursed her lips. "Lucas, you know me by now. I'm going with your men. You can't stop me."

Lucas sighed. "I suppose I do. Nothing you do surprises me anymore."

"It's for the best. I'll be fine with those strapping young fighting men. You've nothing to worry about."

He regarded her and couldn't help but smile. "Maybe it wasn't you I was worried about."

Chapter 37

Provo, Utah

When the Shangri-La group finally arrived at Provo, it was after three weeks of hard travel, and it showed in their faces and their clothes. The procession stopped just outside the town walls, and Elliot wiped the trail dust from his white beard and rode the rest of the way to the main gate, where the guards met him with scowls.

"Quite a collection you've got there," one of them said.

"We've come a long way. We sent envoys to let the council know we were coming."

"The council?"

"Yes. We're all that's left of Shangri-La. You might have heard of it?"

The guard looked to the rest and then back at Elliot. "I'm afraid I can't let you in. I don't know anything about this." His forehead crinkled. "I'll send a rider to the council and let them handle it."

"Fair enough," Elliot agreed.

Forty-five minutes later, Thomas and Duke rode up to the barrier and dismounted. Thomas had a word with the guards, and they hauled the center panel of the barricade aside.

"Welcome. My name's Thomas. I'm the spokesperson for the council. We decided two days ago to invite you to become members of our community, assuming you want to remain with us. If not, we'll do everything we can to help you find suitable accommodations anywhere in our territory."

Duke nodded. "I tried to radio you, but you'd gone dark."

"We had to leave rather abruptly," Elliot said, and shifted his attention to Thomas. "We can't thank you enough. It was a long and arduous ride. Your hospitality is greatly appreciated."

"We've already set aside an area that has been uninhabited since the collapse. But most of the homes are serviceable, and there's water nearby."

"That sounds wonderful. Thank you."

"Tell your people that I'll escort you to the neighborhood that will be your new home – unless you decide you want to set up camp somewhere else."

"That won't be an issue. We're prepared to do whatever it takes to assimilate. We're tired of living apart from our fellow man."

"Good. We'll welcome you with open arms."

Thomas and Duke led the procession through town to a collection of tract homes east of Orem, nestled beneath the foothills that loomed over the city like giant guardians. Curious residents waved to them as they passed, everyone friendly and open. When they finally arrived at the subdivision that was to be their new home, Thomas smiled at Elliot and walked him to the main street of the development.

"Seems fitting you name your new digs as you see fit. I think you'll be comfortable. Once you're settled in, I'll introduce you to the rest of the council, and you can meet your new neighbors in your own time."

"This is a big step for everyone," Elliot said. "We won't let you down or make you regret your decision."

"I'm sure you won't. We can discuss logistics once you've had a chance to move in and rest. There's no hurry."

"I already told them why the move was necessary," Duke said. "They're up to speed."

Elliot nodded. "We covered our tracks as best we could. It's doubtful we'll see any trouble."

"Don't worry about that. We're well fortified against anything man or nature throws at us. Only a fool would attack Provo."

"Unfortunately, as we've all seen, the world's full of fools."

"Too true," Thomas agreed. "Let me take this opportunity to thank you for creating the vaccine and distributing it. Far above any call of duty I can think of."

"No need. We're happy to have been able to avert disaster. This country's been through more than enough."

"Duke can show you where the fresh water is and how the sewage system we've built works. Other than that, again, welcome. We're glad to have you."

Thomas left, and Duke gave Elliot, Arnold, and some of the engineering-oriented a short tour. He finished up by a ranch home that had a fresh coat of whitewash on it. "That one's mine. I've been fixing it up already. It's not bad, especially after living in truck stops and on the run for so long."

"You'll want to get some boards over those windows before winter arrives," Elliot observed.

"Sure. But one thing at a time. There are enough empty houses I can pull some glass from that I'm not sweating it." He snapped his fingers. "Oh, and I reached out to Luis and told him we were going to be resettling here. He's debating making the trip. Should hear back from him shortly."

"They have a radio here?"

"More like a half dozen. They're better equipped than just about anywhere I've been. It's almost like being back in the old world – except for the electricity and gas, of course."

"But they have solar, right?"

"Of course. During the day it isn't a problem, but the batteries are on their last legs. The temperature variations and age haven't been their friend."

"No, I don't imagine they have."

"One thing, though. You're going to have to store your weaponry in their central arsenal. They don't allow guns in the city limits except for hunting, and those you have to get permission for."

"That's fine. A welcome return to civilization."

Elliot smiled at his people, who were already spreading through the neighborhood, laying claim to promising dwellings that caught their eyes. He saw Sierra, Eve, and Tim in the yard of a nearby house, and nodded approvingly. "You know what they say – you can choose your location, but you can't choose your neighbors. Seems like that won't be a problem."

"Everyone's been friendly and helpful. We'll get along just fine."

Elliot clapped Duke on the shoulder. "Of course we will. I want to thank you for riding all the way here and making our case for us. I'm sure it could have gone either way."

"I expect it could. Some weren't so sure this was a good idea, but in the end, they made the right decision."

"Fortunate for us."

"I'd say for everyone. It's a good fit."

Chapter 38

Redding, California

Clark braked the locomotive to a halt at the Redding station, and Lucas and his men descended from the pair of cars they'd occupied on the overnight trip south. It had taken them eighteen hours, the engine maintaining a sustainable twenty-two miles per hour the entire way, and the newly repaired boiler had shown no signs of problems, even as Clark increased the pressure to full intensity. He'd tested it after performing his proposed repairs and had pronounced the system sound, but as with all things post-collapse, everyone had been skeptical until its integrity was proven.

Clark dropped from the cab while the two fireman cleaned up, and walked to where Lucas was waiting with a hundred of his best, all armed to the teeth. He looked around slowly and shook his head.

"The place is a ghost town. They killed everyone. Even the animals they couldn't immediately eat."

"Makes me wish we had time to pay Sacramento a visit to return the favor," Lucas said.

Clark nodded, and the lines in his face deepened. "I'd run you down there myself for free."

"At some point I may take you up on that. But for now, let's stick to the job at hand."

"Agreed."

Lucas had slowly grown to like the crusty engineer, even if he was

208

a self-interested mercenary. He worked long hours without complaint and had a real knack for the mechanical side of railroading, as well as an obvious love for its history.

"This way," Clark said.

"Half of you, stay here and guard the train," Lucas ordered, and the men broke off to take defensive positions around the engine.

"Nothing but phantoms to shoot, I'm afraid," Clark grumbled, and shuffled off in the direction of a low building to the side of the station.

Inside they found a pair of locomotives in disrepair, but not as bad as Clark had made out, at least to the untrained eye. He patted the side of one of the engines with real affection. "This could be the twin of ours."

"Strip it of anything you can. Surely can't hurt to have more spares on the trip."

"Wish we could swap boilers, but that's nigh impossible, given our tools."

"It ran fine. You still concerned?" Lucas asked.

"We're towing two cars. We'll have thirty or more going over the mountains. So yes, I'm going to be concerned until we touch down in Salt Lake."

"That's fair," Lucas agreed. "But so far the repairs have held, right?"

"They have. But my job is to be paranoid."

"You're good at it."

Clark did a walk around, and then they returned to the train to get his tools and several wheeled carts to transport whatever he scavenged. Lucas supervised the unloading and then climbed aboard the second car and lay down across one of the cushioned bench seats to rest. The night had been a sleepless one for him, as he'd kept Clark company on his midnight vigil before moving to the cars to join the men at their final water refill.

Four hours later he started awake to the clank of metal on metal. He sat up and blinked away sleep, and then disembarked and walked to where Clark was measuring the damaged shaft. Another identical one lay on one of the carts, along with a collection of other hardware.

"It'll fit," he said, and looked up at Lucas. "I took your advice and removed all the shafts from both sides in case we have another issue on the way. Once I have this one replaced, I'll see how many of the fittings for the pressure system are usable. Not like we've got a machine shop or a hardware store along the route."

"Probably wise," Lucas agreed, eyeing the new shaft. "That one looks intact."

"It is. We just have to make sure we don't overdo it, and it should do fine." He took a deep breath. "The one I repaired…it was fine for a jury-rigging, but there's no way it would have made it over the mountains towing a full load."

"Hopefully this one's in better shape."

"No way to know without an X-ray, but we'll give it our best shot."

"How long until we can head back?"

"Probably by nightfall."

"Good. That would put us in Salem by…early afternoon tomorrow?"

"Nah. We should be able to go faster with the new shaft. We'll shoot for thirty-five and see what we can do. Should be a piece of cake for her."

"So…morning?"

"That's the plan. Then I want to sleep for about twenty hours while you load up."

"You'll have earned it."

"Damn straight."

True to his word, Clark was finished with the equipment swap and stripping by the end of the day, and they were underway again by dark. Lucas accompanied him in the cab as the firemen stoked the furnace, and soon they were doing well over forty miles per hour with a half head of steam.

"Told you she'd be able to pull her weight," Clark said.

"Never doubted you. But the question is how we'll do with thousands of troops and a full house of animals and gear."

"The shaft should hold. No reason to believe it won't. As long as I did my job right on the boiler, we should be golden."

Lucas's mouth twitched. "Appropriate choice of words."

"Might be time to ask for half, don't you think?"

"Got no problem with that," Lucas said. He fished in his pocket and retrieved two gold maple leafs and handed them to Clark. "But remember there's more to life than money."

Clark smirked. "Right. There's the stuff money buys."

Both men laughed easily as the landscape rushed by. The firemen stoked the flames as the locomotive roared through the night, and for a brief instant, a world where everything worked as intended and disaster didn't lurk around every turn seemed possible, if only distantly.

They arrived as promised in the early morning, and Lucas met with Art to fill him in on his thinking shortly after the train ground to a halt.

"If we can safely pull thirty-five cars, we should be able to bring half the troops, a couple of cars full of horses, and three with weapons and ammo."

"What do we do with the other three thousand?" Art asked.

"They make it to Utah the hard way. Or we can send the train back. Your call."

"I'm for trains. That's a long haul, and a lot of it's pretty unforgiving terrain."

"No question," Lucas agreed. "I'll just have to bribe Clark with more gold."

"It's for a good cause. And it's not like you don't have enough of it."

"True."

"We've been collecting all the weapons we could find. One of the prisoners told us that the Illuminati opened an armory for them. I'd think that was crazy talk if their guns weren't all military issue. And you don't find grenade launchers and mortars in any kind of uniform quantity like they had in a trading post."

"So the Illuminati are gunning for us? Makes sense if they're the ones who sold the country to the Chinese. We messed that up for them, and I'd imagine the Chinese aren't happy."

"Makes you wonder how many of the big gangs they're influencing, doesn't it?" Art mused.

"Probably most. But it won't help them."

"Not if they all fold up at the first sign of a fight like these punks did."

"We can't assume gangs like the Crew are going to be easy to overthrow."

"Oh, I know. I'm just saying that the smaller gangs are nothing more than prison rabble with guns. Not a lot of art to mowing them down with a disciplined force, as you've seen."

"True. But we're eventually going to run up against someone who fights back for real."

"No question. That's why I have all the squad leaders training the men – most are up to speed, but we saw in this fight that some lose it under fire. That's got to change, or they're liabilities."

"Agreed. Does it look like we'll be able to fully replenish our ammo stores?"

Art nodded. "And then some. We're actually going to walk away with about forty percent more rounds than we walked in with. It's turning out well to go up against enemies that don't actually shoot."

"I'm afraid we can't depend on that moving forward."

"I know. We got lucky with the train breaking down. Otherwise it might have gone differently in the valley. I'm not stupid."

"You're anything but dumb," Lucas agreed.

"So the plan is for you to head to Utah with half our fighters, I sit here filing my nails until the train gets back, and then we haul everyone else in one load?"

"That's it. We'll have more confidence in the locomotive after making the trip, and if it can tow more cars, we'll do it. But one way or another, everyone who can fit should."

"What about those who want to stay in Salem? Or the rest of the bunch from Astoria?"

"I'll leave it to you to talk sense into them. Once we pull out, they're essentially defenseless, so if more miscreants decide they want some easy pickings, they're going to be in the crosshairs. Wouldn't be a smart move to stay."

Art grimaced. "You know how the Astoria group can be."

"If they absolutely insist on staying put, leave them enough weapons and ammo to mount a good fight, and wish them well. They're adults."

"I'll do my best."

"Hopefully that'll be enough."

Lucas and Sam spent the day selecting armaments and gear for the trip, and by evening had the boxcars filled and the horses waiting patiently for Clark to show himself. The train still had plenty of coal from the stocks the gang had brought from Sacramento, and the only concern was water for the boiler en route, but Lucas was sure they'd be able to source enough from the myriad streams and rivers they would cross to make the journey without issue – it would be backbreaking labor hauling thousands of gallons in five-gallon containers, but it was necessary and not as bad as it sounded with thousands of helping hands aboard.

Clark appeared as maroon and violet were painting the darkening sky, and Lucas pulled him aside to explain what was expected of him. When he finished, Clark eyed him with a frown.

"It'll take more than four coins to get me to run this all the way back here from Utah and do it all over again."

"Call it eight, then."

"I'm thinking twelve. Got to get paid for the return trip. I don't work for free."

"Call it ten. The return has less risk with an empty train. Although you'll need some gunmen for security."

"You drive a hard bargain. Let's say eleven and get going."

Lucas sighed. "Done."

Clark instructed the men on how to attach more cars, and then jockeyed the locomotive back and forth over multiple tracks to accommodate the new configuration. When they were hooked up, the men climbed aboard, and by ten o'clock at night the train pulled out of the yard, loaded to the brim with fighters and gear.

"You know the route we're going to take?" Lucas asked as the engine eased forward.

"Got a decent idea. Down by Redding, and then across to Reno. From there you don't have a lot of choices to get to Salt Lake."

"We're actually headed to Provo. South of Salt Lake."

"Tracks run there, so not a problem."

"You keep all that up here?" Lucas asked, tapping his forehead.

"There aren't that many routes, to be honest. But yes. I can visualize the route map. Remember, this has been my passion for thirty years."

"Fair enough. I'm just a little amazed by it."

"We all got skills."

"True."

The train picked up speed, and Clark capped their progress at twenty miles per hour, with the pressure at seventy-eight percent.

"Let's see how she holds up doing twenty. If no problem, this should be a cakewalk."

"How long will it take to get to Provo?"

"Four days at least, provided no gotchas. Probably more. We've got to onload water, and that'll take a while, although hopefully we can time it around nightfall so we don't burn through running time. We can't really operate at night once we're on the Redding to Salt Lake stretch – we have no idea what the condition of the tracks is."

"Sounds like a long four days."

"Be five or six times that on horseback. Ten times more on foot."

"Good point."

Clark patted the metal housing in front of him with a calloused hand. "Don't know if you're a God-fearing man, but a little prayer never hurt anything."

Lucas touched his hat brim. "I'll pass the word along."

"Can't hurt."

Chapter 39

Provo, Utah

Elijah and Benjamin studied the barrier that blocked the highway into Provo through their binoculars, noting at least two hundred gunmen lining walls on either side, with four heavy machine guns trained on them from behind sandbagged positions. Elijah's army waited five hundred yards behind them, where it had encamped in the dead of night after being led to the city limits by Leo and his trackers.

Benjamin eyed the machine guns and murmured to Elijah, "Those can fire a thousand rounds a minute. Even at this range they'd cut us to pieces. Serious business. We might want to reconsider a frontal approach."

"We're out in the open now and have nothing to fear. Our fight isn't with these people. It's with the scum hiding behind their walls."

"If they're allowing them to stay, we might be talking about a major fight. They look like they know what they're doing."

"The Lord will guide us to victory, just as He has in every battle so far."

"That was against disorganized amateurs. Look at their weapons. The machine guns. They may also have grenades. This is a whole different level of defense than Colorado Springs or Pueblo."

"We have nothing to fear. We're doing God's work."

Benjamin shook his head. "I have yet to see God stop a bullet."

Elijah turned to glower at Benjamin. "Do you doubt my word?"

"It's not that. We don't want to lose hundreds of men trying to rush a heavily defended access point if we can help it, regardless of how righteous our cause is."

Elijah nodded as though agreeing, but his eyes burned with zeal, telling Benjamin that he hadn't registered a word.

"We'll deliver an ultimatum. Give up the garbage from Shangri-La or face the consequences."

An advance scouting team had taken a young man from Provo prisoner at dawn as he was walking outside the wall that encircled the city, equipped with a slingshot and crossbow to hunt rabbits in the early hours. He'd immediately told his interrogators about the new arrivals the community had taken in, his fear so great he was trembling during the entire questioning. Once word reached Elijah that his targets were within the city walls, he'd become animated and insisted that Benjamin accompany him to demand the citizenry turn the members of Shangri-La over to him or else.

"They might not be receptive to being threatened with death if they don't comply," Benjamin said.

"I don't make threats. I predict the future." Elijah looked over his shoulder. "We have thousands of men. There's no way they can resist us."

"Maybe. But they don't look too worried to me. I'm wondering what else they've got behind that wall."

"We'll ride to their gate and tell them why we're here. God will decide the rest."

Benjamin thought that sounded like a fine way to get shot, but he held his tongue. Elijah had grown increasingly erratic on the trail, and Benjamin didn't trust the man not to lash out rashly if he said the wrong thing.

Elijah raised his rifle over his head in a salute to his troops, and then urged his horse forward, leaving Benjamin to follow in his wake as he rode toward the barrier. They approached at a gallop and slowed as they neared, and when they were close enough to be heard, Elijah reined to a halt in a cloud of dust.

"I am Elijah! I am the Lord's prophet, sent by Him to smite His enemies wherever they are found."

The men at the wall remained silent, apparently unimpressed by the bombastic oratory.

Elijah tried again. "We are on a divine mission from God, in search of a den of murderers and blasphemers who you've taken under your wing – I assume because you know nothing of their heinous deeds. I'm here to ask you to turn them over to us for justice, or be branded with the same curse they are, subject to the same fate."

Benjamin cringed inwardly at the delusional threat in the face of enough firepower to vaporize them both.

"You have in your midst evil of the foulest sort," Elijah continued. "The people of a place they called Shangri-La murdered my father, who was another divine prophet. I'm here to make them pay for their crime."

A voice called from the wall, the speaker sensibly wearing a heavy flak vest and a war-surplus helmet.

"Elijah, is it? My name's Thomas. I represent the people of Provo, as well as our militia, who are sworn to defend the city and everyone in it. We're a God-fearing community and don't take kindly to self-proclaimed prophets showing up at our gates with an army to make threats. So consider this your only warning. You try to do anything besides leave and we'll cut you to ribbons. I don't care how many men you have – we've got more ammo than you've got bodies, and you'll die where you stand if you don't go back wherever you came from and leave us in peace."

Elijah digested the warning and raised his rifle over his head again while he shouted at Thomas, "We have a bioweapon that will expose everyone in your city to a deadly nerve agent if you don't do as I ask. You've been warned. If the members of Shangri-La aren't turned over to us within twenty-four hours, we'll detonate that weapon, and you'll all pay the ultimate price for harboring the forces of darkness. Your guns won't do you any good. I don't want to slaughter everyone, but I will if you don't do as I say." He paused dramatically. "I am Elijah, the sword of God, and you will obey or be smitten!"

Elijah spun his horse around, nearly colliding with Benjamin, and spurred the beast back toward the encampment, with Benjamin riding hard on his tail, fearful of a bullet in his spine at any moment.

Thomas watched Elijah and his man ride away and retreated from the barricade to where Elliot was waiting by a group of militia equipped with grenade launchers and assault rifles.

"What do you make of that?" he asked.

"The man's out of his mind. He sent his people to kidnap one of our children who his father was convinced was foiling his plans for the final apocalypse, and his father, who ran the cult in Denver he's taken over, was killed when we rescued her. Now he's decided he's on some sort of crusade." Elliot shook his head. "Completely delusional. Textbook case of paranoid schizophrenia, I'd wager."

"I meant the bioweapon threat."

Elliot frowned. "I'm not sure what to make of it, frankly. On the one hand, does it make any sense that they'd have followed us halfway across the country carrying a bioweapon with them? Not to me. Then again, he's clearly crazy, so we can't assume anything based on logic. I'd put it at it being possible but highly unlikely."

Thomas sighed in exasperation. "That's my assessment, too. Whatever the case, this is a large area, and I don't for a moment buy that he's got some suitcase nuke, or whatever is the bioterror equivalent, that he's going to release and which will only kill us. So I'll go with bluff. But he's got a substantial army there, and they might be able to do some serious damage to us, depending on how well equipped they are. If this goes to the wire, we've got to be prepared for an all-out onslaught."

"If you're having second thoughts about allowing us in, we can always leave. I'm sure there's some way for us to sneak out during the night without being seen."

Thomas shook his head. "No. We gave you our word and invited you in knowing the risks. I'm just amazed that he led that mob all the way from Colorado on foot to get even with you for killing his father. I mean, it's…nuts."

"Exactly. Which makes him dangerously unpredictable. You can't reason with someone who believes themselves to be Joan of Arc. So we have to expect the worst."

"I didn't see any serious artillery with his group. Just men with rifles. You think he might have more he's keeping out of sight?"

"No way of knowing. I think we have to assume he does."

"Then it would make the most sense to bombard his position while his men sleep."

"Which you won't do. I understand that. You won't attack unless attacked."

Thomas sighed. "Correct. Even though they're threatening us, we're not going to fire the first shots. It's not our way."

"I could argue the wisdom of turning the other cheek against a madman, but I won't."

Thomas nodded. "I'm not saying we'll turn the other cheek. Just wait for him to try to slap it, and then flatten him. We gave him fair warning. The next move is his."

Elliot managed a sad smile. "I'm sorry it's come to this. Honestly, you'd be completely within your rights if you wanted us to leave."

"What kind of people would we be if we threw you to the wolves at the first hint of trouble? After all you've done for us? That's not who we are. We'll stand by you like family, and if anyone tries to harm you, it will be the last thing they ever do."

Chapter 40

Wells, Nevada

The train slowed with a screech of wheels and rolled to a gentle stop at the top of a desert mountain pass, the landscape uninterrupted beige to the distant horizon. When Lucas was sure that the cars weren't going to move again, he leapt from the entrance and trotted to the locomotive, rifle in hand.

"What's going on?" he asked. Three days of travel and there had been no unpleasant surprises, and now, on the morning of the fourth, less than two hours into the trip, they were stopped?

Clark pointed ahead. "There's something across the rails. Looks like logs and maybe an old car."

"Why would anyone bother blocking the tracks? There hasn't been a train on them for...forever."

"Beats me. We can try blowing through it, but I'd hate to find out the hard way that they also rolled a boulder or something onto the rails. I suggest you assemble a crew and go drag the crap off."

Lucas considered the area, slowly sweeping the surroundings with his binoculars, and seeing nothing of immediate concern, returned to the cars and called to the men. "We've got some junk on the tracks. I need a couple of hundred of you out here on the double!"

Terry and scores of men piled from the cars, and when Lucas was sure he had enough help, he led them past the locomotive to where the debris was piled. Clark walked with him, and when they reached

220

it, he scratched his head, perplexed.

"I don't get it. Why would anyone go to all this trouble?"

Lucas shrugged. "Looks like it's been here a while. Probably happened after the grid went down. Those days were crazy. People were doing all sorts of things to try to survive. Maybe some of the locals figured they could hijack a train that never came through?"

Clark nodded. "Probably right. That car's seen better days."

"True." Lucas looked to his men. "All right. Let's remove the logs first, and then we'll shift the car out of the way."

Terry set about organizing teams of workers, and in short order what turned out to be wooden telephone poles were being moved well clear of the tracks by groups of thirty men per pole. Lucas watched as they worked, and then Terry called from near the car.

"Lucas? You need to see this."

Lucas walked over to Terry and stopped when he saw what he was pointing at. Nestled in the debris was a land mine.

"Looks like they were planning to derail whatever came through," Terry said.

"Nice guys." He called over to Clark, "Would a land mine blow a train off the tracks?"

"Maybe. Maybe not. But it sure would destroy the rails, which would effectively do the same thing. Why? You got one there?"

"Yes." He looked to Terry. "You ever disarm one of these?"

Terry looked uncertain. "They showed us how in basic, but that was a long time ago."

"See if any of the men remember. If nobody here does, go back to the cars and ask."

Terry did so, and hiked back to the train when it became obvious there were no takers on his challenge. He reappeared five minutes later with a pair of fighters, one short and muscled, the other lanky and tall as a basketball player.

They studied the land mine for a minute, and then the tall one gave Lucas and Terry a gap-toothed grin. "Might want to move everyone away from here just in case."

"In case?" Terry asked.

The tall one nodded. "In case we have a seriously bad day."

"That's not pumping me full of confidence," Clark said.

"How do you think I feel?" the shorter man asked.

"All right. Everybody back," Lucas hollered. The group edged away until everyone was twenty-five yards from the tracks. "Far enough?" he yelled.

"We'll know in a few," the tall man called, and laughed dryly.

"Good thing we've got some extra rails with us, isn't it?" Clark asked Lucas.

"Foresight's a wonderful thing. Let's hope we're not going to–"

The tracks exploded in a flash of orange, and where the pair of joking men had been, now there was nothing but smoke and twisted steel, the car blown completely clear. Debris rained down from the explosion and Terry shook his head. "Looks like we were far enough."

Lucas sighed at the senseless death and shook his head. "Clark, bring up as many rails as you need. No point in delaying out here all day."

"Sure thing, skipper," he said, and went off at a run to the boxcars, where his tools and the spare tracks were stored.

More men returned toting a pair of rails and a toolbox. Others carried sledgehammers and pry bars and burlap sacks filled with spikes. They wrestled the mangled steel out of the way and then set to work laying a new section of track, reusing the spikes where they could.

When they'd finished and had filled in the hole left by the blast, Clark inspected their work before pronouncing the section safe. "It'd better be," Lucas said. "We're two hundred miles from anything out here, and men have died in the high desert a lot closer to water."

"It'll hold. I was more worried about my trip back. But it looks solid. We'll just go slow, and I'll mark the spot so I'm not going thirty when I hit this section."

"Anyone know those men's names?" Lucas asked.

Nobody said anything, and he nodded. "We owe them."

"Damn shame," Clark agreed. "But we can mourn underway."

Lucas called to the crew, "Back to the train. We're rolling in three."

They carried the tools back and stowed them, and Clark climbed aboard his beloved locomotive and built a sufficient head of steam till the engine lurched forward and inched ahead, rolling so slowly a tumbleweed blowing from the west passed them by on the way to the new section.

And then they were over and slowly accelerating. Lucas checked his watch. By his reckoning, they'd hit Salt Lake in about twelve hours, possibly less, depending on their speed. Clark had warned them that the last section had enough switchbacks and sharp curves to slow their progress considerably, but he expected them to arrive by nightfall – now pushed forward another two hours.

His heart rate increased at the thought of seeing Sierra and the kids again. It seemed like forever since he'd held her in his arms, and he realized it had been. He'd been gone too long, and the prospect of yet more long absences leading the Freedom Army with Art had zero appeal, especially sitting on a cramped train with a hundred other lost souls crammed into the car and a landscape straight out of hell rolling by like an endlessly tedious cartoon backdrop.

Chapter 41

Lucas sat with the radio operator in the rear of the railway car and listened to the shortwave set he'd placed on the seat, an antenna dangling out the window and a solar battery by his feet. They'd been transmitting for an hour on the Shangri-La channel, but with no result other than static and occasional blares of white noise.

The operator removed his headset and grunted. "Sorry, Lucas. Not getting anything."

Lucas leaned closer and frowned. "Try sweeping the dial and see if anyone's on the air. Maybe we can reach someone in Provo who can get a message to them."

"Sounds like a long shot, but you never know." The operator redonned his earphones and slowly turned the dial. Halfway through he stopped and tilted his head, and then gave Lucas a thumbs-up before raising the mic to his lips and pressing transmit.

"Sorry to barge in. Are either of you in Provo?" he said into the mic.

Lucas held one of the earphones to his ear to listen in.

"Roger that. Who is this?" a voice answered.

"We're on an inbound train and want to see if we can get a message to some new arrivals there."

"A *train?* You're shitting me. Ain't no trains running."

224

Lucas motioned to the operator for the mic. He handed it to Lucas, and he depressed the transmit button. "There's one running, because we're on it. Can you get a message to someone there? They should have arrived in the last week or so."

"Oh. Crap. You're serious."

"That's right."

"Look, I can get a message to them, but don't approach the city. We're surrounded by an army. Repeat. Don't come to Provo. We're surrounded."

Lucas frowned. "What army?"

"Some crazies from Denver. There's a swarm of them. Thousands. And they're on the warpath. Threatened us with total destruction if we don't give your friends up."

"Slow down. Tell me what happened. We're maybe ten miles out."

"Then that's where I'd stay." The Provo operator spoke for two minutes, detailing what he'd heard about Elijah's force and his threat of using a bioweapon the next day if they didn't turn over Lucas's people. By the time he was done, Lucas was struggling to keep from screaming in frustration.

"Listen. Can you get whoever is in charge on the horn? I've got a substantial group of fighters myself, and we're loaded for bear. We need to coordinate, and we need to do it now."

"Sure. I can try. Who is this?"

"Name's Lucas. Anyone from your newcomers can tell you who I am."

"Okay. Give me a half hour and I'll see if I can find someone from the council."

"We'll stand by. Over and out."

Lucas tossed the earphones to the operator and stood. "Keep monitoring that channel. I need to talk to my men."

Twenty minutes later Lucas, Sam, Henry, and Terry were seated in the back of the car with the operator. Lucas was explaining what he knew, and Sam and Terry looked ashen by the time he was done.

"So out of the fire…" Sam began.

"Nobody said this would be all martinis and steak," Lucas said.

"Yeah, but heading straight for another battle…"

"Maybe. Or maybe we can figure out a way to work with Provo and stop this before it gets that far."

The operator waved Lucas over, and he hurried to the set, removed his hat, and pulled on the earphones before taking the mic. "This is Lucas. Over."

"Lucas? Thomas. Head of the Provo council and the militia. My man here says you're aboard a train outside town? Did he hear right?"

"That's correct. Nice meeting you, Thomas. We're maybe eight miles out and stopped until we understand what we're headed into."

"Nothing good." Thomas quickly ran down his exchange with Elijah. "How many men do you have?"

"Three thousand, give or take. Some horses. And two boxcars of mortars, machine guns, grenade launchers, and ammo."

A long silence ensued. When Thomas spoke again, his tone had changed. "That could come in handy. We're well outfitted ourselves, and we have more like four thousand fighters here. Between the two of us…"

"That's what I was thinking. And they have no idea we're out here. So maybe we can put that to use."

"I can think of a few ways," Thomas agreed.

"What's this about a bioweapon? Your operator said something about one?"

Thomas explained his sentiment that it was a hollow threat.

Lucas shook his head. "Possibly. But if you're wrong, this could go sideways quickly."

"No question. You have any suggestions?"

"Have you gotten a good look at their camp? We're up north, but do they have any sort of command tent or anything?"

"There's been a lot of activity at one of the big industrial warehouses on the southern end of town, which is where the main body is hunkered down. Then there's a big open stretch where they're camped, but they've occupied some of the warehouses, too.

They've also got men all along the wall and blocking the northern exit, but most of them are on the southern tip."

"Whether they're bluffing or not, if the device is in their midst, there's no way they're going to detonate it."

"Probably not. But the second they see us come out of the gate, it's a different story."

"Right. Which is why the smart thing to do is hit them tonight while they're asleep, or at least groggy from stress."

"We can't even open the barricade without being spotted. They've got most of their men facing us, watching for a move like that. We'd be walking into a chainsaw."

"But if we move on foot in the dark, there's a good chance we could slip past their northern presence and hit them from where they're not looking."

"It's mountains along the eastern wall. We built a ten-foot barrier along that side, and to the north and south. There's not a lot of room to move an army through. Although it's possible, just tough."

"What about to the west?"

"The lake."

"Could we make it along the shore and come up behind them?"

"Again, it's possible. But a lot would have to go right. And you're talking about eight miles of tough slog."

"We've crawled through worse than that."

They discussed possible tactics and terminated with an agreement that Lucas would first try the mountain route, and if that failed, would double back and work his way along the shore. Given how Elijah's army was situated, though, there was a far greater chance of being discovered emerging from the lake area than appearing out of the mountains, which nobody was watching.

Lucas met with Sam, Terry, and Henry for ten minutes, and then they went in search of the squad leaders while Lucas made for the locomotive to tell Clark what had happened, who listened in silence before asking a single question.

"So you want me to power down and wait for the world to end?"

"Something like that."

"Better collect my pay before you disappear, then."

Lucas smiled. "Always the pragmatist."

"Nothing personal. But this ain't my fight."

"No problem. Not asking you to join in. Just to wait to see who wins. If it's us, you've got another round trip coming. If not, get the hell out of here, because you won't want to mess with these nutcases." Lucas handed him another three coins. "That makes five, which is one more than we agreed. So stick around. It'll be worth your while if we aren't all dead by morning."

"You do have a way with words. How can I refuse?"

Forty minutes later, Lucas was on foot and leading his men, who were loaded down with mortars and grenade launchers and crates of rounds in addition to their assault rifles and magazines. They only had five hundred NV goggles among three thousand men, but Lucas wasn't worried – he was planning to use a variation of the strategy they'd put into play in Seattle and Salem, although he couldn't carpet-bomb the encampment like he'd have preferred because of the bioweapon.

Assuming that wasn't a hoax, Lucas couldn't simply lob a few hundred mortar rounds into the camp and target the command building – the risk of detonating the device, or damaging it so that it spread its payload, was too great. Instead, he and the other NV-equipped gunmen would have to do things the hard way and shoot their way to the warehouse before ushering in the second wave of non-NV equipped troops. They could use grenades and launchers to tilt the odds in their favor, but mortars had to be reserved for the periphery of the enemy force and kept well away from its core. Which wasn't ideal, but was the best Lucas could come up with in the time he had.

It seemed like a solid plan as they marched in silence toward the outline of the mountains, keeping well clear of the wall and the tents pitched along it. The enemy troops were largely asleep or watching the town, not the slopes, and Lucas's men were able to skirt their encampment to the north and flank them without them ever realizing that a huge force was making its way past to rain death down on their main body from under cover of darkness.

Henry instructed five of the grenade crews to hold up the rear and set up a firing position so once the attack began, they could target the northern enemy force, and left a hundred men with them to defend their nests while they pummeled Elijah's rear guard.

Then they were working their way along the mountainsides, moving quietly, the only sound other than night birds their breathing and the soft stirring of thousands of boots on the loose dirt along the base of the mountains.

Chapter 42

"What do you think?" Sam murmured to Lucas from a ridge overlooking the enemy camp.

"Let me take another look."

Lucas's NV-equipped troops were with him in an advance formation overlooking the encampment and the warehouses. Lucas switched from his NV goggles to his NV M4 scope and scanned the buildings. One had a contingent of guards and men moving in and out of it even at the late hour, which matched what Thomas had described as the warehouse the enemy was using as its command center.

"You still on for rushing them with the advance group and then calling in the rest once you've taken the warehouse?"

Lucas didn't say anything, but continued to study the building. When he lowered the M4, he leaned into Sam and murmured to him, "I'm not so sure that's the best idea now. Most of the camp's asleep. Only activity is at the warehouse. It might make more sense to take a small squad and penetrate the building rather than five hundred bulls in a china shop."

"If something goes wrong, you'd be dead meat."

"Didn't say there wasn't a downside. But if we could make it in without firing a shot...we could verify whether this supposed bioweapon even exists, which would change our tactics. If it's a bluff, we could just bomb them into the Stone Age and not worry about the fallout. Which would save a lot of our troops."

"Right. But if they sound the alarm…"

"It isn't a perfect plan," Lucas conceded. "But it could work. They're all focused on the city. We come in from the east…nobody's watching for a threat from their flank."

"How big a squad you thinking?"

"Not big. Maybe a dozen of our top men with crossbows."

Sam nodded. "I see your point. Not nearly as messy as a frontal assault. If you can pull it off."

"Which is why they pay me the big bucks. Pass the word to your best fighters. I want to leave in ten minutes."

"Roger that."

Lucas crept down the mountain with his men, all equipped with crossbows and spare quarrels in addition to their usual assault rifles and hand grenades. The camp glowed in their night vision scopes. Nothing was moving as they neared the first of the tents. In the distance, the warehouse loomed large, and a few heat signatures told them where the guards were stationed – not surprisingly, most at the main entrance, with only a few along the sides and presumably some at the rear.

They took cautious steps as they wended between the tents, their weight on the outside of their feet, crouched low with crossbows in hand. The sky was cloudy, no stars in evidence, which played in their favor; without night vision gear, the guards at the warehouse would be largely blind to their approach until it was too late.

When they neared, Lucas gestured for the men to spread out. Six moved to the right side of the building and the others followed Lucas to the left. Both circled around until they were gathered seventy yards from the rear, where only four guards were sitting by a steel rear door, their guns leaning against the wall.

Lucas signaled, and four of his fighters peeled off and crept toward the guards. When they were fifty feet away, two of them fired at the outside guards, and then the other pair did the same with the couple nearest the door. All died silently, the bolts as lethal as they were quiet, and Lucas and the rest rushed to join them. Lucas pointed to the side, and half his men moved to that corner, and he and the rest ran to the other.

Lucas dispatched one of the sentries at the side and his men the other, and then they peered around at the front, where eight gunmen were loitering. The faint glow of lanterns from beneath the heavy front doors lit the NV scopes like neon, and Lucas waited until his men on the far side had time to make it to the front before murmuring to his group, "Make it quick. Overkill. We can take the twenty seconds to reload after they're down. Don't try to save arrows."

The men nodded, and he took a deep breath and rounded the corner with them, crossbows trained on the guards, who didn't register the fighters until they were nearly on top of them.

A hail of bolts winged toward the guards, and all four fell, several skewered by multiple shafts. The other guards turned at the noise, and Lucas's second team took them down silently, all of their quarrels finding home.

The reloading took half a minute, and then they were moving on the front entrance. They were nearly to it when a yell from the camp pierced the night, followed by shooting.

Slugs slammed into the cinderblock by Lucas's head, and he ducked down while simultaneously freeing his M4, the need for quiet now abandoned. One of his men screamed as rounds tore into his hips below his plate carrier, and then Lucas threw the door open and rolled through it, rifle in hand.

A score of startled guards in the warehouse reacted by fumbling with their weapons, but Lucas was already shooting, his three-round bursts loud as a howitzer in the cavernous space. The nearest two collapsed and their rifles clattered against the concrete floor, and Lucas aimed for the lanterns on either side of the warehouse and blew them to pieces.

The room plunged into darkness as more of Lucas's men made it inside, and they stitched the enemy gunmen with continuous fire, killing everyone in sight within seconds. Lucas ejected his spent magazine and slapped a fresh one into place, and then called out, "Everyone inside?"

"We lost five."

"Bolt the door."

The fighters did as instructed; the heavy steel slab would provide a formidable barrier to the enemy – at least for a few minutes.

"Search the place for anything that looks like a bioweapon."

"What are we looking for?"

"Anything bigger than a breadbox."

Bullets pinged off the front door but didn't penetrate, and the men went to work, performing a grid search of the interior with methodical precision. Lucas called out when he reached the rear of the warehouse. "Anything?"

"Negative."

"No."

"Just rifles, ammo, some solar batteries, and a radio."

Lucas nodded to himself. The whole thing had been a bluff intended to force Provo's hand and avoid a real fight.

"All right. Let's head up to the roof."

Lucas scaled a steel ladder mounted to the wall and pushed the hatch above open. He pulled himself through the square gap and ran through the night, groping for the handle of a flare gun in his flak jacket. He found it, oriented himself, and then fired.

The flare streaked into the sky in a blinding blaze of orange, signaling to the rest of the force to begin their attack. Almost immediately the heavy stutter of Terry's .50-caliber machine guns shattered the night, followed by the whump of mortars and grenades being launched from the mountains.

Lucas reached the roof's edge and peeked over as the rest of his men clambered up the ladder, and tossed a hand grenade toward a group of Elijah's fighters that was firing assault rifles at the front entrance. He didn't wait for the detonation and instead retraced his steps to the hatch. "You three, take the rear, and shoot anyone who gets near the back door. The rest of you, we'll do the same for the front. Get moving."

The grenade's explosion lit the night, and Lucas and his gunmen threw themselves down on the flat roof and crawled to the lip. The blast had killed or badly wounded a dozen of Elijah's men, and none of the rest seemed overly eager to take their spot, more concerned with the hail of rounds streaking from the machine-gun nests that were eviscerating them where they stood. More grenade explosions throughout the camp blended with the large blasts of the mortar rounds, overlaid by the agonized screams of the wounded as the Brownings cut them to pieces.

Lucas picked off several gunmen who were foolish enough to attempt another rush at the door, and then the sound of assault rifles filled the air as his NV-equipped fighters joined the fray. When the mortars fell quiet, he could barely make out booms from north of the city, where the troops he'd left there engaged the enemy at the rear barricade with grenades, hopefully with equivalent results to those his frontal assault force was enjoying.

Elijah's men were in complete disarray, and many dropped their weapons and tried running away from the city as fast as they could, hoping to save themselves from what was coming over the ridge. Those who chose to fight were overwhelmed by Lucas's superior firepower and more seasoned troops, and by daybreak the battle was over and the valley floor was littered with the dead and dying.

Lucas descended from his perch and went to meet the heavily armed contingent that had emerged from the Provo barricade.

"You Thomas?" Lucas asked the tall man at the head of the procession.

"That's right. Lucas, I presume?"

They shook hands, and Thomas took in the carnage around him. He shook his head and his face twisted with a look of disgust. "What a...a travesty. Completely avoidable. So much death..."

Lucas gave a small shrug. "They came looking for a fight. We gave them what they asked for."

"And the bioweapon?"

"Complete fabrication."

Thomas looked around. "How many men did you lose?"

"We're still tallying, but fewer than a hundred."

"There must be thousands here."

"A good friend once told me that the point of battle is to win while suffering the fewest casualties possible. Seemed smart at the time. Smarter now."

"Agreed. It's just...such a shame." Thomas paused. "When you're done out here, your people in town are looking forward to seeing you. One young lady in particular."

Lucas smiled. "Glad to hear it. But first I want your help in ID'ing the crazy preacher. Can you take a look in the warehouse and pick him out?"

"Certainly."

They walked together through an ocean of blood and corpses and entered the warehouse. Thomas eyed the dead in the gloom, and Lucas turned over any of the bodies that had fallen facedown. They reached the rear door and Lucas swung it open to admit more light. Thomas joined him and shook his head.

"He's not here."

"What? He has to be. This was the only place there was any activity."

"He's very recognizable. He isn't here."

Lucas's face clouded. "You're sure?"

"Positive."

Lucas stepped outside and waved away the flies – the only beneficiaries of the slaughter – and eyed the horizon, breathing heavily, lost in thought.

Chapter 43

Amber Hot Springs, Colorado

Three men sat at the fire pit, a deck of dog-eared playing cards sitting on the stone. Piles of small rocks from the nearby stream in front of them served as chips. They'd been there for nearly a month, instructed by their leader to remain in place in case any of the Shangri-La stragglers showed their faces, but they hadn't seen or heard a soul the entire time and were now bored out of their minds.

"Hit me," said Joel, a young man in his early twenties with a scruff of wiry beard.

"You're going to go bust again, you moron," answered the man who was dealing.

"Screw you, Gabe. I want another card. You've taken as many of my rocks as you're going to."

"You never learn. Hitting on seventeen? You're giving morons a bad name. How many times have I had to explain this to you?"

"I want a card. You going to give it to me, or do I have to beat it out of you?"

The third man, his head shaved clean each morning with a razor-sharp knife he spent endless hours honing, snorted. "You two need to get a room and work this out. I swear you're worse than my ex-wife, and that's saying a lot."

"You're just pissed 'cause I keep winning," Gabe said. "I'm trying

236

to explain to moron boy here how the game's played, but he's too thick to catch on."

The third man had just opened his mouth to respond when a small hole materialized in his forehead an instant before the sharp crack of a rifle reached them. He fell backward, dead, and Gabe and Joel stared at him in shock.

Another shot rang out, and the side of Gabe's throat exploded in a fountain of blood. His carotid artery showered crimson on the card deck, and he slumped forward as Joel reached for his rifle.

A voice called from the trees, "Don't try it or you're next."

Joel froze, his eyes wide as saucers, and stared at the apparition that emerged from the trees – a lanky man with tattoos covering his face and arms, who was pointing an assault rifle at him. A pair of rough-looking trail bums followed him from the forest, also toting guns.

"You…you killed them," Joel sputtered.

Snake smirked. "The man's a genius." He looked to Eddy. "Take his weapons. Search him good."

Eddy complied and frisked Joel roughly before grabbing his rifle and pistol and tossing them aside.

"What…? I don't have anything to take. A few spare rounds. That's it," Joel said.

"We're not after your ammo," Snake replied.

Joel's confusion deepened. "Then…what?"

"Where are they?"

"Who?"

"Everyone."

"I don't understand."

Eddy's gun butt slammed Joel in the skull so hard his teeth rattled, and he blacked out.

When he came to, his hands and feet were bound, and a small fire was crackling in the fire pit.

"Look," Clint said. "Sleeping Beauty's awake!"

Joel tried to sit up, but couldn't. He looked down at his feet and saw that his pants were stained – he'd wet himself while passed out.

Snake stuck his knife blade in the flames and eyed Joel. "You're going to tell me where everyone went, and you're going to tell me the truth, or you're going to feel pain like you've never dreamed possible – pain so bad that you'll beg for death."

Joel's head swam and his vision blurred. Eddy leaned down and slapped his face.

"Pay attention."

"I have no idea what you want," Joel cried, his eyes tearing from the blow.

"I told you – I want to know where they went."

"Who?"

"Everyone who lived here. Shangri-La. You know damned well who."

"I...I don't know. I swear. All I know is our guys went after them. Followed their trail. That's it."

"What trail?" Snake asked.

"Up past the hot springs. You can't miss it. Looks like elephants went through there."

Snake snapped his fingers, and Eddy took off up the path that led to the springs. He returned several minutes later, just as Snake was removing his knife and admiring the blackened blade.

"He's telling the truth," Eddy said.

Snake resumed. "Who're *your guys*?"

"From Denver. We're part of Elijah's church."

Snake and Eddy exchanged a glance. "A church? Why are you following Shangri-La?"

"Elijah wants revenge on them for killing his father."

Snake stuck the knife back into the flames and leaned forward. "Start at the beginning and tell us what's going on."

Joel tried, to the best of his knowledge. Snake verified that the story didn't change under torture, and when he was through, he wiped the blood-encrusted knife on Joel's shirt and grinned. "You ever been in jail?" he asked softly.

Joel only managed a faint gurgle.

"There's a little initiation for the new meat. That's what they call newbies who've just been locked up. Usually happens in the showers, but sometimes in the cells." Snake grinned again, slid his knife into its sheath, and fumbled with his belt. "You a virgin? Going to hell a virgin's a lousy way to go. But don't worry. Me and the boys will help you out."

A flock of birds rose into the air at the first of Joel's bloodcurdling screams, and then the clearing fell silent, the burbling of the brook in the trees the only sound other than pained gasping from the fire pit and an occasional laugh.

Chapter 44

Provo, Utah

Sierra ran to Lucas and he enfolded her in his arms. Their kiss lasted a small eternity, and when he released her, he looked down at Eve and Tim.

"Miss me?" he asked.

"I told them you'd come back," Eve said. "I don't think they believed me, but I told them."

"That's right. She did," Sierra said, devouring him with her eyes. "Rough time?"

"The usual."

"I figured it had to be you when I heard all the shooting."

"Good guess."

"Where's Ruby?"

"In Newport. She's gone to get that bunch and lead them to safety."

"They're saying a *train* brought you?"

Lucas nodded. "It's a long story."

She stood on her tiptoes and kissed him again. "I've got a lot of time."

He made a face. "I need a bath."

Sierra smiled. "I know someone who'll give you one."

"How have the kids been behaving?"

"They're little angels. Don't change the subject. The train?"

Elliot's voice from down the street interrupted them. "Well, well. The prodigal returns with a bang. Literally. How are you, Lucas?"

"Could use some shut-eye. Other than that, in one piece."

"I hear there's nothing left of Elijah's army except some prisoners."

"That's right. They done kicked the wrong hornet's nest."

"Absolutely remarkable. You have a knack for coming to the rescue just in the nick of time."

"The locals would have fended them off. They were a bunch of disorganized civilians with guns. A mob."

"Mobs can be dangerous," Elliot observed.

"Maybe," Lucas allowed. "So you're settled in here?"

Elliot nodded. "Provo's been nothing but good to us. I think you're going to enjoy living here."

Lucas's eyes flitted to the side and then fixed on Elliot. "May be a while before I can settle down."

Sierra's mouth formed an O and she took a step back. "What are you talking about, Lucas? You just got here."

"I know. I'm just saying there's a lot of moving parts to what we're doing."

He told them about the Freedom Army and the train, and that there'd soon be another three thousand men joining them.

"They can't all stay here," Elliot warned. "The council would never allow it."

"They're not looking to stay anywhere. They're a fighting force. And they've got a job to do."

"What job?" Sierra blurted. "You're talking crazy. Did you get hit on the head? This is over. We're safe. You're back. I…Lucas, I need you here. With me. Your family needs you."

Lucas tilted his head to look at Eve and Tim, and then Sierra. "I know, Sierra. Believe me. We can talk about it later."

"You just got back and you're telling me you're leaving again?" Sierra said, her tone bordering on shrill.

Elliot's cheeks colored. "Sorry to barge in, Lucas. Perhaps you can swing by my house when you have a moment? I'm down at the end of this row. And the house next to mine is Duke's."

"Sure, Elliot. Maybe tomorrow. I'm beat."

"Very well. Nice to have you back," Elliot said, and made his escape as Sierra glared holes through Lucas.

"Okay. He's gone. Time to tell me what's going on, Lucas," Sierra said, making a visible effort to control herself.

"It's complicated."

"I'm a quick study."

Lucas sighed. "Let me get cleaned up and fed, and then I'll tell you everything." He held out his hand to her, and she hesitated before taking it.

"Where's Tango?" she asked.

"On the train. He'll be along shortly, I expect."

She gave him a sidelong glance. "Start with the train, Lucas. That sounds as good a place as any."

He shook his head. "No. Best to start at the beginning. Which I'll do after I scrub the road dust off of me."

"Lucas…"

"Sierra, I know you deserve an explanation, and I'll give you one. But it's going to take some explaining, and right now I haven't slept in about a week, and I can barely hear from rifle fire and explosions. So let me get cleaned up and rested, and I'll tell you everything."

Sierra blinked back her tears and looked away. "I missed you, Lucas. I don't want to spend my life missing you. Is that too much to ask?"

Lucas squeezed her hand. "I missed you too, Sierra. And no. That's reasonable," he said, and it was his turn to look away, his face drawn and his expression fatigued. "Only we don't live in a reasonable world. At least, not yet."

Sierra didn't say anything. Lucas's eyes returned to her profile and he pulled her closer. "I'll explain everything later. Right now, show me our new house and tell me what you and the kids have been up to. We'll have plenty of time to talk later."

Sierra looked unconvinced, but she softened and let her body mold to his.

Eve stared at Lucas with her placid blue eyes, and her lips pursed. "You're not staying, are you?" she asked in a tiny voice.

"For a while, I will," Lucas said, and then tugged on Sierra's hand. "I could sleep for a year, Sierra."

"Then stay and do that."

He exhaled and managed a tight smile. "Come on. Show me our new digs."

About the Author

Featured in *The Wall Street Journal*, *The Times*, and *The Chicago Tribune*, Russell Blake is *The NY Times* and *USA Today* bestselling author of over fifty novels.

Blake is co-author of *The Eye of Heaven* and *The Solomon Curse*, with legendary author Clive Cussler. Blake's novel *King of Swords* has been translated into German, *The Voynich Cypher* into Bulgarian, and his JET novels into Spanish, German, and Czech.

Blake writes under the moniker R.E. Blake in the NA/YA/Contemporary Romance genres. Novels include *Less Than Nothing*, *More Than Anything*, and *Best Of Everything*.

Having resided in Mexico for a dozen years, Blake enjoys his dogs, fishing, boating, tequila and writing, while battling world domination by clowns. His thoughts, such as they are, can be found at his blog: RussellBlake.com

Visit RussellBlake.com for updates

or subscribe to: RussellBlake.com/contact/mailing-list

Books by Russell Blake

Co-authored with Clive Cussler
THE EYE OF HEAVEN
THE SOLOMON CURSE

Thrillers
FATAL EXCHANGE
FATAL DECEPTION
THE GERONIMO BREACH
ZERO SUM
THE DELPHI CHRONICLE TRILOGY
THE VOYNICH CYPHER
SILVER JUSTICE
UPON A PALE HORSE
DEADLY CALM
RAMSEY'S GOLD
EMERALD BUDDHA
THE GODDESS LEGACY
A GIRL APART
A GIRL BETRAYED
QUANTUM SYNAPSE

The Assassin Series
KING OF SWORDS
NIGHT OF THE ASSASSIN
RETURN OF THE ASSASSIN
REVENGE OF THE ASSASSIN
BLOOD OF THE ASSASSIN
REQUIEM FOR THE ASSASSIN
RAGE OF THE ASSASSIN

The Day After Never Series
THE DAY AFTER NEVER – BLOOD HONOR
THE DAY AFTER NEVER – PURGATORY ROAD
THE DAY AFTER NEVER – COVENANT
THE DAY AFTER NEVER – RETRIBUTION
THE DAY AFTER NEVER – INSURRECTION
THE DAY AFTER NEVER – PERDITION
THE DAY AFTER NEVER – HAVOC
THE DAY AFTER NEVER – LEGION

Made in the USA
Las Vegas, NV
21 August 2021

28585700R10146